MURDER
At The Inn

BOOKS BY KATIE GAYLE

MURDER
At The Inn

KATIE GAYLE

bookouture

Published by Bookouture in 2023

An imprint of Storyfire Ltd.
Carmelite House
50 Victoria Embankment
London EC4Y 0DZ

www.bookouture.com

ISBN: 978-1-80314-896-0
eBook ISBN: 978-1-80314-895-3

From Kate to Gail, and Gail to Kate. In celebration.

Julia swore she could see the geraniums perk up before her eyes when the cool water from the hosepipe rained down on them. The lupins, too, seemed to breathe a sigh of relief when she turned the hose in their direction next. The sweet scent of the lavender mingled with the muddy smell of damp earth. The late afternoon sun caught the spray of water, making a fleeting rainbow over the flowerbed.

It was the third boiling day in a row and the whole garden had been gasping for cool and water. So had the chickens. They had spent the day huddled in the deepest shade that they could find. She'd given them a shallow basin of water and ice cubes to paddle in, as suggested in the latest *Chickenews!* newsletter, and filled up their drinking water. An Indian cotton tablecloth printed with blue elephants was draped over one side of their coop to keep the fierce afternoon sun off. She gave it a light spray with the hosepipe to cool it down even more.

Jake, who had spent much of the afternoon in a disgruntled soggy brown heap like a giant melted Easter egg in the shade of the plum tree, sat up and looked in her direction. It is common knowledge that Labradors can't resist water, and Jake was a

particularly Labrador-ish Labrador. He had all their good quali-
ties – a gentle temperament, friendliness, loyalty – as well as all
their less good ones – greed, naughtiness, an inclination towards
chewing your shoes – in great measure.

Jake made up his mind and dashed towards her. He hurled
himself into the spray, his mouth wide open, snapping at the
water. He pivoted and came back for a second pass at the sprin-
kler, his big pink tongue flapping about, trying to slurp the
droplets out of the air. Julia laughed at his leaping and yapping
and snapping, and swung the hose about widely, creating great
arcs of water for his entertainment. He was such a picture of
pure joy that she didn't even mind the droplets that flew from
his fur onto her arms and face as he bounded about.

A lighter brown blur joined the madness. It was Leo, Sean
O'Connor's even-tempered rescue mongrel, followed by Sean
himself, who came into the garden, dressed casually and
laughing at the sight of the three of them enjoying the play. She
turned towards him and sent a small spray just close enough to
his feet to make him jump back and take cover behind the side
of the house.

'All right, enough of that,' she said, dropping the hosepipe
onto the lawn and walking to the garden tap to turn off the
water. 'Let's all calm down, shall we, chaps?'

This suggestion wasn't taken up by the dogs, who continued
to chase each other around the garden, sliding to a skidding
squelchy halt where she had dropped the hose, and rolling
ecstatically in the last of the now-muddy water.

'I think that's a no from the dogs,' Sean said, coming out
from the safety of his hiding place. 'There will be no calming
down, it seems.'

Leo headed off around the perimeter of the garden at speed,
with Jake loping behind him, his big pink tongue lolling from
the side of his open mouth. Leo was slight and swift, nippy
around the corners. Jake was more of a lumberer, but a young

and enthusiastic one. The humans kept close to the wall to avoid being knocked over.

'Shall we go in?' Sean suggested. 'I do rather fear for our cruciate ligaments.'

She looked at him quizzically, while her brain rifled through the part of itself that kept Latin names for body parts.

'Knees,' he said. 'Jake's head to the patella at that speed could put a person in the orthopaedic surgeon's office.'

'Right. Of course, the knees.' As is always the case, the information was familiar once she'd heard it. The frustrations of the middle-aged brain. She hoped she would manage to dredge out *some* facts at the pub quiz.

Sean seemed to read her mind. 'So we're going to go and risk public humiliation down at the Topsy Turnip Inn, are we?'

'We are indeed,' said Julia as they entered the kitchen. 'We are performing a service for the good of mankind – or womankind. Specifically Hayley Gibson. Her work/life balance is shocking and she needs to get out and about more.'

'She is a very hardworking copper, I must say.'

'Well, she needs to find a way to be a dedicated copper *and* have a personal life. That lovely policewoman Lilian Carson had a place free on her quiz team but Hayley was undecided. I met Lilian when we found Ursula Benjamin's body in the maze, remember? She's your patient, I think. Anyway, I said we'd come along to keep Hayley company – Tabitha was keen to put a table together anyhow.'

'It's all right for Tabitha, she's a librarian. She knows every book ever written and every author. And she has excellent recall.'

'I know, she's a wonder, isn't she? A walking encyclopaedia. She was always like that, even when we were at uni. Not only literature, she could recite all the kings and queens of England, and all the American presidents. In order.'

'In order? Oh no, it's worse than I imagined,' Sean said gloomily. 'I am definitely going to be the weakest link.'

'Nonsense, we're a team. And besides, you know lots of things like, um, medical things... The body... and Albert is sure to ask a few of those.'

'Yes, if they ask the names of the valves in the pancreas, I'm the man for the job.'

'Well, I'm going to be a whizz on—'

Julia didn't get a chance to name her preferred categories, because she was interrupted by the dogs who had come into the kitchen trailing mud and water.

She grabbed a round biscuit tin with a grinning collie's face on the lid, and dog treats inside. 'Come on then, out we go!' she said, heading for the door while rattling the tin enticingly. The dogs followed her out, plonked their bottoms down obediently and stared up at her, awaiting their rewards. She tossed a bone-shaped biscuit to Leo, who snatched it from mid-air, and did the same for Jake, whose catching skills were slightly less elegant, in fact non-existent. He snapped at it, missed, and fell upon it greedily when it landed on the ground. 'You can stay outside, chaps. We're off to the pub but we won't be late.'

The sun had finally lost some of its ferocious heat and the twilight was soft and glowing when Sean and Julia arrived at the inn. In the cool, wood-panelled half-gloom of the pub at the Topsy Turnip Inn, the tables had been set up to accommodate six people each. Julia waved at Hayley who was sitting at one of the tables, looking rather out of place next to her colleague and fellow police officer, Lilian Carson.

Tabitha had already claimed a table for their team, it seemed. She caught Julia's eye and gave her a smile of welcome. Next to her, Nicky waved enthusiastically, beckoning them over. As was her wont, she launched into a gabbling monologue as soon as Julia came within earshot. 'Isn't this exciting? I've always wanted to be in a pub quiz team, and now Tabitha's invited me. I know loads of useless stuff, you'd be surprised. Like, did you know that the heart of the shrimp is located in its head? Most people don't. But I've got this book, *Fascinating Facts about Animals*. You wouldn't believe what's in it. Anyhow, my mum said she'd watch Sebastian for a couple of hours, so here we are, aren't we, Kev? A fun night out.'

'Hello, Julia. Hello, Doctor O'Connor,' said Kevin, when

Nicky finally stopped talking. He looked more resigned than excited, and took a long slow sip of his beer before placing the glass down on the table.

'What's your subject area then, Kevin?' Sean asked, making conversation.

'Food and drink, I guess, being in the hospitality game. And sport, I know a bit about football.'

'A bit! Go on, Kevin, don't be modest,' his wife chipped in. 'He's, like, a football *fiend* is Kev. And music! He knows all the lyrics to all the songs of the noughties.'

'Excellent,' said Tabitha. 'It's shaping up nicely. We're just waiting for—'

'Hello!' called Pippa, who was weaving her way through the tables towards them. 'Hello, teammates. Ready for battle? You can count on me for flowers and plants, breeds of dogs and sheep, and the more attractive actors on daytime television.'

Nicky made a delighted noise somewhere between a snort and a laugh, and shrieked, 'We've got this, guys!'

'Well that sounds like a good spread of expertise. Julia and I will be on books and literature. Julia is good on art, too, aren't you? And history. Your degree...' She gave her friend an encouraging smile.

Julia had, in fact, done just one year of art history at uni forty years ago, but she nodded gamely. 'I'm a bit of a generalist,' she said, which was largely true. She did have quite a lot of life experience, and she read a lot.

'An all-rounder is always useful. And then we've got Doctor Sean on science and medicine and so forth,' said Tabitha, sweeping her arm to indicate the great extent of his knowledge.

Sean looked rather nervous, as if he was wondering exactly what 'so forth' encompassed.

Their pregame discussion was interrupted by a loud, 'Attention, please!' from Albert Johns, the quizmaster. He was a short, stocky man with rather bowed legs that resulted in a rolling gait, as if he were striding across the deck of a listing ship. A retired paramedic, he now had various roles around the village. In addition to being master of the pub quiz, he was chairperson of the Berrywick Residents' Committee and – most importantly – the husband of Flo Johns, the manager and part-owner of the local tea room, the Buttered Scone, which was the de facto centre of the universe, as far as Berrywick was concerned.

Albert had an actual gavel that he tapped authoritatively on the table in front of him, which also held a stack of papers and a jar of pencils. It was the same gavel that he used at the Residents' Committee meetings. Julia caught Sean's eye and they shared a micro-smile at old Albert's officiousness.

'Welcome, everyone, to the Berrywick Pub Quiz,' Albert bellowed across the tables. 'It's good to see some new faces here this evening. In a minute, I'll be coming round to collect your entry fees. That's a pound per person to go to charity. And I'll be checking. My dad was a maths teacher, you know. He made sure I knew how to count.'

There was a smattering of laughter, but Albert looked down for a quiet moment and then continued in a sombre tone. 'Before we start, I have an announcement.' He cleared his throat. 'Some of you might have heard the sad news about Monica Evans. She passed away two weeks ago. Peacefully, thank heavens, at home in her own bed, of a suspected heart attack. Monica was, of course, a valued member of Team Smarticus...' He gestured to the team that Hayley had joined. 'And of the quiz community.' His voice wavered and his eyes glistened with tears that threatened to spill onto his cheeks. Julia knew him as a solid, officious sort of man and found it odd and quite disturbing to see him so upset, dabbing at his round red face with a hankie. 'Do excuse me. I'm sorry. So very sorry. It's very sad, very tragic indeed. She will be missed. May she rest in peace.'

Albert took a moment to blow his nose and compose

himself, then continued in his booming voice. 'Tonight's takings
will be donated to the charity Donkeys in Distress, in Monica's
name. As you all know, she was very fond of donkeys.'

There was a general murmur and some tutting from the
seven or eight tables full of quiz teams. A few people raised
their glasses in a toast to the late Monica. Julia had met Monica
Evans once, at a fete, where Monica had been rather aggres-
sively selling jam. She had told Julia a long story about the
plight of the widowed, and how she couldn't find suitable work,
and Julia had found herself walking away with five jars, rather
than the one she had planned on – and unfortunately the jam
had not been very good. She'd avoided the woman's table at
future fetes. Still, she nodded solemnly along with the rest of
the quiz players.

After a suitable pause, and a sip of water, Albert got back to
business. 'As you know, this is the championship round.' Julia
shot Tabitha an exaggerated look of alarm. Her friend just
shrugged and smiled, as Albert continued. 'What that means is
that we'll be playing once a week for the next four weeks,
instead of our usual once a month. The scores will accumulate,
and there will be one champion team at the end who will go
through to the regionals. Everyone got that?'

The players mumbled in assent. He got up and walked
around the room, handing out sheets of paper, one to each table.
'The usual format, eight rounds of ten questions each, with a
halfway break for refreshments. No phones, no googling, no
funny business.'

When he got to their table, he said, 'Ah, we have a new
team. Now, what's the name of you lot?'

'Gosh, do we need a name? I hadn't thought...' Tabitha said,
looking around the table at her team members, who all looked
blankly back, except for Nicky who was never at a loss for
words. 'Agatha Quizteam!' she shouted, to laughter and cheers
from the next table.

'Right, Agatha Quizteam it is. Let's see if you can solve the mysteries of the pub quiz! Now, newbies, the paper's divided into eight rounds, and then numbered one to ten for the questions. You'll soon get the hang of it,' said Albert, and moved off to resume his place at the table, where he took up his gavel and started reading out the questions. Julia felt more comfortable once she found that she knew quite a few answers. The currency of Denmark (the krone) and the previous name of Istanbul (Constantinople) came easily. Others she had to grapple with, worrying in passing about the ability of her ageing brain to serve up facts and figures she knew that she knew.

She drew a blank on, 'What is Britain's biggest carnival?'

But Kevin offered a suggestion. 'Must be Notting Hill Carnival.' There was general agreement and no other contender. Tabitha, as their leader and scribe, wrote it down.

There were medical questions for Sean – the name of the bone in the upper arm (the humerus). Dog questions for Pippa – the other name for German shepherd dogs (Alsatians) – but sadly no questions related to dishy men on daytime telly, yet. Football questions for Kev – the team known as the Red Devils (Manchester United). Tabitha correctly identified Tom and Daisy as the characters from *The Great Gatsby*. Everyone had something to offer.

'Nice work, team,' said Tabitha, when they stopped for a break and drinks after four rounds of questions. 'I reckon we're in with a chance!' A bit of a cheer went round the table. Any anxiety had dispersed, the team members were relaxed and enjoying themselves, and working well together.

Julia wound her way through the tables of teams from the nearby villages, and went over to where Lilian Carson and Hayley Gibson sat. It wasn't easy, in the crush. Quizmaster Albert, who was sitting at the empty table next to them, reading through his list of questions, had to suck his tummy in and shift his chair in to let her pass.

'Having fun?' she asked the DI.

'It's less traumatic than I expected,' Hayley admitted. 'I don't think I've totally humiliated myself. But Monica Evans was apparently an absolute whizz.'

'Well, Monica was the archivist and researcher at the local paper before she was let go, so of course she knew a lot of weird and wonderful things, especially local history,' said Lilian. 'Although we still have Felicity Harbour, who is great at that too, being a historian, but she's sick tonight. But Hayley's been a good addition to Team Smarticus! Major points in geography, I think.'

When Julia had met Lilian before, it had been in the course of a murder investigation. But here at the pub, Lilian was more relaxed, dressed unexpectedly in a pretty frock. Julia had expected her to adopt Hayley's no-nonsense slacks and shirt look. She had a lovely smile, with dimples, and looked more like the sort of person who might make you a delicious cake than arrest you.

'I was six years old when my baby sister came along,' Hayley explained, about the geography. 'Rosie sucked up so much time and energy that nobody noticed me for about three years, and I was left to my own devices. I spent my afternoons with the huge *World Atlas* my parents kept on the tea table. I memorised all the countries and their capitals and I could find them all on the map. It was my party trick. This was before they invented TikTok, you had to make your own fun.'

Julia laughed at the TikTok joke – not that she'd actually perused TikTok herself – and absorbed this rare piece of personal information. Hayley gave out very little, and even though they had become quite friendly, Julia knew almost nothing about her childhood or, in fact, her current circumstances.

'And how are you, Lilian?' she asked.

'Chasing my tail a bit. We've got an arsonist running around causing havoc in Hayfield.'

'Oh yes, I read about it. Someone is setting fire to barns and outbuildings, apparently?'

'Yes, four fires in the last three weeks. No houses, thank goodness, and no injuries. And we're making good progress. I think we'll have our man within the week.'

'Speaking of having our man,' Hayley chipped in. 'We need to commiserate about the early release of that nasty goon we put away five years ago. He should have had another five. His sentence was reduced for good behaviour yesterday. That would be the first evidence of good behaviour he'd displayed in forty-five years.'

'We worked our asses off on that one, didn't we? Young, we were, with plenty to prove.'

'Well, let's hope the run of good behaviour continues,' said Hayley, without much conviction in her voice. 'Do you two want to get a bite after the quiz?'

'I can't,' said Lilian. 'Monica's cousin is here tidying up her place. She says it's a nightmare, all sorts of things squirrelled away, including jars of coins. Anyway, she's got all of Monica's paperwork that she wants to drop off at my place when I get back. Said she didn't know who Monica was doing what for, and could I take a look at it and see. She said that Monica had been so pleased to get some professional work, and that she'd seen it as a turning point. All for nothing, poor thing. The cousin seemed to think I would be able to sort the papers out, because I'm police. Not like it's got anything to do with a crime – but I suppose when I have some time, I can go through it all. Monica was an odd woman, but a good neighbour to me. Always willing to lend a cup of sugar, despite how tight things were for her, or watch the kids. Monica's cousin certainly didn't want to help with *that* – I had to get a local teen.'

'Lilian left her car at my place and we walked here. It's not far and I planned to have a beer or two.' Hayley lifted a half-full pint glass to illustrate her point. 'We won't hang about when the quiz is over – just long enough to collect our vast winnings. A hundred grand, didn't you say, Lilian?'

'Oh at least. I'll be taking David and Stacy to the Bahamas on my share. You could come with us, Hayley. The kids love you.'

'Discerning people, your kids. Although I think it's mostly because of my magic trick.'

Lilian turned to Julia to explain. 'Hayley can magic a pound coin out of the kids' ears.'

'The genius part of my plan is that I let them keep the pound.'

'Mercenary little things, children.' Julia laughed.

Albert hmphed from behind them, gathering up his papers, then stood up and walked over to his podium, where he started hammering and tapping the mic.

'Judge Judy is ready with her verdict,' Hayley said, which made the other two women snort.

'Chat in the week. Maybe make a plan for supper,' Julia said, and went back to join her teammates.

There was a woman in her seat, but she jumped up when she noticed Julia. 'Bye then, Doctor Sean... Or should I say Doctor No?' she said with a tinkling laugh, clutching his shoulder. 'Isn't he just the spitting image?' she asked Julia. Without waiting for an answer, she shook her honey-gold curls and said with a flirtatious wink, 'Good luck, 007.' Then she glided to her table with a sway to her hips that Julia felt sure was for Sean's benefit.

'Who was that?' Julia asked, deliberately casual.

'A patient, she came to say hello.'

She noticed a light blush on his face. He appeared mildly flustered, something she had no intention of mentioning. 'She's with the Trivia Newton-John team,' he said, which made them both smile, and broke the whiff of awkwardness that had crept in between them.

The questions were a bit trickier in the second round, and there were a few they had to take wild fliers at. The number of keys on a piano. The nickname of the golfer Ernie Els. It was soon time to wrap up.

'Don't forget to write your team's NAME on the top of the answer sheet,' Albert instructed, with a smack of his gavel to emphasise key words. 'And pass your answer sheet to the table to your RIGHT. Your team will mark the answer sheet from the team on your LEFT.' Agatha Quizteam did as instructed, sending their answer sheet to The Master Minds, the team from Edgeley, and accepting the meticulously neatly completed sheet from Quizards, who hailed from even further away, Hayfield. As team leader, Tabitha had the job of marking their papers and tallying the scores.

'RIGHT.' Albert stood to his full height, which wasn't very high, but was somehow quite imposing, armed as he was with the hammer. 'I am going to read out the answers, and you will mark each question either correct or incorrect.'

As Albert read each question, and then – after a short pause for dramatic effect – the answer, the room reverberated with delighted 'yeses', and disappointed 'aaahs'. There were more yeses, it seemed to Julia. Certainly, their team seemed to be doing quite well, although the number of piano keys is apparently eighty-eight in number, not ninety-two, as per their educated guess.

'What is Britain's biggest carnival?' Albert asked, and paused dramatically before answering. 'The Badger.'

The Agatha Quizteam members frowned, and looked at Kevin enquiringly. He was no help. 'The Badger Carnival? Never heard of it.'

Tabitha looked up from Quizards' paper, pencil in hand. 'This lot got it right!' she whispered to the rest of the team.

'How come none of us has ever heard of such a thing? How can it be bigger than the Notting Hill Carnival, this Badger Carnival?'

Pippa started to laugh. 'Carnivore!' she said. 'Britain's biggest carnivore! The badger.'

As each team member twigged, they started to laugh until the whole table was jiggling and giggling with mirth.

Albert looked over to them. 'You all right there?'

'Fine, thanks,' Tabitha said, getting a grip on herself. Nicky gave one last high-pitched whoop of laughter, Sean patted his eyes with his hankie, and they all settled down.

Tabitha took the completed form over to Albert who added it to the pile so he could check the answers and tallies.

'Imagine, a badger carnival,' Julia said, her body still ringing from the good feeling of a big laugh.

'I'd like to see that,' Kevin said, with a chuckle. 'Them all dressed up in their finery, parading through the streets with their badger brass bands.'

'Glitter on their stripey little faces,' Julia added.

Albert cut short a further descent into hysteria by rapping his gavel and announcing, 'We have a winner!'

An expectant hush fell on the assembled quiz teams. Albert milked the anticipation for a minute longer than strictly necessary, Julia thought, before announcing, 'Team Smarticus!'

3

The contraption looked like some mediaeval torture device, with its ropes and its pulleys. Something to wring a confession from a witch, perhaps, or convert a recalcitrant heathen. Except that the bed was shiny silver and made up in crisp white hospital linen. Hayley's right leg rested on a raised platform, bandaged from hip to foot. Her toes peeped from the cast, the nails – to Julia's mild surprise – meticulously painted a deep-metallic green.

Next to Hayley's bed sat Lilian, in a smart dark suit and sensible work shoes. There was no sign of the floral-dressed, dimpled woman of the night before. This Lilian looked tired and anxious.

'Oh my goodness, poor you!' Julia started as if to hug Hayley, but stopped herself. She wasn't sure that the detective inspector would *like* a hug, and besides, she might have other injuries. Also, Julia had a voluminous velvet bag over her shoulder and was holding a slim glass vase of roses that she'd picked that morning. It was all a bit awkward.

She settled for putting the vase down on the bedside table,

and giving Hayley a gentle pat on the shoulder and Lilian a similar squeeze.

'How are you feeling, Hayley? Are you in pain?'

'I've got meds,' said Hayley. 'Good meds.' There was, indeed, a gentle lilt to her voice that was not ordinarily apparent. She tended to be brisk and forthright and not at all lilting.

'Well, that's good. What about you, Lilian?'

'Just a bit bruised,' said Lilian. 'My body and my dignity.'

'How *did* it happen?' said Julia, turning from one police-woman to the other. 'I mean, I know you were hit by a car, but...'

'Lilian and I were walking home after the pub quiz. We were on Peony Lane, and this car came from behind us. It must have been travelling pretty fast, and you know how narrow those side roads are. It seemed to come from nowhere. One minute I was on my feet, next minute I was lying on the side of the road with Lilian peering down on me and shouting my name. And my leg at a very unusual angle.'

'It's all my fault,' said Lilian. 'I should've pulled Hayley out of the way.' She looked like she might cry.

'You would have if you could have,' said Julia decisively. She knew that in situations like this there was no good served by people feeling that they could have changed things. Even if they could have. 'I am sure that Hayley doesn't blame you at all.'

'Of course not. You were just a bit quicker than me and managed to jump out of the way of the car,' said Hayley, not giving Lilian a chance to start berating herself again. 'Very lucky you did. You would have been right in its path. You would likely have been killed. Imagine if you had died, Lilian. Because of one careless driver. Thank goodness you jumped out of the way.'

A nurse came in, carrying a clipboard and pen.

. . .

'How are we feeling, then?' she asked, with a bright smile for Hayley, ignoring both Lilian and Julia.

'Okay, thanks, not too bad, thanks to this,' Hayley said, pointing at the drip that snaked into her arm. 'Just a bit throbby.'

'That's to be expected. We just have to be patient, don't we? Take it easy and let the body do its work.'

Julia noted the inclusive plural pronoun that carers tended to use, as if the nurse, too, was laid up with a broken leg, possibly the same one.

The nurse fiddled about, checking Hayley's heart rate and adjusting a drip. 'And remember what the doctor said – no moving about. We have to keep it nice and still for a few weeks, don't we?'

'How long will she be here, Nurse?' Julia asked.

'That's for the doctor to say,' the nurse replied, pursing her lips a little as if to indicate that she wouldn't be sharing any confidential patient information, and didn't appreciate the question.

'He said likely a week,' Hayley said. 'I'm hoping less. I've got a lot of work on my desk.'

'Now let's not be worrying about that now,' the nurse said, smoothing down the detective's blanket. 'Let's just relax, get some sleep. I'll be around a bit later to check on you, but you know where the bell is if you need me.'

They listened to the rhythmic squeak of her foam-soled shoes grow fainter as she left the room and proceeded down the passage.

When the shoes finally faded to silence, Julia spoke. 'She seems attentive and nice. I'm pleased to see they're taking good care of you.'

'Oh, they're all lovely,' Hayley said with a sigh. 'It's just that I hate being fussed over. And I hate being dependent on people.'

'Of course you do. But, you know, you have to be here now while you heal, so you might as well enjoy the rest.'

'That's just it, I don't *like* resting.' After she said it, she gave a long, wide yawn which rather contradicted her words. 'I like working, Julia. It's what I do.'

Julia knew how she felt. She'd been like that herself for all those years as Head of Youth Services. She didn't even much like holidays, really. A week or so and she was itching to get back to her job. It had been a sore point between her and Peter – her reluctance to embark on a two week cruise of the Nordic countries, or a three week South American adventure. It was amazing how she'd settled into life in Berrywick, and how full her days were with the house and garden, Jake and the chickens, her volunteer job at the charity shop, and the small busyness of village life.

'Is there anything I can do for you? Water your plants? Check on anything at the station?' said Lilian, her blue eyes wide. She seemed desperate to help.

'I don't intend being in hospital a minute longer than I have to. I intend to be home in a couple of days. There's no reason I can't lie around there as well as here.' Hayley looked quite fierce about this. 'Anyway, Lilian, you need to focus on your arson investigation. You're about to crack it, and it needs all your focus. Don't worry about me. I'll be out of here in a jiffy.'

There was the small question of the mediaeval contraption, but Julia saw no point in arguing with Hayley about that.

Hayley turned to Julia. 'Lilian's putting on a brave face for you, but she walked away with some bruised ribs and about a thousand scratches from the brambles she fell into. She shouldn't be at work this morning, but she's like me. We don't let anything stop us.'

'And what do you know about the driver?'

'Didn't even stop.'

'How disgusting! What is *wrong* with people? Probably

under the influence and didn't want to be breathalysed. What was it? Nine o'clock?'

'Yes. We only stayed ten minutes or so after the quiz – had to celebrate our victory. So it was about nine. He was coming from the same direction as us, so he could even have been coming from the Topsy Turnip. Honestly, this time of year the roads are so dangerous. It's all the tourists who don't know the roads and who drive too fast. You know Peony Lane. It's just a little country lane, quite dark and a bit windy – although we weren't even on the bend when he hit us. It was a perfectly straight bit of road.'

'Well, I hope they catch whoever did this.'

'Walter's on the case.'

There was a brief silence, the three women acknowledging the fact that the effectiveness of DC Walter Farmer, Hayley's right-hand chap, didn't match his enthusiasm and goodwill, and he usually required a fair bit of bossing around from Hayley. His being on the case wasn't altogether reassuring.

'I wish I could help him,' said Lilian. 'But the bloody arsonist...'

'I'll be on top of it, don't you worry,' Hayley said. 'Walter will keep me briefed and I'll make sure he investigates the heck out of this one.' She gave another long, wide yawn, and added, 'Once they turn down the meds and I'm not so sleepy all the time.'

'I'm sure you will. Hopefully there's camera footage or something. Did either of you...?'

Lilian sighed. 'We didn't see a thing. He came from behind, it was dark. I heard the noise and just dived for the verge completely by instinct. I didn't catch so much as a glimpse.'

'And I think I might have passed out for a moment,' said Hayley. 'I didn't know where I was for a few seconds, and I was in no state to notice anything. I just wish I could remember more.'

Lilian stood up. 'I'd best be off, Hayley. Fires call. But I'll pop in and give Walter a pep talk, and I'll be back. Nice to see you, Julia.'

Julia stood up, and this time she hugged the younger woman. 'You should be resting,' she admonished.

Lilian smiled. 'Maybe once I have my guy behind bars,' she said.

Once Lilian had left, Julia turned back to Hayley.

'I'm worried about her,' said Hayley. 'She feels everything deeply, that one.'

'Well, there's not much you can do about that now. You need to concentrate on getting better. Is there anything you need? Oh, I nearly forgot, I brought you these.'

Julia reached into her big bag and pulled out three paperbacks. 'I didn't know what you read, so I brought some options. This one here, *Girl in the Attic*, is a psych thriller. I think the title tells you all you need to know about that set-up. Then there's a police procedural – I wasn't sure if you like reading about cops solving crimes, or if that might be a bit like a busman's holiday. And then this is a romcom about a forty-year-old woman who gets divorced and goes on holiday to a Greek island and meets—'

'I'll start with the... what did you call it? The romcom. I've never read one.' Hayley held out her hand and took the book, then turned it over and examined it, as if it were an object of great curiosity. Julia couldn't believe it.

'You've never known the pleasure of a highly improbable romance between ill-suited strangers in a beautiful locale?'

'Nope. I don't read many novels. I used to, but, y'know, work...' Her voice was languid and her eyelids heavy. 'Now I mostly read case notes and coroners' reports. And the dusty yellowing files from the pre-digital era.'

'That is very sad, Hayley. But on the upside, you are in for a *treat*. And the books come as a package, with this.'

She reached into her bag again and pulled out a large slab of hazelnut chocolate.

'Do you have a rabbit in there?' Hayley asked, through another yawn.

'I think you're thinking of hats. That's where rabbits come from. Magicians' hats. Either way, I don't have one, but if you'd like one I'll bring you one next time.'

'The books and choccies are probably better anyway for now.'

'You look tired, I'm going to be on my way. Give me a ring if you need anything else, and I'll pop over.'

'I am a bit tired. The drugs. But thanks, Julia, I appreciate it all. You're a good friend.'

'You're welcome. Now get some sleep.'

4

DC Walter Farmer was sitting alone at the table, having folded his lanky body into the very chair that Hayley had occupied just a week before, and sipping morosely on a beer clutched between both hands. His face lit up when he saw Julia enter the pub, with Sean following behind.

'Mrs Bird! Julia,' he called, motioning her over. He looked relieved to see a familiar face, and patted the chair next to him, saying, 'Sit a minute.'

Sean gave her a smile and nodded in the direction of the Agatha Quizteam table, then set off towards it. Julia sat down and took off her cardigan for about the fourth time that afternoon. It was one of those unpredictable days when she was constantly too hot or too cold.

'Hello, Walter. I didn't expect to see you here. Have you been deputised to handle the Thursday Night Pub Quiz, as well as Hayley's other investigations?'

'Yes, I have.' He did not look happy about it. 'DI Gibson insisted, she's been very...' He stopped himself. 'Never mind. The thing is, I've never been at a quiz night before and I always forget things when I'm nervous. Can't even remember my own name.'

'I'm the same, but I think you'll be fine. Last week was my first quiz and it was great fun once I got going. I mean, apart from...'

'Of course, yes, poor DI Gibson.' He smoothed over her embarrassment.

'How *is* Hayley today?' asked Lilian, who had taken the seat next to Julia and caught the conversation. When she unzipped her black jumper and pulled it off her arms, the scratches from the brambles she'd fallen into the week before were visible on her hands and forearms. She wore her dark hair loose and hanging into her face, instead of in her usual low ponytail, half-hiding the small scratches to her left cheek.

'Much better, she's healing well. She's going home tomorrow, thank goodness,' said Walter. 'Being in the hospital doesn't agree with her. Not at all.'

'When I visited yesterday, I thought she was going to send the nurse out to question witnesses.' Lilian laughed. 'She really hates it.'

'Yes.' Walter did not elaborate, but Julia could see the desperate look on his face.

'I'm sure she'll be much happier once home,' she said brightly. 'Although she told me she's booked off work for another week at least.'

'It's a complicated break. The doctors want her to keep the leg raised, so she has to lie down or at least sit with it up.' Walter sighed and stared into his beer.

'Any news on the car that hit us?' asked Lilian. 'Any leads on the driver?'

'I'm working on it,' said Walter grimly. 'Unfortunately, there are no cameras on that road.'

'The ones on the main road are not much use – too much

traffic, going in too many different directions,' agreed Lilian. 'It takes a lot of manpower to go through them all.'

'We're on it,' said Walter. 'It takes time, though.'

'I wish one of us had caught just a glimpse of the car. Two police, and not even one bit of detail. It just happened so fast. It's a complete blank.'

'It's not at all surprising that you didn't see or don't remember anything,' Julia said kindly. 'He was coming from behind, and it must have happened in an instant. Thank goodness you managed to get out of the way of that car.'

'Yes, I still can't explain how it happened. It was luck and instinct, really. I'm just sorry I didn't manage to pull Hayley out of his path.'

'It must have been very scary for you. I hope you've been taking good care of yourself.' Julia thought about what Hayley had said, that Lilian felt things deeply.

'Oh, I'm fine really,' Lilian replied, with a toss of her shoulders that revealed a rash of small scratches on her neck.

'You've been through something traumatic, though,' said Julia. 'It's not just the physical scars that a thing like that leaves. It's a huge shock. I hope that you're looking after yourself.'

Lilian leaned closer to her, away from Walter and said quietly, 'Actually, you know, you're right. I was quite shaken. I am surprised by how nervous I've felt all week. Playing it over in my head, you know, what might have happened. I could have been killed.'

'You had a terrifying experience. A near miss that could have gone the other way. I'm not surprised that you feel very unsettled.'

Lilian nodded and continued, eager to have someone to confide in. 'I mean, my kids. What would happen to them? I couldn't stop thinking about it. They'd go to their dad, of course. We're recently... well, I suppose you'd call it separated. But he's not very... I mean, I wouldn't want... Even leaving them with him tonight...'

She had worked herself up into a state just at the thought of it. Julia put her hand gently on Lilian's arm. 'But you're here. You're okay. You're alive, and your kids will have you for a good while yet.'

Lilian laughed, a short hard laugh that broke the confiding moment. 'Listen to me! Good heavens. What a lot of drama over a few scratches. I'm completely fine.'

'Good, but do take care of yourself. Do you need a lift home after the quiz?'

'No, I decided to give myself a treat and stay over at the inn. I was a bit nervous about being out on the streets after last week, and the kids are with their dad anyway, so it works out for the best.'

'All right then, enjoy the alone time.'

'I intend to. After this I'm going to have a lovely steak dinner in my room and I've taken the morning off work tomorrow. That arsonist just keeps slipping through our fingers – it's like he knows where every camera in the Cotswolds is – and I just need a break. At nine o'clock, when the other coppers are starting the morning meeting, I will be starting my one hour full body stress release massage. There's someone who comes to the room.'

'That sounds wonderful. Have to say, I wouldn't mind a massage.' Julia rolled her shoulders back and moved her head from side to side, unleashing a little clatter of clicks. 'Good luck for the quiz. See you soon.'

'Next week, for sure. The semi-finals, if I'm not mistaken.'

'That it is. Bye then.'

'Bye, Julia.'

Julia joined Agatha Quizteam, where Nicky was in fine good humour, regaling everyone with tails from Sebastian's nursery. Julia arrived in time to catch the punchline of a story.

'And would you believe, he'd eaten the glittery crayon, and when she went to change his nappy, let's just say it was Christmas in there!'

Tabitha and Pippa laughed heartily. Kevin gave a brief grunt of amusement – Julia suspected he'd heard that story a few times. Sean was not much of a laugher, he was more given to an encouraging smile and a chuckle.

Albert's gavel got everyone's attention. 'Right, quizzers, let's settle down,' he said. 'Take your places, please.' There was a bit of movement as people returned to their seats. The chirpy blonde from the Trivia Newton-John team patted Sean's shoulder as she passed by on the way to her table.

'Hello there, Doc. Feeling clever this evening, are you?' she said, with a twinkly smile. 'You'd better bring your A game, because you've got some *hot* competition.' And she sashayed away, tossing her curls.

Julia was surprised to feel a little flush of annoyance and, yes, a teeny tiny – really, barely noticeable – flash of jealousy. She liked to think of herself as 'not the jealous type'. She'd never worried about Peter, even though he, too, was an attractive man, and would have had the opportunities, had he wanted them. It was her belief that people would either cheat or they wouldn't, and worrying about it didn't help. Peter never did, not as far as she knew. He simply fell in love with Christopher, after thirty years of marriage, and that was that. No amount of fretting and suspicion on her part would have made any difference.

Sean appeared not to notice his patient's flirtatious tone. He turned back to the table and said earnestly, 'It's true, the competition will be serious. We need to keep our wits about us.'

'I've been swotting up on celebrity news,' Nicky said.

'What she means is, she's been lying on the sofa reading *People* and *Hello!*,' said Kevin, giving her an indulgent smile.

'Homework!' she said, and swatted his shoulder playfully. 'Any you've been glued to the footie doing your own research.'

She made air quotes around that last word.

'I personally spent most of Sunday watching the History Channel, armed only with a cup of tea and a Chelsea bun, on behalf of the group,' said Tabitha, joining in the fun. 'Anything you want to know about the polar expeditions – north or south – the First World War, prehistoric—'

Another thump of wood on wood put an end to their banter. The papers were distributed and they were off.

On their second time out, Agatha Quizteam was comfortable, focused and in the groove. The nervousness had dissipated and they worked together efficiently. The mix of questions played to their strengths. Sean got a few sciencey ones – the chemical symbol for iron – and Kevin came through with some sports trivia. Julia acquitted herself well, remembering what 'my true love gave to me' on the fourth day of Christmas, as well as the other name for baking soda.

Albert asked his last question, and instructed the players to swap papers. As he read out each answer, and Kevin marked the paper that had been handed to them, Julia and her teammates kept a mental tally of their own score. Right, right, right... She noticed Sean nodding at each answer, too. It was looking good for Agatha Quizteam, with just a couple of snags.

Albert read the last answer – yes indeed, bicarbonate of soda was the other name for baking soda, Julia was pleased to hear – and came round to collect the scored papers.

They had pipped The Master Minds to the post.

5

Flo came over with a menu. It was largely redundant, as it wasn't overly long or complicated, and like all the regulars, Julia knew exactly what was on it, and had sampled most of the fare. She took it anyway.

'Hello, Julia. Coffee is on the way.'

'Thanks, Flo. How's life at the Buttered Scone? Are you well?'

'That I am. It's crazy season of course, summer, but I never complain about that! Lots of lovely customers, from all over the world. Yesterday we had someone from Belarus, a tour group from Germany, and a lovely fellow from Namibia. Imagine that, over here in my little tea room in Berrywick.'

'It's the United Nations around here these days, isn't it?' agreed Julia. 'I met a sweet young couple from Venezuela on the footpath this morning. They'd got all turned around and asked for directions.'

'Venezuela? Well, I never. Sounds like the answer to one of Albert's quiz questions.'

Their chat was interrupted by the arrival of Jane, a fellow

book club member, who stopped at Julia's table for a hello. Because of Jake, Julia always took the table just outside the door. As a result, anyone she knew stopped for a chat. Jane had hardly said hello, before she was enfolded in Flo's enthusiastic embrace. Flo let out a shriek. 'Jane! Congratulations, I hear your Hannah's expecting. How exciting for you, your first grandchild!'

'Ooooh, I couldn't be more delighted, you know how I love babies.'

'Oh, I know, but then who doesn't love babies, the little darlings?' Flo asked rhetorically.

Julia felt mildly ashamed of herself for not loving babies quite as much as she might. Give her a smart five year old any day.

It was Jane's turn to shriek joyfully, 'And congratulations to you too! Your Fiona, about to be elected as leader of the Cotswold District Council. Imagine that. Lord help me, but when I look at her I still see that girl five years old dragging that stuffed rabbit all over the village.'

'Funny Bunny. She wouldn't leave the house without it for a year. Drove us mad. It was forever getting lost, and then you don't want to know the drama. Eventually it got lost for good somewhere on one of the footpaths on one of our walks. We scoured the area but never found it.'

They laughed some more. 'Well, whatever happened to Funny Bunny, your Fiona's got over it. She's going places, that girl. Ah, there's my cousin Moira, she's already here. She'll be getting tetchy, waiting. I'd better go in.'

Flo turned her attention back to Julia.

'Sorry about that. Jane really can talk, can't she! Good heavens. Now, what are you having?'

'A banana muffin, please. And the coffee.'

'Right you are. And congratulations to you too, by the way. Albert tells me you won the pub quiz last night.'

'We did! We're the newbies on the block, so it was quite unexpected. Beginner's luck, I suspect.'

'Nonsense! You've got some good people on that team. Well deserved.'

'Ah, that's kind of you to say. And what lovely news about Fiona – I couldn't help but overhear. I didn't know she was running for some sort of public office. Gosh.'

Flo looked a little bashful. 'I don't know where she gets it from. She's so driven. Wants to make a difference, she says. Even when she was at school, she was on this and that committee, library monitor, a prefect, all of that. And now she's standing for the leader of the council, and she's not even thirty. Albert says she'll be prime minister before we know it. And he's only half joking! He's dead proud of her.'

Flo went to place Julia's order, with only a minor detour to check in on how Mrs Blundell's mother was doing after her op, and a nip past Table 9 to see if the Americans were enjoying their scones. Jake looked up hopefully as she arrived back with her tray – after all, there was a real possibility of a rasher of bacon or crust of toast coming his way – but settled down with a sigh when his nose told him it was only coffee and something baked with *fruit*.

A chilly breeze had got up, sending the up-and-down weather, which had been lovely and balmy since last evening, on a distinctly downward trajectory. Julia reached into her basket for her jersey, muttering darkly to Jake, 'Since we *must* sit outside.' He had the good grace to look apologetic, or perhaps that was just confused – hard to tell. She slipped on the cardigan and realised it wasn't hers. It was black, like hers, but it had a zipper instead of the gold buttons that looked like knots of rope. She thought back to when she'd last worn her jersey. Was it last night? Yes, she'd taken it off at the pub. And she hadn't worn it again, it had been so warm when she and Sean walked home. She realised she'd picked up the wrong cardi when she'd left Walter and Lilian's table. She remembered Lilian taking off her own black jersey when she'd arrived, and deduced what had happened. She reached for her phone and then remembered she didn't have Lilian's number, and there was no point in phoning the police station. She'd be at the inn, probably finishing up her massage. 'Not to worry,' she told Jake, who wasn't worried in the least. 'We'll drop it off at the inn on our way home.'

The timing worked out perfectly. They arrived at the inn a few minutes after ten, just in time for the end of Lilian's massage.

'I've got something for one of your guests, Lilian Carson. Could you ring the room?' she asked the receptionist, a fresh-faced girl with a pixie haircut and huge green eyes fringed with pale lashes. She looked to be about fifteen, but was no doubt twenty-something. This was one of the hallmarks of ageing, Julia had discovered. Young people always looked so improbably *young*.

'With pleasure, she's in room eight,' she said, picking up the phone and dialling.

'No answer,' she said, after a minute or two of waiting.

'Ah, she did say she was having a massage, so perhaps that's running a few minutes late,' Julia said. 'I can just leave it here then.'

'Oh, she didn't have the massage. The masseuse arrived but there was no answer. I rang the room and we even went up to knock, but she wasn't there. The masseuse went home. She wasn't happy, I'll tell you that.'

Julia frowned. This seemed very odd. Lilian had been so looking forward to the massage. Why would she not be there? The kids, that's why. She was uneasy about leaving them with her husband, maybe she'd gone to fetch them.

'Could she have left early?' she asked.

'My shift started at six, and I haven't moved. So unless she went out before dawn...'

Julia didn't like this situation. It didn't make any sense, and besides, it was giving her a funny feeling. Not a nice funny feeling.

'I'm Julia, Julia Bird. I should have introduced myself.'

'Bella Brown.'

'Pleased to meet you, Bella. Now, let's go and knock on the door,' she said.

'I don't like to disturb our guests.'

Julia gave the receptionist a hard look which caused her to get up from behind the counter. 'The dog...' she said, hesitating. 'They're not allowed.'

'We'll only be a minute, and he can't wait by himself, can he?'

'No dogs. We can't take him to the rooms.'

Julia took Jake outside, attached his lead to the bicycle rack and assured him of her imminent return. He seemed unperturbed, and lay down for a nap. He really was growing up.

Julia followed Bella down a corridor with four wooden doors on either side, odds on the left, evens on the right. The girl stood in front of number 8 at the far end and rapped sharply on it, leaning in to speak loudly into the keyhole. 'Ms Carson? Sorry to disturb. It's Bella here from reception. Are you in there?'

No sound came from the room. Bella knocked again, harder this time, and looked at Julia expectantly. Julia didn't know what to do.

She reached into her basket, past Lilian's black jersey, and took out her phone.

'Hayley,' she said, without so much as a greeting. 'Can you give me Lilian Carson's number?'

'Sure. What's up? You sound odd.'

'I'm at the inn where she's staying. The one above the pub?

She's not answering the room phone or the door. I thought I'd phone her mobile but I don't have it.'

'Open the door.' Hayley spoke quickly and authoritatively. 'Get the hotel to open it.'

The receptionist was close enough to hear her. 'I am not allowed to.'

'She says—'

'I heard. Put me on speaker.' Julia did. 'This is Detective Inspector Hayley Gibson. This is an urgent police matter. Please open the door. Now.'

The young woman went a ghostly white and stood rooted to the spot.

Julia spoke calmly and firmly. 'Do you have a key to the room?'

The girl nodded.

'Go and fetch it right away.'

'Right, right, okay,' she said, coming out of her daze and setting off at a run in the direction of the reception. She was back in a minute.

'Here, it's the master key,' she said, handing it to Julia. Julia took it somewhat reluctantly, wondering how it came to fall on her to open the door. She knocked again, hard and loud, making the door shake in its frame.

'Lilian?' she called, and when there was no answer, slid the key into the lock, turned it, and pushed the door open.

Bella screamed, a blood-curdling, ear-splitting shriek, just centimetres from Julia's head. Julia was stunned silent – by the scream and by what she saw on the carpet in the middle of the room. Lilian Carson was sprawled face down, and a tendril of her blood had seeped across the patterned carpet, entangling with the pink roses and their pale green stalks, studded with thorns.

6

The front door opened, setting off a cheerful tinkling bell that was at odds with the glum scene in the foyer. A tall man in police uniform entered the Topsy Turnip Inn. Julia knew all of the local Berrywick police, having found herself entangled in a number of investigations, but this thin, sandy-haired man was not familiar to her. He walked over to DC Walter Farmer, and they had a brief conversation.

As they spoke, the new policeman's eyes flicked over to Bella, pale-faced and shaken behind the reception desk, and then Julia. Julia was sitting in a big overstuffed tartan-covered armchair, one of two such, on either side of a small table furnished with a stack of *Homes & Gardens* magazines and a bowl of individually wrapped peppermints. She had told Walter Farmer her story, but was waiting to give a formal statement to a more senior police person who was on their way. She suspected that this tall fellow was him. A kind receptionist had bought her a cup of sweet tea, which had slightly helped with the terrible shock that was making her hands shake. She could not get over the sight of poor Lilian, sprawled on the carpet, dead.

The tall man nodded, and turned and strode across the small foyer toward her, his large black shoes and determined tread causing the floorboards to tremble. DC Walter Farmer followed a step behind. The unfamiliar policeman planted himself six inches in front of Julia and looked down at her, engulfed in the tartan and cushions.

'Mrs Julia Bird? Superintendent Roger Grave,' he barked, by way of introduction, hands on his hips. 'You found Constable Carson's body?' It was something between a question and a statement. His manner was brusque, just on the edge of abrasive, and she was annoyed to find herself feeling like she might cry. She stood up, so at least she was vertical and he wasn't towering over her.

'Yes, I'm Julia Bird. We found Constable... We found Lilian. Me and Bella, the receptionist. We opened the door.'

'And why were you visiting her? What was your relationship to the constable?'

'I didn't know her very well. We were acquaintances, I suppose. But I liked her. She was a kind woman.' Julia took a deep breath. This wasn't the information that the policeman needed, and the look on his face made it clear that he shared that view. Julia knew she had to tell the story clearly. 'I picked up her cardigan last night, by mistake. We were at the quiz night here in the inn and by coincidence, we both had black cardigans. I put it on this morning – you might remember that it got rather chilly after the boiling weather last week – and I realised I'd taken the wrong cardigan. I wanted to give it back, and see if she had mine, and I knew she was staying over at the inn, so I came here to drop it off.' Despite her best intentions, Julia could feel herself starting to babble. There was something very unnerving about Superintendent Grave.

Superintendent Grave's eyes started to glaze over at 'cardigan', and by the time she got to the next sentence, and the phrase 'quiz night', his interest had dwindled to next to nothing.

Mention of the changeable weather sealed the deal. He vacated the conversation.

Julia knew this scenario, this progression – what she was watching was the process of an alpha male writing her off as an insignificant older woman whose piffling issues were of no interest to him.

'A cardigan, you say?' he said, looking around the room as if eager to move on to something or someone more interesting. 'All right then.'

But Lilian deserved better than that. Julia needed to tell every detail of the story, because – as she had learnt in the last year – you never knew which detail might be the key to the whole thing. She said firmly, 'Yes, I came with the cardigan, but when I got here, she didn't appear to be in her room. The circumstances seemed odd. She had missed an appointment.'

'An appointment?'

'Yes, with a masseuse. She had booked an appointment for a massage.'

'A massage?'

'Yes. I found out that she didn't answer the door when the masseuse came. No one at the hotel had seen her, and she wasn't answering the phone in her room. I thought it odd. We went to the room to check. No answer. I was worried and asked DI Hayley Gibson for her mobile number. Hayley was concerned too, so we opened the door.'

'You phoned DI Gibson?' he asked, momentarily interested in Julia.

'She is a friend. I'm a retired social worker and we've worked together on—'

The door gave another merry tinkle. Grave's gaze left her face and moved on to the forensic team. Three figures dressed in white overalls had arrived in the little lobby of the inn, which was already full to overflowing with the two policemen and the two witnesses, and the two very large chairs on either side of a small table.

This was clearly the someone or something more important he'd been waiting for. 'Farmer, take a formal statement, will you? This one, and then from the receptionist,' he said, and set off in the direction of the forensic team. Two steps away he remembered her, and half-turned to say, 'Thank you, Mrs, er, Bulb. The DC will take it from here.'

Walter looked at her apologetically and let out a small sigh. He gestured to the armchairs, and the two of them sat down. 'He's from regional headquarters,' he said, as if that explained everything there was to know about him. Walter took his notebook and pen from his pocket, flicked to a blank page and said, 'Now, tell me again what happened. Let's start with the pub quiz?'

Julia ran him through the whole story again, more slowly this time, while he took detailed notes – Lilian's nervousness after last week's accident, the night away, the massage, the cardigan, the door, the phone call, the master key – and the body.

'And there she was. Lying face down on the carpet. Her feet were near the door, and her head near the bottom of the bed. I could see the blood on the floor, but not the weapon until I moved a bit closer and to the right. That's when I saw there was a knife in her neck. The black handle was sticking out. It looked like the sort of knife you'd have in your kitchen. Not a dagger.'

'Yes. She was stabbed with a steak knife from the hotel kitchen. It was either a lucky blow...' He stopped and blushed, then coughed and continued, 'I mean not lucky, of course, not for DC Carson. What I mean is, either the killer knew what he was doing, or he accidentally hit her carotid artery when he stabbed her. There was only one wound, as far as I could see without moving the body. It was a direct blow to the carotid, and she would have bled out very quickly.'

'Poor Lilian, how terrifying and brutal. It's unimaginable, a nice young woman like that, her whole life ahead of her, and a young family. She had two children. Do you know how old they are?'

'Stacy and David, they are eight and six, I think. Somewhere around there... I haven't seen them in a while, the Christmas before last I think, we had a—'

'Are we done here, Constable?' Grave interrupted, addressing Walter Farmer as if Julia were invisible.

Walter got to his feet. 'Yes, sir. I've taken the statement.'

'Good, now get over to forensics and see what they need. And you're going to have to get in touch with the family—'

It was Julia's turn to interrupt. She stood up and spoke firmly. 'Speaking about the family, there's something you should know.'

Grave turned to her, as if surprised to discover she existed at all. 'You're a social worker you said?'

'Yes, retired.'

'Well that might be handy, I believe there are children.'

'Indeed, there are. Two. But I'm more interested in the husband at this point.'

'You are? Well, I'm sure you can have a chat with him once we've finished.'

Walter's eyes were fixed firmly on the ground, blushing at his superior officer's series of patronising blunders.

Julia tried again, drawing her shoulders back, looking the superintendent in the eye, and speaking slowly. 'Lilian Carson was recently separated from her husband. You might want to look into that.'

Grave looked at her as if for the first time. 'I might, might I? Well, all right then, Mrs Bert—'

'Bird. It's Bird, you know, robins, starlings and so on. Birds. But in the singular. Mrs Bird.'

'Right, Mrs Bird, well DC Farmer is going to be in touch with the family today, break the sad news.'

Poor Walter looked stricken at the prospect of speaking to the family.

Julia pushed on. 'I mean to say, that her husband should be considered as a possible suspect, at least until he's accounted for his whereabouts. Lilian mentioned to me just last week that she wasn't keen on leaving the children with him. So as far as interviews go, he should be top of the list, surely.'

'Now, let's leave that to the police, shall we, Mrs Bird? We know what we're doing, and of course we'll speak to the husband. Standard procedure. DC Farmer, I'm going upstairs with forensics. Come up when you're done with the family.' And off he strode, floorboards shaking under his size twelves.

'I will speak to her husband. Charles is his name,' Walter said, apologetically.

'Do. As I said, it seems their break-up was recent, and it didn't sound particularly amicable. She was eager to get back to the kids when they were with him. It was as if she didn't trust him. What sort of man is he?'

'I don't know him well. Just met him once or twice at social things. He does something in insurance, I think. Nice enough chap, it seemed. Certainly wouldn't have thought of him as a... as a killer. But who knows?'

'No one knows, Walter. No one ever knows.'

'It's my first time telling someone, telling the family. It would usually be DI Gibson's job,' he said. 'They're sending someone with me, though. There's always two officers. She's more senior, so I'm hoping she'll know what to say.'

'Well, I'm sure you've both been trained. Just be direct, tell him straight, and quickly.'

'Will do, Mrs B. I'll be getting on then.'

'Can I leave, do you think?'

'Yes, I've got your statement. I'll be in touch if I need anything else.'

'Thanks. And good luck, Walter.'

It was a great relief being out of that stuffy foyer, brimful of cops and death and soft-furnishings. But away from the ritual of the police protocols, she was also struck by a wave of sadness. A woman – a *good* woman – had died, and now her children were motherless. Julia closed her eyes and filled her lungs with the cool fresh air and took a moment to feel the weak morning sun on her face. *In the presence of death, one had to appreciate life,* she thought, *the pure, physical and spiritual privilege of being alive in this world.* A profound insight that was interrupted by a tap on her shoulder and a question.

'Is that your dog?'

Julia opened her eyes to meet those of a young woman wearing a bicycle helmet.

'What dog?' she asked, although she knew full well without even looking that the correct answer to her question would be 'Yes'.

'That-there brown one, with his nose...'

She turned her head slowly, reluctant to see whatever it was that that-there brown one was up to.

'Oh for heaven's sake, Jake. Sorry.'

Lord knows how, but he had entangled himself in the bicycle rack and his velvety muzzle was wedged between the wheel and the frame of its only bicycle inhabitant. Fortunately, he wasn't leaping about in a panic, but simply looking at her with a sheepish expression and pleading eyes, as if to say, 'If I could get a little help here?'

'He seems to be stuck,' the woman said, taking a sip of the straw sticking out of a takeaway cup. 'I hope he's all right. He won't have been there long. I was only gone a few minutes.

Dropping off the insurance paperwork about my shed that burnt down with the police.'

'He's fine, I just need to untangle him.' Julia spotted the source of the problem right away. On the other side of the wheel was a large, soft potato chip, presumably an escapee from someone's fish and chip takeaway, and Jake's intended morning snack. In his effort to reach the chip, he had pushed his head between the spokes of the bike, and then snagged his collar on the rack. She knelt down and disentangled Jake's collar from the rack, and Jake from the whole contraption. He gave a happy shake, enjoying his freedom.

'Thank you,' said the cyclist, lifting the bike off the rack.

'I'm sorry, he's a youngster, and he does get into rather a lot of scrapes.'

'Ah, he's all right, isn't he? Aren't you a lovely boy?' She patted Jake who looked very pleased to be so appreciated, and gave her a wide grin before lunging for the chip that was accessible now that the annoying bicycle was out of the way.

'Thanks for your patience,' Julia said, as the cyclist got on her bike.

'No problem.' She waved as she pushed off and pedalled away.

Julia knelt down, and buried her face in Jake's fur. She needed the comfort of his warm, chocolatey body after her shock of the morning. She needed a moment to collect herself.

Lilian. Dead. She just couldn't believe it.

7

Julia had been surprised to discover, when she retired and moved to Berrywick, that cooking could be soothing. For most of her life she had found it dull, at best, or, at worst, actively stressful. Why was the sauce lumpy? How long would the chicken take to cook? Was the oven on the right setting? And how much, exactly, was a dash? These were the questions that vexed her.

Her ex-husband Peter had been chief cook in their household, specialising in simple and tasty meals which, because he was a determined keeper of his slim figure, were light and healthy. Julia had supplemented his thoughtful cooking efforts with less impressive efforts of her own, as far as possible consisting of good bread, deli meats and cheese, and salads. She was good at salads.

Living alone, she realised that there's only so much bread and deli you can eat. Or serve to your new friends. She made a fine Spaghetti Arrabiata, but she could hardly serve pasta and tomato to everyone she knew for the rest of time. Her move to Berrywick had come with a vow to embrace new experiences and try new things. Julia reasoned that while she might not be a natural, neither was she an idiot. She could *learn* to cook well and confidently. From a book. And so she did. Her repertoire now included curries, stews and soups, as well as scones and cakes. And she actually enjoyed it.

This morning, she was making a frittata to take to the incapacitated DI Hayley Gibson. After the shock of yesterday's grisly discovery, she found the simple, rhythmic tasks involved in cooking soothing. Collecting the few implements and ingredients she would need. Cutting a large potato into even cubes. Putting the potato cubes on to parboil. Then chopping an onion.

She left the onions and the boiled potatoes frying gently in the pan, while she took her little basket and went out of the kitchen door and into the garden to gather the rest of the ingredients.

'When life gives you eggs, make Spanish omelettes,' she said out loud to herself. She had been having rather a lot of omelettes – Spanish, and regular old cheese and tomato, and an interesting Asian flavoured one with soy sauce and spring onions – as well as scrambled eggs, lemon curd and meringues. The chickens were prolific in the warm weather.

She reasoned that the frittata was light and nourishing, and could be easily managed in a semi-prone position. The two of them could eat it warm for lunch, with a salad, and the leftovers would do Hayley for another meal or two. Plus, it would use up six of her seemingly endless supply of delicious fresh eggs. This kind of high-level strategic domestic thinking was new to Julia and made her rather happy.

'You see, you can teach an old dog new tricks,' she said, addressing Jake, who was in the shade between the chicken run and the azaleas. 'It's the young dog who seems not to learn terribly fast.' She smiled at her own little joke as she snipped thyme, oregano, chives and basil from the pots at the kitchen door. 'Only joking, Jake. You're actually coming along very well for a dog who failed guide dog training,' she said.

. . .

Twenty minutes later, she was in the car, the golden omelette in its cast-iron skillet next to her on the seat, wedged into a big flat basket lined with a tea towel, the smell of hot oil and sweet onion and fresh herbs filling the air. Next to it was a small steel bowl of tomato and basil salad with a fitted plastic lid that she hoped was watertight, and a bar of hazelnut chocolate for dessert.

'Good heavens, look at that,' Julia said to herself, as she drove up the rise that took her towards Hayley's part of the village. She slowed the car, and pulled to the edge of the lane, looking through the windscreen at the wreck of a building, its timber frame a blackened skeleton. She'd heard about the arson, of course, but she'd not seen any of his handiwork. It was one thing hearing about an act of destruction, and quite another seeing it. It was a shocking sight, brutal, violent. And even through the closed window she caught the faint smell of burnt timber. It had been the prettiest barn. The beams freshly painted, and rambling roses around the front. And look at it now. Destroyed. What for? After the tragedy of the previous day, this felt like one thing too much. Even though no one had been harmed when the barn was set on fire, death and destruction seemed to be stalking the streets of Berrywick.

'I don't understand people, Jake. Honestly I don't.'

Ten minutes later still, she was at Hayley's house. Hayley had left the front door, which was painted a rather scuffed and tired red, unlocked, as arranged. Julia opened it and let herself into a small hallway with a table topped with flyers and letters. There was a stairway ahead of her, and two doors, one on the left, one on the right. As instructed, she opened the one on the left.

'Hayley? It's me,' she called, and stepped gingerly into the sitting room. It was odd letting herself into a strange house. She and Hayley had known each other for almost a year, but this was the first time Julia had visited her at home. When they met, Hayley came to Julia's house, or they went for coffee at the Buttered Scone, or out for a meal somewhere, or – it had to be said – they were at the police station or at a crime scene. There had been more than a few crime scenes.

She had called Hayley yesterday as soon as she got home. The detective had already heard about Lilian's death from Walter, and Julia had expressed her condolences. Lilian was a friend of Hayley's, and Hayley had been uncommonly subdued on the phone. 'I just can't believe it,' she kept saying.

The visit this morning was really to see if Hayley was okay, if she needed to talk, or even a shoulder to cry on. Julia had to admit that this might work both ways.

'Hi, Julia.' Hayley was sitting in a wing chair, her foot resting on a kitchen chair in front of her. The large bay window that looked out onto the road also let some sun into the room, and Julia could imagine that Hayley might spend a lot of time in this armchair, even when she was healthy.

The décor was much like Hayley herself – largely sensible and functional, but as Julia looked around her eyes found some small quirky touches that hinted at hidden depths. There was a particularly beautiful set of prints framed on one wall, a quirky sculpture of a duck angled so that it looked out the window, and a pillow embroidered to say, 'Leave Me Be'. Julia imagined the latter must have been a gift from someone who knew Hayley rather well.

Hayley's leg was horizontal, and heavily bandaged. A pair of crutches leaned against the side of the chair, at the ready. She was dressed in black sweatpants and a T-shirt saying 'Police'. Even off-duty, Hayley looked like she might leap up and chase down a criminal at any moment.

'How are you feeling?' Julia asked, putting the frittata in its basket onto a small square dining table, surrounded by four chairs.

'Oooh, that smells good. Thanks for bringing lunch. I'm okay. The leg is healing well. It's not even sore as long as I keep it up and don't move around too much.'

Hayley's cheerful answer was somewhat belied by the bruising under her eyes – a lack of sleep, or perhaps from crying. A half-empty tissue box close to Hayley's chair confirming this impression. Julia had seen this a lot in her work – strong women dealing with the loss of a friend in their own quiet way.

'Have you got someone to help you get around? Bring you food and so on?'

'My sister, Rosie, has been threatening to come up from London and look after me,' she said with a dramatic shudder, as if being looked after was the most awful fate imaginable. 'I think I've managed to fend her off, thank goodness.'

'Are you sure you don't need the help?'

'I can stagger around the house when I have to, and there's a health visitor who'll be coming by every day. And we do live in the era of food delivery, even in Berrywick, so I won't starve. I'm all right, really. Fine.' She gave a stiff smile, but Julia could see how hard Hayley was working at presenting a calm and accepting demeanour. Julia knew Hayley better than to fall for it.

'Are you going mad?' Julia asked.

'Absolutely, completely insane.'

'I'm sorry, Hayley, it must be very hard being stuck at home, especially now.' It hadn't escaped Julia that both she and Hayley had skirted around the elephant in the room, and the grief in their hearts. She knew that they both needed to talk.

'I can't believe it, Julia,' said Hayley. 'Lilian. Stabbed at the Topsy Turnip Inn. One of ours. A colleague. A friend. And I'm stuck here like a bump on a log.'

'I know,' said Julia. 'She was so full of life. It just doesn't seem real.'

'I should be out there, finding her killer,' said Hayley. 'It's the least that I owe her.'

'Well, if it's any consolation, the investigation seems to be well under way. The forensics team was there. I'm sure Walter will update you.'

'Sure, but I want you to tell me what you saw. Everything. Minute by minute. Don't leave anything out.'

'I'll give you every detail, promise. But let me serve lunch first and we can eat while we talk. Can you sit at the table?'

'Yes, the doc says I can sit up for short periods with my foot on the floor. Kind of her.' Hayley's grimace showed how much she liked taking instruction.

'Wait there, and I'll get the lunch set up.'

Julia found plates and cutlery in the little kitchen that led off the sitting room, and set the table. Hayley directed operations from the sofa, giving instructions. 'The drawer on the left' and 'Salt and pepper by the stove.' Julia noticed how sparsely the kitchen was equipped, four of this, five of that. Three cutting knives and a bread knife took up a whole drawer. It was safe to assume that Hayley wasn't hosting dinner parties.

She located a cupboard housing six or seven unmatched glasses. She took the two that did match, filled them with water and set them down on the dining table. She went to help Hayley up.

Hayley used her hands to lift her leg slowly from the kitchen chair and place it carefully on the floor. She sat up straighter in the armchair and said, 'If you can just give me a bit of a pull?'

Julia helped her to her feet and handed her the crutches. 'Are you steady?' she asked.

'Yes. I've got it.'

Julia walked behind the detective as she manoeuvred

herself awkwardly to the table, but she didn't fuss around her or try to help or take her arm. She had learnt as a social worker not to take over, fussing and fixing, but to stand close by to help if needed. The detective inspector, in particular, was not someone who would take well to being incapable, or being helped.

Julia served up the omelette and salad, and handed Hayley a plate.

'Thanks. This looks great. Now tell me everything. Right from the beginning.'

Julia did, starting with the pub quiz. She stuck to the facts, without offering opinion or conjecture. Hayley let her talk, forking pieces of omelette into her mouth and chewing thoughtfully. She listened with a look of deep concentration and interrupted only occasionally with a question – 'What time was that?' and 'Who else was on the team?' and 'Did she leave alone?'

When Julia had finished relating the evening's activities, she turned to eat her own lunch while Hayley mused on what she had heard.

'So she stayed over because she was nervous after our hit-and-run?'

Julia swallowed. 'Yes, and I think she wanted a break, and her husband was with the kids,' she answered. 'They had separated, I'm sure you know.'

'She said it was over. Quite recently, by the sound of it. I don't know the details though. She was a private person, like me, and I knew she would tell me in her own time, when she was ready. That's how it was with us. I didn't like to push.'

Julia could well believe it. She had known Hayley for a year, and remarkably little about Hayley's life. The DI didn't offer much of a personal nature, and answered direct questions with only the necessary information. Perhaps Lilian was similar in that regard.

'I went to their wedding, back when Lilian and I worked

together,' Hayley continued. 'They were love's young dream, back then. I remember being struck by how devoted and attentive he was. I thought their marriage was one of those "made in heaven" sort of things. And when I've visited over the years, things seemed fine. I thought that they were one of the couples who would make it. But it seems it didn't last. Never does, I suppose.'

There was a note of bitterness in that last sentence which made Julia wonder again about Hayley's romantic history. She knew she had never been married, but not much beyond that. Had she had some spectacular failure of a relationship that she didn't want to talk about? Julia thought of her own marriage as expired rather than failed. It had been fresh, then a little stale but not toxic, then over. When Peter met and fell in love with Christopher, she'd been surprised, but not devastated.

Hayley's voice brought Julia out of her musing. 'To be honest, I don't think it's the husband. I've got another theory. But first, finish your story. I want to hear how you found the body. Why did you go to see Lilian?'

Julia picked up the account again, from Friday morning. Hayley was much more interested in the cardigan and the massage and the unanswered phone than the annoying superintendent had been. When Julia came to the opening of the door, Hayley slowed her down with questions.

'Where was she lying, exactly? Were her feet pointing towards you? How many metres from the door?'

Julia's memory of the morning was fresh and sharp, she could picture the scene clearly – the angle of the body, the feet near the door, the knife.

'What kind of knife?'

'It looked like a kitchen knife, not a dagger or anything. It had a black handle. You see that sort of thing everywhere. Walter Farmer says they think it might be one from the pub kitchen. But there are photos, of course. You can see for yourself. I'm sure Superintendent Grave will share them with you.'

'Roger Grave? Is that who they sent?' Hayley gave a brief, involuntary roll of her eyes.

'Yes. He's a big cheese apparently.'

'They'd be bringing out the brass on account of it being a police officer killed. I worked under him when I was first on the force. Right after graduation.'

'What's he like?'

Hayley paused to eat a forkful of tomato salad and then answered, 'You know what we used to call him? Shallow Grave. No depth. He always talked a big game and impressed the top brass but never actually seemed to do much.'

Julia snorted. 'He certainly didn't question *me* very closely.'

'And you actually *found* Lilian.'

'Exactly. He was eager to talk to the forensic team, though.'

'Hhhmph.'

'I did try and tell him about Lilian's husband, the estrangement. I got the impression he thought I wasn't much in the way of a witness. He discounted me as largely irrelevant. I'm used to it as a woman of a certain age, but I would think a policeman might know better.'

Hayley's narrow face contracted further in a grim frown and she exhaled a small exasperated *ppfff* from her lips.

Julia continued. 'Anyway, Walter Farmer should be able to update you on everything. He was going to break the news to Charles Carson, the husband, and ask him some questions.'

'Oh dear, poor Walter.'

'Yes, he was not looking forward to it, as you can imagine. I wonder how it went. You haven't heard from him?'

'No. Could you get me my phone?' Hayley gestured to the little table next to the wing chair. On it a phone and a notepad and pencil. Julia fetched both and put them on the dining table next to the detective. Hayley was all business now. She made a call and waited, then spoke. 'Hi, Walter, I'm just checking in about the investigation. How did it go with Lilian's husband? Call me back as soon as you get this.'

She killed the call and made another impatient puffing sound. Hayley was not one who liked to sit around twiddling her thumbs.

'I'll phone the station,' she said, and made another call. 'Hello, Cherise... Yes, fine, thank you, coming along. Yes. Thank you. I'm hoping to be back soon. Very soon. Maybe even next week. Is Walter there? Oh, okay, not to worry, I'll get him on his mobile. And, Cherise, please can you send me a phone number for Superintendent Roger Grave, he's from regional... Oh, he is? Oh, in *my* office? Well could you put me through?... Oh, well, could you ask him to ring me as soon as he's finished the meeting. And if you could send me his mobile number in the meantime. Okay, thanks.'

She put the phone on the table. In a moment it gave the little ping of an incoming message.

'Grave's number.' Her face relaxed a little in relief. She called and spoke in a brisk professional clip. 'Good morning, Superintendent, it's DI Hayley Gibson calling to check in on the investigation. I'm housebound for a day or two, booked off with the leg, but I'm feeling fine and I'm eager to be of assistance in the investigation. Please give me a call as soon as you get this message.'

Hayley put the phone on the table and drummed her fingernails. Julia could feel the waves of frustration coming off her. It was intolerable for her to be stuck at home and out of the loop on such an important investigation, so close to home. Well, presumably Walter or Superintendent Roger Grave would call her soon and fill her in, and she could put that brain of hers to work.

Ping.

'Ah, there it is.' Hayley visibly lightened when she heard the message arrive on the phone. She picked it up and played a voice note. 'Hello, DI Gibson, it's Cherise here. The superintendent asked me to call and tell you he is busy with the investigation and can't return your call at this time. He says, um, that you should rest up that leg and, er, not worry about what's going on at the station. He's got it all under control. He'll be in touch if he needs you. Bye then. You take care.'

Hayley hurled her phone across the room and onto the sofa.

8

Julia broke out the hazelnut chocolate, and passed a square to Hayley who was in her armchair, her leg once again elevated on the kitchen chair. She looked pale and worn out, her head resting heavily against the back of the chair. A cup of tea, made by Julia, steamed on the table next to her. Hayley put the block of chocolate next to it, and left both untouched.

'Now then, Hayley, you've only been out of hospital for a day or two. You need to rest and look after yourself.'

'I don't want to rest. I want to help solve Lilian's murder. She was a colleague, a friend. I can't just sit here.'

'Superintendent Grave is busy with the investigation, I dare say he'll be in touch when—'

'He won't. I tell you, I'm being cut out. Typical Grave. He'll cut corners like he always does, and he doesn't want me to notice.'

'Well, you were booked off to recover. Perhaps he just wants you to relax and get well.'

'He wants to swoop in and solve this himself and get a big win against his name. Believe me, Julia, I know the type. And I know *him*. He won't take my calls or hear what I have to say.'

Julia was horrified to hear the catch in Hayley's voice. She looked up and saw her struggling to hold back tears. It was so unlike the detective that Julia was shocked. She patted her arm and said, 'Tell me. Tell me what it is you want him to know.'

'I've got a possible suspect – and his motive.'

'You do? Who? And why?'

'It's a case Lilian and I solved when we were working together up in Colchester about six years ago. We put away this tough guy, Nico Gordon. I think I mentioned it?'

'You did, yes. The other night at the pub, on the first quiz night. He'd just been released.'

'Right. He got ten years, served five, and now he's out. He was released from custody less than two weeks ago. That seems like too much of a coincidence, wouldn't you say?'

'I would. What was he in for?'

'He put a rival tough in hospital. Lilian and I worked the case – successfully, as it turned out. Nico Gordon was convicted of assault. He was facing a tough time in jail; his victim had some associates, so to speak.'

'Do you think he'd kill Lilian for revenge?'

'I wouldn't put it past him. A thoroughly nasty fellow. And the timing...'

'Why Lilian, though? Surely there was a team on it?'

'Yes, of course. But she was the one who put the cuffs on him. It was her who gave testimony. It's my theory that he felt Lilian was the one responsible for putting him away, and when he got out he came to Berrywick to kill her.'

'How would he know where she was?' Julia asked. It was just one of about six questions she had about this theory, which didn't hold up particularly well, to her mind.

'It's not hard to find out where she works. And then, I don't know. He could have followed her, I guess.'

Julia got the fizzing feeling she got when there was something not quite right, something her unconscious brain had picked up on before her conscious mind.

'Hayley! The hit-and-run.'

'What about it?'

'Maybe it wasn't an accident. Maybe it was the first attempt on Lilian's life. She was on the side of the lane closest to the cars, and she jumped to the kerb, out of harm's way. Do you think whoever stabbed her had first tried to run her down?'

There was no sign of Hayley's pallor and tiredness. She sat up, alert, her eyes bright. 'How could I not have thought of that? Julia, you are brilliant. I think you're right. It could have been Gordon's first attempt. It would have looked like an accident, a hit-and-run – except she jumped out of the way and he hit me instead. Now I really need to get hold of Grave. I'll send him an email, at least.'

'You do that. I'm sure he'll want to talk to you when he hears your hunch.'

'Can you pass me my laptop, please?' She gestured to where the laptop lay on a small table next to the sofa. It shared the table with an empty vase.

'Sure,' Julia said, walking the few steps across the rug to fetch the laptop. Hayley took a sip of her tea and popped the square of chocolate into her mouth. She held her hands out for the computer, ready for business. Julia handed it over, saying, 'I know you don't like to take advice, but, please, don't overdo it. You know what the doctor said – rest, and keep that leg up and still. Maybe let your sister come and help you? And just write to Grave and leave it to him. Take the weekend to relax. I'm sure Walter will phone you and fill you in on everything that's going on. You'll be kept in the loop. And I'll give you a ring on Monday and see what you need, okay?'

Hayley was already tapping away. She entered the password to unlock her computer, and brought up her Gmail.

'Sorry, what? Oh yes, thanks, Julia.' She dragged her attention back to Julia. 'Really, thanks. You've been great. As a friend and... you know. Your ideas. I'll email him now, let you know what he says.'

'And then rest.'

'Yeah, yeah, sure...' Her eyes were already back on the screen.

'Hayley, I'm going to go. I'll fetch my pan and my basket and I'll let myself out. Leave you to it.'

'Bye.' Hayley's mind was miles away, deep in her email. Julia could have grown two extra heads and Hayley would not have noticed.

Her tap, tap, tap receded as Julia shut the door behind her.

As she drove home, Julia considered Hayley's theory. She respected Hayley's experience and instincts, but she had her own experience and instincts, and they told her that this Nico Gordon fellow wasn't a good bet for Lilian's killer. Sure, the timing was suspicious, but the logic didn't hold. Julia reckoned a guy who'd had the good fortune to be released early on good behaviour would lie low for a bit, not come running to Berrywick to kill a police officer two weeks after his release.

For a start, the injury or death of a police officer attracted a huge amount of attention and generated a lot of action – and any criminal would know it. The force would throw resources at the case like nobody's business. There would be police all over it like a rash, starting with Superintendent Grave from Regional Head Office. They'd get anything they needed. Forensics would be prioritised at the lab. It just seemed like too much heat. And for what?

Julia was surprised to find herself turning into Slipstream Lane. It was a little alarming that her mind had been so taken up with Nico Gordon and Lilian Carson that she barely remembered the drive. Even on a Saturday afternoon in the Cotswolds when the traffic was light, it paid to keep your wits about you. A cyclist could come out of nowhere, she told herself sternly, or a dog might have run into the road.

Speaking of dogs, there was no chocolate brown welcoming committee hurling itself at her when she opened the front door. This was unusual. Jake must be napping. She deposited the basket in the kitchen, and stood at the kitchen door looking into the back garden for her faithful companion. There was no sign of him.

'Jake!' she called. 'Where are you, Jakey boy?'

Nothing. Could he have gotten out and wandered off? Had he been stolen, perhaps? Her heart rate spiked alarmingly at the thought.

Calm down, you are being ridiculous, she told herself walking out into the garden. People did not steal dogs in Berry-wick. And even if someone had decided to suddenly take up dog thievery, they wouldn't start with a dog widely acknowl-edged as being the naughtiest dog in the county.

She heard a rhythmic rustle as she neared the far end of the garden. She walked towards it and, peering closer, she saw Jake, lying in the shade of the rhododendrons. The rustling noise was his tail sweeping against the leaves. He looked up at her with an odd expression that seemed to combine pleading, pride and a dash of embarrassment.

'Are you all right?' she asked. It wasn't like him to lie quietly when she came out into the garden. His usual place was right next to her, at her heels – or, quite often, in front of her and in the way. Jake wagged his tail again, but didn't move. What was wrong with him? Was he injured?

Julia looked closer. She couldn't believe her eyes. Snuggled up against Jake's underside was a chicken. If Julia wasn't mistaken, it was Penny – short for Henny Penny – the biggest and bossiest chicken of the lot. Penny was the hen she thought of as the matriarch of the group, keeping everyone in line with an officious bustle. The chicken lifted her head and looked at Julia, then settled back down, tucking herself closer into the space between Jake's chest and his front leg. Jake moved slightly to accommodate her more comfortably. She rested her head on his leg.

'Are you all right?' she asked again, but to the hen this time. Julia's first thought was that the hen might be injured, although she seemed quite calm. Perhaps Jake had chased her and hurt her. It wouldn't be the first time that Jake had chased a bird – far from it. Julia squatted down on creaking knees. Penny looked at her with her clever, beady eyes and stood up, looking mildly irritated as if Julia had ruined a special moment. There seemed to be obviously nothing wrong with her – other than the fact that she was allowing herself to be cuddled by a Labrador, which was unconventional chicken behaviour, to say the least.

Julia picked up Penny, using both hands to pin her wings to her sides. She liked the heft of the bird, its strong shoulders and its solid compact body. Penny was fine, as far as Julia could tell. She tucked her under her arm and carried her to the coop, slid the bolt and put the chicken on the ground. Penny turned her fluffy rear to Julia and shook out her feathers.

Jake had followed Julia. Through the fence, he watched Penny meltingly as she trotted helter-skelter towards the back of the coop where her five friends gathered round inquisitively. They clucked and fussed around her as if enquiring after her adventures.

'How did she get out of the chicken coop?' Julia asked in the direction of Jake. Living alone, much of her talking was to herself and her non-human companions, or into a space in between. She checked the perimeter of the coop, but there was no sign of a breach. No gaps under the walls or holes in the wire fence. 'The coop door must not have been latched properly,' she answered herself. 'And it was a bit windy, it must have blown open and closed.'

Jake said nothing, of course. He simply gave a little sigh, sent one last lolling pink smile in the direction of Henny Penny, and followed Julia into the house.

9

Hayley had not rested on Sunday, it seemed. Or at least not willingly.

Julia had planned to phone around lunchtime on Monday to check in with her, but she didn't have to. Hayley called at nine, and she was spitting.

'Not a word from Grave,' she said, without even a hello. 'I sent the email, as you know. I told him all about Nico Gordon. He didn't even reply.'

'It was the weekend,' Julia said, in what she hoped was a calming tone. 'Perhaps he took time off and didn't check his mail.'

'Roger Grave does not observe the Sabbath, I can tell you that much. And *no one* takes a day off when a police officer has been killed. Believe you me, everyone would have been on the case and at the station yesterday, but no one's talking. And with Robert Grave in charge, that isn't necessarily a good thing. All I want is that Lilian's killer is caught, and from experience I know that Grave is not necessarily the best man for the job.'

'That must be terribly frustrating, Hayley. But you know what? Maybe it's for the best – you need to rest. I was thinking,

would you like me to pop by the library for you? I'll ask
Tabitha for some recommendations and bring them round later
this afternoon. A good book will take your mind off things for a
bit.'

'I don't want to take my mind off things. I want to put my
mind *on* things,' Hayley said desperately. 'On Lilian Carson's
death.'

'Well, maybe you'll hear from Roger Grave today. Or you
could give him a call, it being Monday.'

'I sent three text messages and a voice note yesterday,'
Hayley said. There was a pause, and she added, somewhat
shamefaced. 'I couldn't just sit here.'

'You could and you should,' Julia said firmly. 'You are meant
to be recuperating.'

'I can recuperate and make a phone call,' Hayley said
grumpily. 'Which I did, but he didn't even have the courtesy to
respond.'

'That *is* strange. What does Walter Farmer say?'

'Walter!' Hayley spat out the word. 'Walter, my colleague,
my sidekick who I've trained and mentored for *three years* – and
I have *not* been working with the most promising material,
between you and me – is not taking my calls either.'

'Really?' This was a surprise. Walter Farmer's mission in
life seemed to be to please – or at least not displease – his boss.

'He sent me a message saying he'd been instructed not to
speak to anyone who was not working directly on the investigation.'

'Including you?'

'Specifically me. Grave mentioned me by name.'

A strangled breath became a sob on the other end of the
line, and after a minute Hayley took a deep breath and said,
'Sorry. Just a bit emotional. Tired. I had a bit of a bad night with
the leg, truth be told. It was aching something horrible, and I
can't stop thinking about poor Lilian.'

'Have you spoken to the doctor? Maybe you can increase the painkillers.'

'I can't take the heavy painkillers, they make me dull and I need to be sharp. I'm reading up on what Nico and his lot have been up to since he went away. I've been making notes. A list of key players in that gang, following them up. They are still active. Drug running, robbery.'

Julia knew this, but she didn't let on that she, too, had spent part of the supposed day of rest googling Nico and his mates. In fact, his round, flat face with its round, black eyes and blob of a nose had visited her in her dreams on Sunday night. And not in a good way.

'The problem is there's not a lot in the public record,' Hayley continued. 'I need access to the police database, which I don't have from home.'

Julia cut her off. 'You need to take the pills, Hayley.'

'Yes, well, of course. You're right. I will. Maybe this afternoon when I've—'

'Hayley Gibson, listen to yourself.'

There was silence on the other side of the phone. 'I'm going crazy here, Julia.'

'I know, it's hard. But you need to let that leg heal and that means rest. And taking your medication and getting a good night's sleep. The sooner you get better, the sooner you'll be back on the case. In an official capacity.'

'Maybe a book or two would be nice, thank you,' Hayley said meekly. 'If you're going past the library.'

'I am indeed. I'm planning to go later anyway. Now I want you to promise me that when you put the phone down you'll take your meds and you'll go and have a nap.'

'Yes, as soon as I've—'

'Now. Meds and nap. And I'll be there around lunchtime.'

'Any time, I'm not going anywhere,' she said gloomily and after a pause added, 'Thanks, Julia.'

'My pleasure. Message me if there's anything you need from the shops and I'll pick it up on the way.'

'Will do, thanks.'

'Sleep well.'

Julia set off for the library. After a bit of dithering, she had decided to take Jake for the walk. She felt some trepidation after Friday's bicycle debacle. He would have to sit outside the library, briefly, but she would make sure to avoid any moveable objects when attaching his leash to an immovable one. It was another lovely summer's day, and she took the river path into the village in order to enjoy the dappled shade of the trees and a light breeze. The river sparkled in the morning sun. A duck family – Mum and Dad and three babies – paddled upstream in descending order of size, as if auditioning for inclusion in a children's picture book. The early mornings and late afternoons were busier with dog walkers and runners, but in the mid-morning, the path was almost empty. She let Jake off the leash so that he could run about and investigate the sights and smells.

Auntie Edna tottered towards them. She always looked impossibly frail and unstable, like a bundle of sticks upended and swaddled in shawls and scarves, but Julia had come to realise that she was sturdier and stronger than she appeared. Physically, at least.

'Out and about, up and away of a winter's day,' Edna said politely – if meteorologically inaccurately – as she passed them.

'Good morning, Edna. Lovely day indeed.'

'If you say so. Watch out, there's a dog.'

She pointed to Jake, who looked mildly affronted, as well he might – Edna usually treated him as a dear friend.

'Thanks, Edna, he's my dog, so it's okay. Enjoy your walk.'

'Likewise, I'm the dog,' she replied, and they went on their way.

Julia left the river path and headed into the village along a little road lined with cobblestone pavements and the golden sandstone row houses that appeared in the calendars and postcards of the area. In fact, there was already a large fellow with a big hat and a professional-looking camera blocking the pavement as he squatted down framing a shot of the houses with a stand of glorious pink hollyhocks in the foreground. She waited until she heard the click of the shutter, and moved past him with a cheerful, 'Morning. Excuse me.'

'Why good morning, ma'am,' came the reply, in an American accent that she thought of as Texan. It was rather odd and charming to hear it in Berrywick. He even tipped his hat! 'And to you, good dawg.'

They were nothing if not polite, the American tourists. The clicking resumed and receded behind them as they went on their way, and then turned right into the main road towards the library.

'Here you go,' Tabitha said, setting a pile of books on the table with a thud that set her bangles jingling, and their teacups clattering gently in their saucers. The library cat, who was lying on the table in a little beam of sunlight from a high window, opened her amber eyes and gave the women the feline death stare. 'Sorry, I didn't mean to disturb you, Too.' The cat was called Too – short for Tabitha Too, on account of the librarian and the library cat coincidentally and confusingly sharing a name. Julia stroked her warm and shiny coat of gold and brown stripes, and Too settled back into her nap.

Tabitha picked the first book and held it up as if she was a host on a TV show, turning towards the camera. 'This one's been very well reviewed. It's about a very cool, older black female PI in New Orleans – in fact, you should read that, being an older female solver of crimes and mysteries yourself.'

'Only by accident. And I notice you skipped the "very cool" part of the descriptor,' Julia said in mock disappointment.

'And the black part,' said Tabitha.

'Well, if you combined the two of us we could be the very cool, older female black New Orleans PI.'

They laughed at their own banter and Tabitha continued, while Julia sipped her tea. 'This is a police detective novel set in Barcelona – it's translated from the Spanish actually. And then there's a newish Reacher novel, published a year or two back, I think, and lastly, for some retro appeal, an Agatha Christie. A classic Christie, and nicely relaxing.'

'Brilliant, thank you,' Julia said. 'I'll take all four if that's okay. It will give her some options.'

'Of course. Poor Hayley. She isn't exactly made for bedrest, is she?'

'That would be an understatement. But the doctors are adamant that she needs to rest that leg or it won't heal.'

'Well, let's hope these help,' Tabitha said, stamping the books with the date stamp, and pushing the pile towards Julia, who put them into her basket. 'Give Hayley my best and ask her if she'd like a visit.'

'Will do. Come for supper during the week?'

'Love to, thanks. We'll make a date.'

Honestly, village life was a lot more tiring than city people imagined, Julia mused as she set off for home. There was the livestock management – she had already given the chickens and Jake their food and water before she went out – and then there was the walking to and from the village, which Julia enjoyed no end, but which took up a fair amount of time. Then there were the missions of mercy, or friendship – fetching and dropping off library books, for example. Not to mention the gardening, cooking, cleaning and solving of occasional crimes.

'I'm too tired to make lunch. Let's get a sandwich from the café shop and eat that out in the garden. A little picnic,' she suggested to Jake. 'And then I'll drive to Hayley's to drop off the books.'

Jake wagged his tail and grinned to show that he loved this idea. *Loved* it! He loved all of her ideas. That was one of the nice things about him. He thought everything that came out of her mouth was brilliant. Except for 'Stop' and 'Leave' and 'No', of course.

She left the shop with a tomato, roasted red pepper, cheese and basil on a baguette for herself, and the same for Hayley. She would drop it off along with the books. Her chosen filling wasn't very Jake-friendly, so she bought him a small packet of fancy dog treats to keep him occupied while she ate it. She knew from experience that if he didn't have a snack of his own, he either stared mournfully into her face while she ate, or slammed his heavy paw hard and insistently on her knee, occasionally diving for microscopic or imagined particles of bread that might have fallen to the ground. It wasn't very relaxing.

The familiar figure of DC Walter Farmer came into view as she neared the police station. There was a little patch of green next to the station, with a bench and some grass. He wasn't sitting on the bench, but lurking next to a hedge of large rhododendron bushes, which half obscured him.

'Walter!' she called. 'What are you doing in there?'

As he turned to face her, a puff of smoke exited his astonished lips.

'Are you *smoking*? You don't smoke!' she said, noting the shrill disapproval in her own voice.

He dropped the cigarette in the dirt and stomped on it, like a schoolboy cuffed by the head teacher.

'Gave up seven years ago,' he muttered, grinding it under his foot. She gave him a stern look and he bent down and picked up the cigarette butt with the tips of his fingers. 'I cadged one off the fellows. I don't know what came over me. It's the stress,' he said.

'Lilian Carson?' she asked.

'Yes. Well, her and her family, of course, and Superintendent Grave. The whole package. And without DI Gibson, it all just seems so...'

He looked skyward, the dusty fag end still hanging from his fingers, and continued. 'Just so *difficult.*'

'How's the family? Charles and the children.'

He glanced wistfully at the squashed cigarette as if he'd like to take another puff. 'It was awful. This other officer and me, we had to knock on the door and tell him. Straight to his face. I can't even...' He shuddered, and his voice wavered. 'I can't tell you the sound he made. It was the sound of pure pain. And then the kids...' He shook his head and let the sentence trail off.

'That is a horrible, horrible task, Walter. I've had to do it myself, accompanying a police officer. It's one of the most difficult, painful things I've ever had to do. I'm sure you did your very best, and did it with dignity and kindness.'

He nodded in acknowledgement of their shared experience. 'And then he's a possible suspect, too. I mean, it's usually the husband, isn't it?'

'That's what they say. What was your impression of him?'

'Like a man in shock and grief.'

'I wondered... Hayley said when she knew them he was extremely devoted and attentive. Strikingly so. I wondered if he was an obsessive, jealous type.'

'I wouldn't know about that. Honestly, he seemed absolutely gutted, distraught. Which doesn't mean he didn't do it, of course. Superintendent Grave is on a different tack, and I don't want to be coming on all heavy, accusing the grieving husband. DI Gibson would know how to handle things. But I'm not allowed to speak to her. Superintendent Grave says it's too high profile, the case, and we can't talk to anyone outside of the team working on it. Oh, gosh, I suppose I shouldn't be talking to you!'

'Oh, don't worry about me, I'm just a civilian, a social

worker, retired and raising chickens,' she said with a laugh. 'And besides, you haven't told me anything you need to worry about!'

'Well, yes, so the superintendent is running the investigation himself, and it's all very need-to-know. And Lilian's partner, DI Paul Bend, obviously, because she was working with him on the arson case. So he's nervous, of course, I mean, who knows if he's—'

'The arson case?' The connection wasn't immediately apparent to her.

'You know, setting those fires. Lilian and Paul were close to cornering him, apparently. That's the tack the superintendent is following. That's why he...'

Walter stopped, his face grey. Julia followed his gaze. A tall, slim man with a shock of black curls springing straight up off his head walked slowly towards them. He held a child's hand in each of his, a boy on one side, a girl on the other.

'Mr Carson,' Walter said, dropping the cigarette end and taking a step towards them.

'Oh, hello, DC...' The man seemed stupefied, unable to recall Walter's name, through shock, exhaustion, grief or medication, Julia couldn't say, but she'd seen that look before, of someone moving as if through mud or water, their movements slow, their voice too. He dropped the children's hands and pushed his wireframed spectacles up his nose.

'DC Farmer,' Walter replied.

'Of course. Um, I was looking for you. To talk. About Lilian. About something I saw. Or rather someone hanging about...'

'Certainly, sir. Let's go to the station, shall we? We can talk there.'

Charles Carson looked back towards the station house. 'Yes,' he said, and then looked at the children in a puzzled sort of way. 'Err, kids, can you wait here?'

The boy, who was the younger of the two, grabbed his hand and whispered, 'Dad.'

The girl said, 'It's all right, David. We can stay here.'

The boy started to cry gently, which attracted the attention of Jake. In spite of being a clumsy galumphing nutter, Jake was very sensitive to unhappiness and did his best to help and comfort the sufferer. He put his large brown head very close to the boy and looked into his eyes, then nudged him gently, encouraging a pat. The boy sniffed back his tears and stroked Jake's silky ears. 'What's his name?'

'He's Jake and I'm Julia.'

The boy squatted down, put his arms round the dog's neck and rocked himself gently, muttering softly into his fur while he stroked Jake's head. He grew calmer with each rock, and every stroke.

She could see that Charles Carson was torn between his eagerness to get to speak to Farmer, and his wanting to see the boy soothed.

'Jake and I aren't going anywhere. We could just sit here on the bench for a few minutes and let Jake and David get acquainted, if you'd like to have your chat inside,' she said.

'Mrs Bird is a social worker,' Walter Farmer said, as if that explained everything, and justified leaving his children with a complete stranger.

Charles Carson ran his fingers upwards through his dark curls, while he looked at the station and back to the bench, then back to the station, as if he was deciding what to do.

'My name's Julia. I knew Lilian a little. I'm very sorry for your loss,' Julia said.

'Thank you,' he said, in a formal tone. She wondered how many times he would have to thank some well-meaning person for that exact expression of sympathy.

'If you want to go inside with DC Farmer, I'll keep an eye on the children. And you can keep an eye on all of us from the window.'

'That's very kind of you. Is that all right, kids?'

David nodded without lifting his head from Jake's neck.

'Stacy?'

'It's okay, Daddy.'

'We won't be long,' Charles Carson said, patting the girl's shoulder. 'Thank you, Mrs Bird. If you're sure?'

The two men nodded to each other, and walked towards the door. Charles gave a final worried glance towards them, and disappeared into the station.

'Do you have dogs at home?' Julia asked, making conversation.

David's answer was muffled. 'Yes, we have Ragnar. He's a mutt, Dad says. A cross shepherd.'

'Our mum died,' Stacy said flatly, rejecting the small talk.

'I heard. I'm very sorry, Stacy. That's terribly sad and painful for you and David.'

'And for Dad. He cried and cried. Dad never cries.'

'And he forgot to give us our breakfast,' David said, lifting his head. 'He said we were going out to see the policeman, but he forgot we hadn't had breakfast.'

Julia held up the paper bag. 'I've got sandwiches. Do you like cheese?'

The boy looked up at her and nodded eagerly.

'Excellent, we'll share. And there's something for Jake too. When you've had your breakfast, maybe you'd like to give it to him?'

The baguettes were divided amongst the humans, and the bag of dog treats given over to the children for distribution. They relished the power that came with this possession, instructing Jake to sit and stay, and then rewarding him with a little bone-shaped biscuit when he complied. It would have been quite a cheerful little scene, if not for the reason for their presence outside a police station.

'Dad is staying at home again,' Stacy said, in between bites.

'He was away for a bit, staying at Auntie Carol's house. That's his sister. But now he's home.'

Ah, the separation Lilian had spoken of. She wondered how long 'a bit' was, and when he'd moved out. Tempting as it was, Julia didn't like to pump grieving children for information, so she just said, 'Well, it's good that you're all together now.'

'All of us except for Mum,' David said in a wobbly voice. Julia wanted to kick herself for that last remark. 'We will have to remember our own breakfast now.'

'Daddy isn't good at remembering things like that,' Stacy said, by way of explanation. 'He has his head in the clouds, Mum says. Used to say. And she said if his head wasn't screwed on, he'd have lost it.'

'She called him Mr Scatterbrain,' said David, and took the last bite of his half of the baguette.

Mr Scatterbrain came through the glass doors of the police station, as if on cue, and walked towards them. 'You didn't have breakfast,' he said, when he saw the children eating their sandwiches. 'I completely forgot... I'm sorry, did you give them yours?'

'It's no trouble, I had extra,' said Julia.

'My mind is all over the place.'

'Of course. You've been through a terrible shock. It's normal.'

'I guess. But the kids... I can't believe I didn't give them... Lilian would...'

'It's okay, Dad.'

'I was in such a rush to get here, to talk to the DC. I thought I saw a chap hanging about outside the house. Just a feeling of being watched, and then a glimpse, him disappearing around the corner. Thought it might be connected.'

'Well, that's completely understandable. You wouldn't want to waste a minute if it was going to help in the investigation.'

With a deep sigh, Charles sat down next to her on the bench.

'Look, Daddy, look at the clever dog.' David was standing in front of Jake like a small lion tamer in a circus. He raised his hand commandingly. 'Sit!'

Jake plonked his bottom on the ground, his eyes fixed on the little bag of dog treats in David's other hand.

'Good boy. Lie down.'

Jake did as he was bidden, without letting the bag out of his sight.

'Good boy!' David handed Jake a treat and patted and stroked him.

A trace of a smile crossed Charles' face, the first she had seen there. 'Very clever. Very obedient.'

Julia reflected that this might be the first time anybody in the history of his short existence had called Jake obedient. Was it a sign that Charles was a very nice man, or a person with terrible judgement?

The children's attention was on Jake now. Stacy was trying to convince him to roll over. Jake had no idea what she was on about, but was happy to be rolled about by four little hands and accept treats.

Charles turned to Julia. 'Thank you for keeping an eye on them. I hope it wasn't too much trouble.'

'None at all. They are lovely children and Jake enjoyed the company.'

'They are. They're lovely kids and their mum... This is the first time I've seen them having fun since we got the news about Lilian. I haven't told them... how. How she died. That she was stabbed. I know I'll have to, but I haven't. I can't. I'm no good at that sort of thing, Lilian was the one who knew what to say and how to say it, and not mess things up. Lilian was the one who knew everything. She wouldn't have forgotten to give them breakfast. I don't know what I'm going to do.'

He dropped his forehead into his hands and breathed deeply in and out, trying to calm himself. The breath came faster, and noisier. He rubbed his hands over his face and then put them to his chest. 'I'm just... I can't breathe...' he said. His face was pale and sweating and his hands shook.

'I think you're having a panic attack,' she spoke quietly, to calm him and not to alarm the children, who were fortunately still preoccupied with Jake. She handed him the paper bag the baguettes had come in. 'Breathe into this. That's it. Try to slow your breathing. Now focus on something else. The birds on the bird feeder, look.' She pointed towards a little bird table where two robins were pecking and fluttering. 'Look at that red breast, that must be the male I think... Now breathe slowly in for the count of four... Good and now breathe out... Keep it up.' The bag inflated and deflated. The rasping had stopped. 'And don't worry, you're safe here with me. And look at the robins, that's it. Pretty little things, not a care in the world...'

The colour came back to his face, as the panic left it. He breathed more slowly, then lowered the bag to his lap. She felt his shoulder relax where it touched hers, and he said, 'It's okay, it's getting better. I'm sorry about all that, I just lost it there for a minute.'

'It's hardly surprising, with what has happened. You've suffered a huge loss and an enormous shock. You need to be gentle with yourself, and take care of yourself – not just the children.'

'Right now, I hate myself. I'll never forgive myself for what I did.'

This was so unexpected, that Julia didn't react. Was this some kind of confession? Had her original hunch been right after all? She waited silently for Charles to explain himself.

'I moved out. These last few weeks we were separated. We'd been getting on each other's nerves – or more like I was getting on her nerves. It was my fault, I was so distracted by my work and my own projects. She had a big job herself, and this arson case was really high profile and stressful, but she carried the load at home. I was all over the place, dropping balls at home, not being responsible, or helpful, or present for the kids.'

So that was what Lilian was worrying about, when she said she was nervous to leave the children with him – that he'd forget something.

'She was right, I wasn't practically or emotionally available. And the last two weeks I was sleeping at my sister's place. The last two weeks of my wife's life, I wasn't there.'

10

Wilma's blonde bob swung and brushed her shoulders, left right, left right, as she walked towards Julia and Diane, who were waiting on the doorstep of Second Chances. Wilma was close to Julia's age, and the assisted blonde was streaked with silver, but she was slim and fit – not without effort – and moved efficiently, and with a youthful bounce.

Wilma's energetic manner did not translate into punctuality. She was almost always five minutes late and sometimes ten to open up the charity shop that she managed, and where Julia volunteered on Wednesdays. The keys were already jangling in her hand when she stopped in front of the door with a cheerful, 'Good morning!' and opened the lock.

'Morning,' said Diane. 'Everything all right?'

Julia smiled inwardly at the little scene that played out regularly between the two women – Diane never voiced her irritation at Wilma's tardiness, but she usually made some sly little reference to it with a seemingly innocent enquiry. 'Traffic bad outside the school this morning?' or 'The daylight saving always takes a bit of getting used to, doesn't it?'

Luckily for Julia, she herself wasn't irritated enough to make anything of it. And besides, it wasn't as if there was a queue forming outside the shop on the dot of nine. They usually had time for tea and a bit of a catch-up before the first customer came strolling in.

Diane never held on to her tetchiness and was soon pottering around in the back room that doubled as a storeroom and a little kitchen. 'What are the plans for today, Wilma?' she asked, over the noise of the water filling the kettle.

'I think it's time for a tidy of the book section, it's got rather out of order. People don't put things back properly. And they could use a wipe down, too, some of them.'

'I'll do the books,' Julia said quickly. She enjoyed perusing the odd selection of donated books, and she liked creating order from chaos – this task was right up her alley. 'I'll take them out in sections, dust them off, and put them back in the right section.'

'Would you? Thank you. I'll take care of the customers,' said Wilma, ignoring the fact that there was not one customer to be taken care of. 'The window display needs a bit of a cheer-up, too. I'll try and get to that later this afternoon, if there's time. So if you have anything fun and summer-themed, please keep that aside.'

'Will do.'

'I'll give you a hand with the window, Wilma,' said Diane. 'But tea first!'

While Diane fussed about with the mugs and the milk, Julia moved towards the bookshelves at the back of the shop. She decided to start with the non-fiction books. Second Chances was the beneficiary of downsizing, divorce and death – 'The three Ds', as Wilma always said. The bookshelves provided evidence of the leisure pursuits of the residents of Berrywick, particularly the older residents – gardening, walking, bird-watching, cooking, baking, knitting, dog training, and so on.

Julia picked up a book entitled *Birding for Beginners*, wondering idly whether its owner had abandoned the pursuits, or got so proficient that they had moved on to a more advanced book, or moved on up beyond the realm of birds to the realm of angels. It was the kind of mildly morbid and slightly amusing thought that she could share with Tabitha or Sean, but not with her colleagues at Second Chances. She smiled to herself, dusted the book off with a kitchen towel, put it on the floor as the start of the 'dust-free' pile, and picked up *Birds of Southern England*.

The tinkle of the bell of the front door came just as the kettle whistled, to a rather startling effect.

Wilma welcomed the day's first shopper with a bright and breezy, 'Good morning. Welcome to Second Chances. How can I help you?'

Julia zoned out the chatter, concentrating on the third book, and then the fourth. She had just picked up the fifth – the cheerfully exclamatory *Know your British Birds!* – when a woman came over to peruse the vases and jugs in the cabinet next to her, chatting over her shoulder to Wilma. 'Oooh, I like the colours on this one, but it might be a bit big...' Her voice was familiar. Julia couldn't remember where she'd heard it, but it was recent. She looked up. It was the blonde woman from the pub quiz, the one who'd been so chatty with Sean. A patient of his, if she remembered rightly. A very friendly, possibly flirty, patient.

'Oh, hello,' Julia said, looking up at the woman, who was now right next to her.

She blinked in confusion. 'Sorry, do we...? Have we...?'

'I saw you at the pub quiz last week,' Julia said. 'My name's Julia. We met briefly, I think.'

The younger woman pushed her blonde hair out of her face in an embarrassed gesture. 'Oh, I'm sorry, yes, of course, you do look familiar now you mention it.' Although her face told another story: *never seen you in my life.* 'I'm Gina, Gina McFarlane.'

'Pleased to meet you, Gina.'

'Oh you're pub quiz friends, are you?' Diane said, misinterpreting the overheard conversation and coming over to join in. 'I rather fancy a pub quiz, but Mark wouldn't hear of it. He hates all that sort of thing.'

'You should come without him,' Gina said, picking up a cut-glass vase. 'I'm in a team with friends, you don't need a partner to join in. In fact, I thought it might be a good way to meet someone. And someone who's not an idiot. Someone who knows the capital city of Italy, at least. Not like the last fellow I met on Tinder. He thought the capital was Pisa, named after the actual pizza.' She laughed, and the others joined in.

'Gina's right, Diane, you really don't need a partner. If there's a gap in the team I'll let you know, you can come and try it out,' Julia said.

'You're in a team with Sean, though, aren't you?' Diane asked.

'Yes, we are both in Agatha Quizteam with Nicky and Kevin, and Tabitha.'

'*Doctor* Sean?' Gina asked.

'That's right, Sean O'Connor,' said Diane.

'Oh yes, of course. I saw him there last week. Isn't he just a dead ringer for James Bond? Always had a soft spot for 007. And for Doctor Sean. He's my doctor. Lovely chap. Good hands, too.' She gave a bit of a suggestive giggle.

'He's a good friend of Julia's,' said Diane, with a bit of emphasis on the word *good*, presumably to ward off further discussion on the attractiveness of Dr Sean.

'Really?' Gina looked at Julia properly for the first time, lowering her hands with the vase to get a better look at her. 'Quiz friends, hey?'

'Quiz friends, walking friends, what have you...' Julia said.

She didn't feel she needed to explain her relationship to Gina, and was, in fact, keen to move on to other topics. Like vase shopping, for example. 'What are you looking for, specifically?'

'Oh you know, just someone kind, and solid. And, of course, you need a spark, don't you. I mean, if there's no spark...'

Diane was turning an ever-darkening shade of pink at the turn the conversation was taking.

'Oh!' said Julia, with an awkward laugh. 'I meant for the vase!'

'Oh, good heavens!' Gina said, embarrassed. 'Of course! And here I am going on about Doctor Sean.'

Julia did not know quite what to make of that.

'Don't worry, Julia's not the jealous type,' said Diane.

'Jealous?' Gina asked with a frown.

'About Doctor Sean.'

'Why would she be jealous about Doctor Sean?'

Gina looked from Diane to Julia and back again. Julia realised with dread that Gina had not caught on to the fact that Julia was more than quiz friends with Sean.

'No reason at all!' she said. 'Now, about that vase?'

She saw the realisation come over Gina's face, as if in slow motion – confusion, then dawning comprehension, a dash of denial, and finally embarrassment. 'Oh, goodness, you're not... Are you...? I mean you and Doctor Sean, you're a couple? Gosh, I'm so sorry, I didn't realise. I just didn't think. How stupid.'

The embarrassment and the blushing had caught up with all three of them now. There was no escape.

'Well, this is the one, I think,' Gina said, looking at the ugly cut-glass vase. 'Thanks for your help.'

She walked to the counter and put the vase down. 'Five pounds, is it? I've got it right here,' she said to Wilma, opening her bag. She took out a five-pound note, which she handed over, and turned to go without waiting for her to ring up the sale.

'Bye, thank you,' she called over her shoulder, and with a tinkle of the bell, disappeared into the road.

That left two blushing, embarrassed people in the shop.

'Goodness, she was a bit strange,' said Diane, breaking the awkward silence. 'You get all types in here, don't you?'

'That you do,' said Julia. 'All types.'

Diane wandered off without saying anything to try to make the situation better, which Julia appreciated. She picked up another birding book, and as she wiped it softly with the cloth, she was surprised to find her throat feeling tight and her eyes sting with hurt and shame. Gina had not even considered that Sean and Julia might be a couple. That's why she had flirted openly with him at the pub quiz. And why she'd stumbled around, putting her foot in it today. Julia and Sean were of an age – in fact, Julia was six months younger – but Sean was considered a sexy older bloke, by a woman at least ten years their junior, while Julia was considered... Well, she wasn't considered at all. She was as good as invisible. Gina didn't even remember meeting her.

Julia put down the book on the pile of bird books. She took a minute to compose herself before starting on the next category, gardening. Through the window, the main road was a-bustle with morning shoppers and the earlier-rising summer tourists. A man stopped outside on the pavement, examining the window display. He raised his eyes and they met hers. It was an awkward moment. Julia felt as if she'd been caught staring, and she could only assume he felt the same. She gave him a tiny smile in recognition of their shared discomfort. No answering smile twitched the thin lips in the round, flat face, and she realised that he couldn't see her. He was looking into his own reflection, and not at Julia at all. She realised something else, too. That she'd seen him – or someone very like him – before. And recently. But she couldn't place him. Had she seen him on her walks? At the library? The pub quiz? The supermarket?

The answer hit her with such force that her heart thumped about like a startled bird in the cage of her ribs. She had seen him not in any of those places, but in a picture. A photograph on her computer.

Unless she was very much mistaken, the man was Nico Gordon.

11

Gina McFarlane had thought her invisible, thought Julia. Well, now she would put that to the test. Julia joined the ambling tourists and the somewhat more purposeful shoppers heading in the direction Nico Gordon had taken. She kept the back of his head in sight quite easily – it was early, after all, and the pavement wasn't too busy. It bobbed along in front of her like a bouncing ball on the choppy sea. She had excused herself from Second Chances, rather to the surprise of Wilma, saying she had an errand to run, and dashed out of the door. He was five shopfronts ahead of her by the time she exited the shop, and she walked briskly to catch him up a little.

In her mind's eye, she conjured up the face from the photograph taken at the time of his sentencing – the round face in the round head, and the small round eyes – and compared it to the one long look she'd had of him before he had turned and continued down the road. Doubt began to creep in. Was it really him?

Hayley had been set on Nico as a suspect. Julia hadn't bought her rationale at the time, and now she wondered whether Hayley's opinion had made her imagine the likeness.

Or was it him, but changed? He would be five years older now than when the photograph was taken. Five hard years in prison will change a man. She needed to get a better look.

She was a few feet behind him now, and had him well in sight. She slowed to match his pace, and calmed her breathing. She realised that she didn't actually have a plan, other than to study the man and confirm to her satisfaction whether or not he was who she thought he was. If it was him, what was he doing in Berrywick? That was the next question. He wouldn't be up to any good, that's for sure. But she'd put that out of her mind for now, and focus on getting a good look at him. She wished she could take a photograph to show Hayley, but couldn't imagine how that would be achieved without detection.

Maybe-Nico turned into the hardware shop. Julia hesitated a moment, and went in after him. After all, he didn't know Julia or have any reason to suspect that she was following him. She could simply check him out, buy a packet of nails or a tube of glue, and leave. It was a nice simple plan.

He was perusing a rack of tools on a side wall. She studied his profile – the round head, the flat face. His nose was small and his ears large and fleshy. She tried to imprint the shape of him into her brain. She was able to stare long and hard, as he seemed engrossed in his choice of tools, lifting them and examining them. He picked up a long metal thing with a flattened end, a tyre iron, and felt the weight of it in his hand. He put it back and tried another. He paid no attention as Julia walked behind him, glancing into his basket, which contained nothing but a coil of blue and white rope. She studied a shelf of glues and rolls of tape, trying to find something that she might actually need.

'Can I help you?'

Julia jumped about two feet off the ground and landed to the sight of a skinny, pimpled youth, right next to her.

'Sorry, miss, didn't mean to startle.'

'Not at all,' she said. 'I was lost in my thoughts. I've found what I need, though, thank you.'

She grabbed a bottle of wood glue and held it up like a prize. *A prize for being a twit*, she thought.

'Anything else I can help you with, you let me know,' he said, edging away from her, towards the man who might or might not be Nico Gordon, who was walking towards the till. Julia allowed herself a peek. The mystery man was almost full face in her direction, although he wasn't looking at her. She studied him carefully. He was similar to the man in the photograph, that's for sure, but was he the *same* man? She couldn't tell. Hayley would know, of course. If only she was here. Or if she could just get a photograph. She reached her hand into her bag and felt for her phone. There might be a way.

He had paid now. The cashier put his goods – the tyre iron and rope, as well as a roll of heavy-duty duct tape – into a carrier bag. As he came towards her, she slipped into the aisle between the paint cans, her phone in her hand. Perhaps if she pretended to photograph the paint tins, or something. She fished for her glasses so she could unlock the screen.

Too late. He was out of the door. She put down the wood glue and followed him out, the wraith of a salesman staring balefully after her.

The mysterious Maybe-Nico was on the move, back towards Second Chances. Julia ducked her head as she passed the shop, hoping that Wilma and Diane wouldn't spot her. At the exact moment she passed the window, Diane looked up, her mouth a surprised 'O', but Julia couldn't stop. She was tailing the man. As they passed the bakery, the warm sweet smell of fresh pastries made her mouth water with desire. *A chocolate croissant would be nice*, she thought. *Or perhaps an apple Danish.* She remembered that she had a sandwich in the little fridge at the back of the shop. A nice one, egg and lettuce, home-made, but perhaps not as nice as an apple Danish.

She was so busy pondering her choices in the category of baked goods, that she almost walked straight into her quarry, who had stopped in front of the police station. Julia walked past him and made her way to the bench where just days ago she'd spotted Walter Farmer having a sneaky ciggie. She watched the birds on the bird table squawking and fighting over a crust of bread. From the corner of her eye she could see the man who might be Nico Gordon watching the police station, his hands on his hips. He seemed to be making a decision. His tough, rather ugly face seemed soft and sad and his chest puffed up and then out in a long slow exhale. He made his decision. He walked into the police station.

'Julia!' It was Nicky, with little Sebastian in tow. 'What are you doing here?'

'Looking at the birds,' said Julia quickly. 'What are you doing here?'

'Oh, wouldn't you know, there was a bumper bashing over on Flannery Avenue, and the man didn't stop. Smacked into the back of some poor old fellow in a hundred-year-old Morris, green it was. Admittedly going about five miles an hour but still, look where you're going, why don't you? Anyway, I was on the way to school with Sebastian, and I saw the whole thing. Got his licence plate. I'm going to hand it over to the authorities. That'll teach him. I'm in a rush though, I've got an appointment down in the village, and it's almost noon—'

'Where's naughty Jake?' Sebastian asked, interrupting the torrential flow of his mother's words. Quite a feat, in Julia's view.

'Jake's at home, love. You must come and visit him, he'd like that.'

'Can I, Mum?'

'Of course. Sometime. But right now I need to go and talk to one of the police.'

Through the door, Julia saw Maybe-Nico on a chair in the

waiting area. She was almost sure she could see the shadow of Roger Grave through the frosted window to Hayley's office. If the shadow was anything to go by, his feet were up on the desk.

Maybe-Nico was the only person in the waiting area. Why was he there? What did he want? Did he have a parole officer or some such to see? If only she could hear.

Nicky tugged at Sebastian's hand.

'Mum... I need a wee...'

'Didn't you go before we left home like I told you?'

He shrugged.

'I'll take him to find the loo and wait outside while he goes,' Julia said, brilliantly happening on a solution that would help Nicky get to her meeting on time, and let Julia eavesdrop on the conversation in the station.

'Good one, thanks,' Nicky said.

It was all Julia could do not to stare at the man waiting on the row of plastic chairs. In her peripheral vision, she saw his knee bobbing up and down in a nervous manner. Nicky sat down a few chairs away from him. A second glance in the direction of Hayley's office confirmed Julia's suspicions. She could make out the outline of Grave with his feet on the desk – he certainly wasn't out investigating anything.

The door to the restrooms led off the waiting area.

'Come on,' she said to Sebastian, opening the door for him.

'I can do it myself, wait there,' he said imperiously, and then added, 'Please, Auntie Julia.'

'I'll be right here,' she said with a smile.

'How can I help you?' Cherise, the desk sergeant, asked Nico.

He came up to the counter just as a young policeman came through the door behind the desk sergeant. The second man called Nicky.

Julia was trying to catch what Nico was saying, but it was hard to hear because Nicky was telling the car story all over

again, word for word, it seemed, because Julia overheard...
'Smacked into the back of some poor old fellow in a hundred-year-old Morris...' Despite the carrying quality of Nicky's voice, Julia managed to catch another voice over hers.

'I'm afraid DI Gibson is not at work today.'

Julia abandoned her pretence of not listening and whipped round to see Cherise addressing the round-headed man. 'What's it in connection with, sir, could someone else assist?'

'No, I need to talk to her in person,' he said. 'When will she be back?'

'She'll be out all week, I'm afraid. At least a week, I think.'

Nicky's voice cut over them. '... I saw the whole thing. Got his licence plate...'

'No, no message. Could you perhaps give me DI Gibson's phone number?'

'... That'll teach him...' Nicky said, with satisfaction.

'I'm afraid I'm not at liberty to give out personal information about police officers, sir.'

'As I said, it's a message that needs to be delivered in person.'

Sebastian burst into the room. 'All done!' he said proudly.

'I'll have to come back,' the man said dully to the desk sergeant. 'When are you expecting her?'

'I have to make a written statement,' Nicky called to Julia, her voice tinged with self-importance.

Julia took Sebastian's little hand in her own trembling one, and said, 'We'll wait outside. We'll go and see the birds.'

Julia hurried out, aware of the man at the counter behind her abandoning his mission to see Hayley Gibson. She positioned herself at the bird feeder and got out her phone. A couple of starlings swooped down and tore into what was left of the bread. As they did so, the man who now seemed almost certain to be Nico Gordon, pushed the glass doors open and came out. He rubbed his hands over his face and gave a sound between a groan and a sigh.

'Let's get a nice picture of the birds for Mummy,' said Julia, raising her phone. Nico Gordon's round, pale moon of a face with its wide, flat nose, filled the upper half of the screen, above the flutter of starlings fighting over the crust. Julia clicked and clicked again.

'There we go, I think I've got it,' she said, smiling down at the little boy at her side.

12

'It is him, right?'

'It's him. Look at his eyes,' Hayley said, her eyes scanning Julia's phone screen, and then flicking back to her own phone for comparison. 'Although you're right, he looks different. It's the nose. It looks as if it's been broken.'

'He must have broken it in prison. Or had it broken.' Julia sickened at the thought of a fist connecting to the fragile bone, the septum splintering under the punch.

'Yes. It's definitely him. Five years older, and with a broken nose. Have to say, I'm impressed at your investigative skills. Tailing someone undetected isn't easy for an amateur, let alone getting a photograph,' Hayley said. There was a wistful edge to her voice, as if she would like to have been out in the world tailing and photographing criminals, instead of in her flat with her foot propped up on a cushion.

'I pretended I was taking a picture of the birds.'

Hayley nodded her admiration. 'That was a genius move.'

'Yes, well, thank you. A bit of luck, too,' Julia said quickly. She was eager to move on to more important topics – like Hayley's safety.

Hayley leaned in closer. 'I recognise that bird feeder, isn't that the one by the station?'

'Yes. That's what I came to tell you about. I'm worried. When I saw Nico, I followed him, and where should he go but—'

'Here we are then!' came the cheerful lilting voice of Rosie, Hayley's younger sister. It had been she who had opened the door for Julia, welcoming the visitor with a big smile entirely at odds with Hayley's pale face, which could be seen glowering from the sofa. When Rosie had retreated to the kitchen to make tea, Hayley had hissed under her breath, 'She's come to *help*. Arrived yesterday, and she's driving me mad already.'

Now, here she was again, a tea towel over her arm, bearing a tray of tea and biscuits which she set down on the table. She poured three cups of tea and handed them round. She offered the plate of biscuits. 'Jaffa Cakes, they were our favourite when we were little, weren't they, Hayley? We only got them on special occasions, of course. What a treat they were! I got some because I thought they'd cheer you up.'

'Thanks, Rosie, I do love Jaffa Cakes,' Hayley said, some of the tension and irritation dissolving from her face. She picked one up and took a bite.

'Remember how we used to eat them, first round the edge, and then separating the sponge from the jam?' Rosie said. She demonstrated, nibbling at the edge of the biscuit with her straight white teeth which were the exact same size and shape as Hayley's, although the sisters couldn't have been more different. Rosie was plump and creamy, compared to Hayley's leaner build and darker tones. Julia wondered if one looked just like Mum and the other like Dad, or if the difference between them was simply the result of the vagaries of genetic selection.

'Don't let me interrupt you,' Rosie said, into the awkward silence that followed the distribution of the tea.

'Oh, we were just chatting,' Hayley said quickly, with a flick of a warning look that told Julia that their previous conversation was not appropriate for the company.

'Tell me what the doctors said,' Julia said. 'How's the leg doing?'

'They're happy enough. It's healing fine and I don't need to keep it elevated all the time.'

Her foot was resting on a cushion on the floor, rather than a chair, which was progress – if slow progress.

'Any idea when you'll be up and about?'

'I am allowed to move around now. I could probably go—'

'Just a bit, a few minutes at a time, the doctor said,' Rosie chimed in. 'And no weight on that leg.'

'I've got crutches. I'll need them for a little while, they say. Really, I could go back to work, at the desk at least.'

'Oh, you!' Rosie said, giving her sister's arm a playful swot with the tea towel she had carried with her from the kitchen. Hayley cringed from the blow, but in irritation, not in pain. 'Absolutely not! You've been booked off for two weeks, with strict instructions to rest the leg. That's why I'm here. To help you, and to make sure you take good care of yourself. And besides, didn't the superintendent say—'

'Grave!' Hayley spat his name out. 'That man. He won't even let me help out with desk research from *home*. I just know he's messing the investigation up.'

'Rosie, do you think we could get a spot of hot water to top up the tea?' Julia asked.

'Of course!' Rosie got quickly to her feet, eager to be of assistance. She took the teapot and disappeared into the kitchen. Julia heard the sound of the running tap, and leaned forward to speak to Hayley.

'Hayley, we need to talk about Nico Gordon.'

'That we do. What was Nico Gordon doing at the police station? I mean, if he killed Lilian, that's the last place he would be.'

'That's what I've been trying to tell you. I think you're in danger, Hayley. Let me tell you everything from the beginning, and then we need to phone Grave.'

Rosie came back with the teapot.

'Thanks, Rosie, you've been such a help,' Hayley said, with real softness in her voice this time. 'Would you mind giving us a couple of minutes? Julia needs to talk to me about a case. She's a social worker.'

'Of course. I've got to finish unpacking my suitcase anyway. My, but it's a mess in there! You shout if you need me.'

'Will do. Promise. Thanks, Rosie.'

'And thanks for the tea and biscuits,' Julia added.

'No trouble,' said Rosie, with a smile.

As soon as her younger sister left the room, Hayley spoke. 'She's always been such a helper, that girl. From when she could walk, it was like she's been trying to make it up to me for being born. Makes me feel bad, I was so resentful of her as a child.' Julia was quite startled – this was possibly the most personal sentence that Hayley had ever uttered. But before Julia could ask more, Hayley seemed to pull herself inwards again. 'Right, tell me everything, from the top,' she said.

Julia started the story from the moment she spotted Nico through the window of Second Chances, and set off after him, tailing him through the village.

'He didn't spot you?'

'No. It was busy. Nice day, a few people out. I followed him into the hardware shop.'

She hesitated a moment and told Hayley about his purchases.

'A tyre iron?'

'A long metal thing with a flat end. I googled it, it's used for—'

'I know what a tyre iron is, and what it's used for. It just seems odd.'

'I've been thinking, Hayley. A tyre iron and a rope. That's the shopping list of someone with bad intent, if you ask me.'

'Let's not jump to conclusions. There could be another explanation,' Hayley said, although her voice sounded unconvinced.

'Let me finish my story,' Julia said. 'So after he left the hardware store, I trailed him all the way to the police station, and inside.'

Hayley looked thoroughly bemused by this turn of events. 'It doesn't make sense. Why would he go into the police station if he killed Lilian?'

'I don't know. But, Hayley, the thing is, he was asking for you.'

That stopped Hayley.

'For me? And what does he want with me?'

'He said he had a message for you, one that had to be delivered in person. All I can say is, I don't like the look of this situation. I agree it seems crazy for him to go to the police station. But if Nico killed Lilian, I think you are in danger.'

Hayley's pale face went a shade paler. She shifted uncomfortably in her chair, rattling the teacups in their saucers.

'But he was going to deliver this message there in a police station, where there are actual police who would nab him in a minute if he tried anything.'

'Maybe he's so angry he doesn't care about the consequences.'

'That would be unusual for a newly released prisoner. And as for the tyre iron, what was he going to do, smack me with it? It's not exactly the ideal weapon.'

'It's clear that he doesn't have access to a gun. He's winging it, as far as weapons are concerned. Lilian was killed with a steak knife.'

'Now, Julia, let's not get ahead of ourselves. As far as we know, there is no evidence at all to link him to Lilian's murder.'

'That's why we need to get this info to Superintendent Grave asap,' Julia said, cringing somewhat at the term asap, which wasn't really her. 'He can cross-check his fingerprints with the murder scene. Get in touch with Nico Gordon's parole officer. Muster the resources of the British Police to get to the bottom of it.'

Hayley sighed. 'All the things I could do myself if I wasn't on the bench like some lame duck,' she said. 'A literal lame duck. And with a stern warning from Shallow Grave to keep my nose out of the investigation.'

'We have to tell him that Nico Gordon's in town, and that he was looking for you... It's not interfering in the investigation, it's just what I happened to see, as a concerned citizen out and about in Berrywick. And, Hayley, the fact is you are in danger. You need protection.'

'I'll make the call, tell him you came to me with the information. Tell him everything I know.'

'Right, do it now,' Julia said.

'He probably won't be in the office though,' said Hayley. 'And they certainly won't give me his mobile.'

Julia thought about the shadowy Grave, so at home in Hayley's office and so clearly not doing much work.

'I'd put good money on him being at the office,' she said, making an executive decision not to worry Hayley any more than necessary.

13

Driving home, Julia's brain was occupied with a hundred questions and worries. Her biggest worry was Hayley's safety. Hayley had phoned the station, but Superintendent Grave was not taking calls. Or, perhaps more accurately, he was not taking calls from DI Hayley Gibson. Hayley left a message with the desk sergeant and sent Grave a text message, both asking him to please phone her urgently.

'I'm sure he'll ring me back any minute.'

Julia wasn't so sure. There were a lot of things she wasn't sure about, including Superintendent Grave. What was up with him? Why was he cutting Hayley out of the investigation? Was he even investigating? Was it, as Hayley believed, that he didn't want to share the glory when the case was solved? Or was there some other explanation?

She had come to no useful conclusions by the time she arrived home. As always, she felt a sense of peace in her homecoming. The little house was so dear and pretty, so welcoming and safe. The summer garden was positively riotous with blooms and the bees that attended them. And her faithful animals were always eager to welcome her home.

Julia went straight to the kitchen. She opened the door out to the garden and called, 'Hello, Jakey, I'm home.'

She was starving. A rummage in the fridge turned up a cold sausage, a bit of good cheddar, and a handful of little tomatoes which, together with a slice of sourdough bread, made an excellent meal. She had a funny, discomfited feeling of being watched. She remembered what Lilian's husband, Charles, had said, that he'd felt someone watching him, and seen someone hanging around his and Lilian's house. She glanced up from buttering the bread to see Jake observing her from the door, willing her to share the sausage. 'Oh, there you are. You'll get a bit, don't worry,' she told him. 'You wouldn't believe the day I've had. I've had nothing but a Jaffa Cake since breakfast. The nice egg sandwich I made for my lunch is still in the fridge at Second Chances.'

There she was, explaining herself to the dog. Classic batty old lady behaviour. But she did have some explaining to do – to Wilma and Diane. She sent Wilma a text message, apologising for running out, and giving a vague sort-of explanation that something rather urgent had come up, and she had had to dash.

Sitting at the kitchen table, she cut a slice of sausage for herself and one for Jake. She held it out to him, where he hovered in the doorway.

It was not like Jake to be so reticent when it came to snacks. He was more of a snatch-your-hand-off sort of eater. If a sausage was in the offing, he might take your arm too.

'Come on, here's yours.'

He sloped in, with a quick look back to the garden. Behind him – much to Julia's astonishment – strutted Henny Penny. The visitor's beady little eyes darted left and right, checking out the kitchen with interest. Jake looked at the hen, and then at Julia and the sausage.

'Both of you, out,' she said, holding out the sausage and leading Jake to the door. He followed her, and Penny followed him. Julia tossed the sausage to Jake, who snapped it out of the air and swallowed it whole.

'Silly boy, you can't even taste it.'

Penny found her own lunch, a snail that had, in turn, been lunching on the tomatoes planted in the pots outside the kitchen door.

'There's a good girl, you eat them all up.' She would bring the hen into the coop later, seeing as she was obviously in no danger from Jake.

Back at the kitchen table, she thought about Charles. Could it have been Nico Gordon hanging about outside his house? Had Walter Farmer got a description of the loiterer? She finished her lunch and phoned the DC.

'Now, you know I can't tell you that, Mrs Bird,' Walter said apologetically. 'It's a police matter.'

'Of course, I quite understand. It's just that I saw Nico Gordon in the village – you know, the man who Lilian and Hayley put behind bars five years ago? He has recently been released. I was thinking it might have been him who was prowling around outside Lilian's house, and him who was behind her death. Taking his revenge. He went to the hardware shop and then to the police station, looking for Hayley. I'm worried he could come after Hayley next.'

'Well, that is rather a coincidence, but you can rest easy on that score. It wasn't Nico Gordon that killed Lilian.'

'It wasn't? How do you know?'

'We've got a suspect in custody.'

'You have? Who?'

'Now, Mrs Bird...'

'Julia...'

'You know I can't give out that sort of information.'

'I understand, but will you at least talk to Hayley about it? She's very concerned, as you can imagine.'

There was an uncomfortable silence on the other end of the

line, before Walter Farmer said miserably, 'I'm in a tricky situation, Mrs... Julia. Superintendent Grave was very clear, the whole investigation is under wraps... We're not to share information with anyone, anyone at all.'

'Even with a fellow police officer? A colleague?'

'Yes, even fellow officers. DI Gibson was mentioned specifically, in fact. But there will be an official announcement tomorrow morning, Superintendent Grave is going to brief the press at the station. It'll be in all the papers.'

No doubt it would, if Grave had anything to do with it. That man loved the limelight, from what she'd seen and heard.

She hoped that Walter was right, that the suspect was behind bars, and Hayley was safe. Anyway, there was nothing to be done this afternoon. She would just have to wait for tomorrow's big reveal.

Trailing about Berrywick after a murder suspect had tired Julia out. She looked at her watch. Quarter to five. She would put her feet up for half an hour, take Jake for a short walk, and then get on with making supper for Tabitha. She woke in the twilight to the sound of knocking. She sat up, sending the book that was lying on her chest crashing to the floor.

Her head was befuddled and her heart racing.

'Coming,' she yelled, staggering to her feet.

Tabitha, as always, arrived with a basket of goodies. A paper packet of red and yellow baby tomatoes from her garden. Half a bottle of Chardonnay from her fridge. A book that she had finished and enjoyed. Julia put a carton of six eggs into the basket in return, and transferred the wine to her own fridge.

'Were you sleeping?' Tabitha asked, taking in her friend's rumpled hair, the creases on her face.

'Just for a moment. I dropped off on the sofa.'

Why, Julia wondered, is it so shameful to be caught napping? Why didn't she admit to her oldest friend that she had more than dropped off, she'd fallen into a deep, heavy slumber for at least half an hour. She pushed her fingers through her hair, fluffing up the flat bit at the back, and then ran her hands over her sleep-creased face. 'Gosh, I haven't even fed Jake.'

'I'm in no rush, just do what you need to do,' Tabitha said, following her out of the kitchen door.

Julia took a scoop of dog biscuits from the tin she kept outside the door, and poured them into Jake's bowl. The rattle of biscuit on bowl drew him out from the bushes. Without so much as a hello to Tabitha, he fell upon his supper snuffling his velvety snout deep into the food. His big pink tongue flashed and his head bobbed, sending pellets all over the place.

'Savouring every morsel, I see,' Tabitha said dryly.

'Oh yes, he's a true connoisseur. A fine palate.'

Tabitha pointed in the direction of the bushes. 'One of your chickens is out. You'd better hang on to Jake.'

Henny Penny strutted confidently towards them.

'No need, he doesn't chase her.'

'The terror of the birds of Berrywick doesn't chase this particular chicken? What, is he scared of her?'

'She is actually the bossiest of the chickens. But it's not that. Jake and Henny Penny have a special relationship. He seems a bit soft on her.'

Henny Penny stood next to Jake and pecked at some bits of pellet that he'd ejected in his enthusiasm for his meal. Jake lifted his head to give her better access to the food, and gazed down at her proudly.

'Weird.'

'Yes.'

Tabitha watched the animals for a few more moments, while Julia picked basil leaves, snipping them off with her fingers. She'd not had time to think about food, let alone buy or make anything. It would be pasta for supper tonight.

The women returned to the kitchen, followed by Jake, and

then Penny. 'Now that's far enough,' Julia said from the doorstep. 'We can't be having the chickens in the house.'

Jake looked at her, and then back at the hen, and then back at Julia, pleadingly. She shook her head. 'No.' Jake sighed, and flopped down on the threshold, his front paws and wet black nose in the kitchen, his shiny chocolate-hued body and his new best friend outside. The chicken hopped on top of him, ruffled her feathers and settled down contentedly.

'Weird,' Tabitha said again.

'Yes, very.'

The basil filled the kitchen with its deep, fresh fragrance, soon accompanied by the smell of garlic cooking slowly in olive oil. The baby tomatoes gave off their own fresh-from-the-plant scent as Tabitha cut them in half. Julia drained the boiling water from the linguine, and tossed everything together with salt and pepper, another glug of olive oil and a grating of Parmesan.

'Perfect,' Tabitha said, twirling the pasta round her fork. 'Nothing better than a fresh and simple pasta. Remember the wonderful pasta we had in Rome?'

They reminisced for a while, turning over old memories of a trip they took together after they'd graduated and before they went off and got jobs and husbands. A precious fortnight, the two young women degreed and unencumbered, exploring, eating, laughing, talking.

'Who would have thought that forty years later we'd still be friends, and living in a village in the Cotswolds?' said Julia.

'I'd have hoped we'd still be friends, but I wouldn't have put my money on village living.'

'I'd have been horrified at the thought. I was such a city girl. I thought I'd be in London for ever. Saving people and changing the world.'

'And yet here you are, living in a charming cottage and raising chickens and basil in the back garden.'

'As you see me.' Julia swept her arm around the room, encompassing the whole scene – their bowls with the last strands of basil-flecked linguine, the twilit rectangle of garden through the open kitchen door, Jake and Henny Penny dozing on the doorstep.

'Well, I thought I would be the first Ghanaian-Welsh woman to win the Booker Prize for my brilliant and genre-breaking novel.'

'And here *you* are, running the library, growing tomatoes, and using your brilliance to smash the opposition at the pub quiz.'

They laughed at themselves, and each other. Their lives might be smaller and their achievements more modest than they'd imagined, but by many measures they were full and rich. Julia experienced one of those rare moments of knowing herself to be happy. With the cottage, the chickens, the basil, the friendships – all of it. It seemed enough, more than enough.

Tabitha interrupted her little gratitude moment. 'Speaking of the pub quiz, I saw on a message on the group that it's still happening tomorrow night.'

'Yes. It seems a bit odd, after everything, doesn't it?'

'"We must carry on," is Albert's view, and I suppose he's right. If we cancel our plans and lose our pleasures and rituals, the bad guys have their way, don't they?'

14

'Turn on the TV. The breakfast news on the local station.'

Hayley's voice came forceful and urgent through the phone, above the sound of the television in the background.

Julia dropped the knife on the plate, next to her half-buttered piece of toast, dashed through to the sitting room and grabbed the remote control. The television flickered to life and Superintendent Grave's narrow shoulders and angular, handsome face filled the screen. The camera zoomed in closer, and Julia saw the tracks of his comb in his sandy-coloured hair. He was standing in front of some sort of lectern in front of a small crowd, the backs of whose heads filled the bottom of the screen. Grave was mid-sentence '... residents of Edgeley and Hayfield can sleep easy tonight, knowing that the arsonist who has terrorised the area for the past month is safely behind bars. This dangerous criminal set fire to four dwellings and outbuildings, causing hundreds of thousands of pounds worth of damage. It is only by great good fortune that the residents escaped with their lives, and no one died as a result of his heinous crimes.'

A photograph flashed across the screen – smoke curling from blackened timbers that lay higgledy-piggledy across the charred remains of brick walls, windows broken, only a chimney stack standing tall and proud above the carnage. It appeared to be the remains of a barn, a horrifying scene of destruction, improbably surrounded by a beautiful Cotswold meadow worthy of a picture postcard, vivid green scattered with white, blue and yellow flowers, a horse grazing peacefully in the distance.

The picture disappeared, to be replaced by Grave's image.

'No effort was spared to track him down. Once it was clear that these were the acts of a determined arsonist, I was personally deployed from District Head Office to lead the investigation last Friday. I'm pleased to say that, less than a week later, and with the good efforts of local police, a suspect is in custody.'

A burble of questions and a few hands arose from the assembled in front of him. Grave held up a palm to silence them. After a pause – seemingly for dramatic effect – he continued. 'I have further positive news on a related investigation.' Grave's smug expression reminded Julia of someone, but she couldn't think who. After a moment it clicked – he reminded her of Henny Penny, after she'd laid an egg.

'The suspect we have in custody is also the chief suspect in the murder of DC Lilian Carson, who was stabbed last week at the Topsy Turnip Inn. DC Carson was involved in the arson investigation at the time of her death, and we have reason to believe that her murder is connected. It is my intention to bring charges against this suspect as soon as we have the evidence required to do so.'

So this was what Walter Farmer had referred to! It wasn't Nico after all, who murdered Lilian. It was this unnamed arsonist fellow.

The questions this time were closer to a roar than a burble. Grave looked over the sea of hands and pointed. A man that Julia immediately recognised stood up.

'Jim McEnroe, the *Southern Times*. What can you tell us

about the suspect? Can you give us a name? Anything about his background?'

'Not at this stage, Jim. I don't want to release any information that might jeopardise the ongoing investigation. Suffice to say that this is a very dangerous, destructive individual, who I'm pleased to say is now off the streets and in the cells of the Berrywick police station.'

It was strange seeing an interaction that she'd seen a hundred times in American cop shows – a scene she thought of as Top Cop Fields Questions From Reporters – and knowing both the top cop, whom Julia had met at the Topsy Turnip Inn, and the reporter, Jim McEnroe, who she had come across in a previous investigation into the death of Ursula Benjamin at the village fete.

Grave looked over the raised hands, but before he could take another question, Jim pressed on with one of his own.

'Are you saying that DC Carson was killed because she was investigating the arson cases?'

'That is our hypothesis at this stage, yes,' said Grave, rather pompously. 'As I said, there are a few i's to dot and t's to cross.'

Jim tried to voice a third question – Julia heard him say something about Lilian's partner, and caught the name Paul Bend – but Grave had moved on to the next journalist.

Question time was overall quite unedifying. Grave stood in front of the cameras and took questions to which he didn't provide much in the way of answers, but he seemed in no hurry to vacate the lectern.

'All the information we are able to share at this time is in the press release that DC Farmer will give you as you leave. I know this is a big story for all of you, so rest assured, I'll keep you updated as soon as we have more.'

She caught a brief glimpse of Walter with a small stack of papers, before the programme switched back to the news anchor who promised 'regular updates on this important developing story', and moved on to the next news item of the day, a large pothole that was inconveniencing motorists on the road between Edgeley and Hayfield.

Julia waited long enough to see a picture of the aforementioned pothole, which was indeed impressively broad, taking up more than half the road. A small gathering of people, as well as a sheepdog, gazed into its centre, which was filled to the brim with water from a recent rainfall. An ancient man in what appeared to be pyjamas and work boots poked a stick into it and lifted it up triumphantly to demonstrate the depth of the hole, grinned up at the camera proudly, then repeated the motion. She made a mental note to avoid the road for the meantime.

Her toast was cold by the time she got back to it, but she smeared on a layer of blackberry jam and ate it anyway while the kettle boiled for tea and then dithered over the bread bin, trying to decide whether or not to have a second slice of toast – on the grounds that the first was not entirely satisfactory, being cold. She decided against it. Instead, she would get on with the day.

Her goal for the week was to sort out her little spare room. She wanted everything spick and span for her daughter Jess, who would be arriving for a visit before the end of the year, she hoped. Jess would be the first visitor to the spare room, whose only occupants so far had been the last few boxes from her move. They lurked behind the bed, still taped up, making her feel mildly guilty whenever she thought about them. She thought about that famous tidy-upper – Marie someone, was it? – who said something along the lines that if an object wasn't useful or didn't spark joy, it should go. It was clear that the contents of the boxes were not essential – she had not missed them in over a year. And it was highly unlikely that anything she unearthed would spark joy. She would open the boxes, pack away anything she needed, or wanted to keep, and give whatever else was in there to Second Chances.

It wouldn't take long, and she would just get down to it. She would sort out the boxes this week, as promised. And the week was drawing to a close, so she'd better get a move on.

Much as she tried to buck herself up, her heart sank at the thought. She felt her resolve slipping. Perhaps another slice of toast and cup of tea would give her the boost she needed to get started. *And started I will get!* she told herself sternly, dropping a slice of bread into the toaster and pushing down the handle. *Before lunchtime*, she added, narrowing down the goal and flicking the kettle for tea. *Or at least I'll have it done before I leave for the pub quiz.* She gave herself a tad more wiggle room.

She was pleased to have negotiated successfully with herself and reached agreement with herself on this task. As the kettle boiled for tea, her phone rang. Not surprisingly, it was Hayley Gibson.

'Isn't Grave just unspeakably annoying? The grandstanding. Honestly.'

This wasn't at all like Hayley. She took her work very seriously, and didn't share frustrations about her colleagues or the police establishment. Also, she almost never phoned Julia. In fact, she never spoke on the telephone if she could help it. A terse text was more her style. But she had more time on her hands now, being booked off work.

'He did seem rather pleased with himself, I must say,' Julia agreed tentatively.

'Lilian told me that she and her partner, DI Paul Bend, were about to make an arrest. They would have done all the groundwork on the arson investigation. And he just stepped in and took the credit. It's...' Hayley struggled for the right word and failed, ending with, 'It's *rude*.'

'Well, the good news is—'

'And he didn't offer any explanation of how they nabbed him. Or what evidence links the suspect to Lilian's murder. It was a total fluff fest!'

'Is that a police term?' It was rather apt.

'No, I just made it up right this moment, especially for Shallow Grave's so-called press briefing.'

'But it's good news that they have the arsonist in custody. And murderer. You no longer have to worry about Nico Gordon.'

'I suppose so,' said Hayley grumpily. 'I just wish... I mean to say... I'm just not sure... Oh, never mind. Okay, bye.'

And with that, Hayley ended the call. From anyone else, this might have seemed rude, but from Hayley it was all perfectly normal.

Julia took a light jacket from the hook by the kitchen door and grabbed the blue-rimmed white enamel bowl of kitchen scraps. She stepped out into the cool morning air to feed the animals. Henny Penny was wandering around the garden free as a bird – so to speak. She seemed to have permanently flown the coop – so to speak. But when Julia unlatched the door of the coop and stepped in, and the potato peelings slithered out of the bowl, followed by a couple of too-soft strawberries and some other odds and ends, the hen dashed in after her to join the fray.

Jake was just as delighted to see his dog pellets. Chickens and Labradors had that in common, Julia thought – they fell upon any morsel of food as if they'd not eaten in weeks. She watched them affectionately, all the little heads and Jake's large one bobbing up and down contentedly.

She sat down at the little outside table and took her mobile phone from the pocket of the light jacket she was wearing over her pyjama trousers. She wasn't procrastinating, she told herself. Just checking her emails to get that out of the way and clear the decks so she could get stuck into the boxes.

HAYFIELD ARSONIST NABBED – EXCLUSIVE DRAMATIC
FOOTAGE!

She clicked through to the Facebook page of the *Southern Times*. It usually served up tales of distinctly local interest. The journalists reported on new shops opening, and old ones closing. Flower shows and fetes. It seemed every second week there was a story about the money raised for charity in a school's Big Walk or raffle. If they were lucky, there might be a mugging or break-in. Last week's big story was of a 'miracle sheep' who had found her way home two weeks after getting separated from the flock. She had travelled tens of miles and safely crossed the A424 to rejoin her friends. It had been, Julia had to admit, a very gripping tale.

But this week, there was a genuinely big local news story. The arsonist who had terrified the villages had been caught – and the *Southern Times* had the video.

Julia clicked on the link and leaned into the screen. A shaky camera had captured a scene.

A still figure in sweatpants and a dark hoodie stands in front of the dark shell of a barn, his hands in pockets. The left side of the barn has burned to the ground, leaving a dark jagged hole. To the right, a wall of blackened planks and a door, still showing flecks of red paint amongst the blisters.

A shout. The figure turns to the source of the shout, not far from the camera to reveal a face – a young man, his mouth open in shock.

'No, no...' he cries, falling to his knees.

More figures come into the frame, shouting.

The young man crouches, his hands covering his head as it shakes back and forth.

One of the figures resolves into a policeman, a baton in his belt. He lunges at the man who is writhing on the floor, crying and screaming. The policeman grabs him and hauls him to his feet. The young man – almost a boy, from what she sees – is babbling and sobbing. It's mostly incomprehensible, but she catches snippets. 'I just wanted to see...' and 'Everyone's fine. It's all okay if everyone's fine...'

The policeman turns to the camera. 'Oi, you, put that away...' he snarls.

The screen wobbles, and the wrestling policeman and sobbing boy tilt to the diagonal.

Their heads disappear from the frame as their feet loom large.

The screen goes black.

15

Tabitha was sitting alone at the table in the corner of the Topsy Turnip Inn when Julia arrived. They caught sight of each other at the same moment, and Tabitha smiled and lifted her hand in a little wave. The place was quiet, and more subdued than the previous quiz nights, which had a happy buzz about them – shouted greetings to new arrivals, joking and joshing of opposing teams, the little crush at the bar to order drinks. *Perhaps it's because I'm early and the place is only starting to fill up*, thought Julia. Although more likely, the hit-and-run, and the subsequent murder of Lilian Carson were on people's minds. They were certainly on hers.

'How are you?' Tabitha asked. Somehow, the way she asked the question made it more than the customary greeting.

'It's weird being back here, I must say. I was just thinking of Lilian, sitting over there.' She gestured towards the empty table traditionally occupied by Team Smarticus. 'And Hayley, the week before. Both of them, now, well...'

'It's awful. Just awful.'

Julia felt the horror of it come rushing back, followed by a flashback of the scene at Lilian's hotel room, the knife, the blood. She shouldn't have come. It was a mistake.

'Good evening, teammates.'

They hadn't seen Sean approaching from the side. She looked up, pleased that he was there.

'How are you?' he said, sitting down next to her. Like Tabitha's, Sean's question carried genuine concern and interest. He knew that she'd been uncertain about coming to the pub quiz at all, and could no doubt read the discomfort on her face. He put his arm across the back of her chair and leaned in towards her. The smell of the fresh, piney soap he used was familiar and comforting.

'I'll be all right once we get going,' she said.

Kevin and Nicky arrived just then, with Nicky in mid-story, as usual. 'So I said to him, "Well, if you're going to be like that about it, I'm not interested," and can you believe, he said, "Suit yourself." Suit yourself? I'm the customer, aren't I?' She stopped her story when she got to the table. 'Hello then, Agatha Quizteam. How's everyone? Did you get the message from Pippa? She can't come. The dog's sick. Or she's as sick as a dog. Or did she say she was sick *of* the dog? Something like that. Anyway, she can't make it tonight. Maybe we can find a stand-in?'

There was a desultory murmur of response. No one felt much like tackling that team management issue.

Julia saw Gina McFarlane, the flirty blonde who had come into the charity shop, enter the pub. *She'd be a willing stand-in,* Julia thought. She'd love the chance to sit next to Sean and laugh at his jokes, and congratulate him when he got an answer right. The woman recognised her this time – unlike the last time they'd met – and gave her a small embarrassed smile and nod before continuing to her own table.

DC Walter Farmer came through the door next, rather to Julia's surprise. He looked at the Team Smarticus table – still empty – and wavered, as if he wasn't sure what to do with himself.

'Walter!' called Julia, waving him over.

He hesitated, and then moved towards her. 'Oh, hello, Julia. I wasn't sure if I still had to come. I was standing in for Hayley, you know. I didn't want to let her down. Or let the team down. But it seems like no one else from the team has arrived. I mean, not Lilian, obviously. Or Monica Evans... And I suppose Felicity thought—'

'I suppose Felicity and the others are too scared to come. It's like the team's cursed, or something, isn't it? First Monica, then Lilian...' Nicky gave a dramatic shiver.

Walter turned pale, and stuttered, 'Well, Monica was a heart attack, it's not as if the curse—'

'Not you, of course. You're a substitute,' Nicky said confidently, as if she knew exactly how curses worked and he was in the clear. Walter Farmer did seem to relax a bit once that was cleared up.

'I'll be going then, if they don't need me.'

'Hang on a minute,' said Julia. 'Pippa's not coming and we need a stand-in. Why don't you join Agatha Quizteam?'

'I don't know...'

'Course you do, come on then.' Nicky patted the seat between her and Julia, and after a moment's hesitation, Walter sat. Kevin, who had been following Nicky's instructions for some years, sent Walter a sympathetic look.

Julia was pleased to see Walter. She liked the chap, sure, but also she had questions. Questions about the arsonist.

She leaned in close and spoke quietly. 'So, you've got your guy on those arson cases. You must be pleased.'

'Oh yes,' he said with a smile. 'It's celebration time down at the station, I tell you. No more fires, I promise you. And no more big brass and local politicians breathing down our necks.'

'Great news. Really, a huge relief for everyone. Well done.'

He took her congratulations with an awkward smile and a flush crept over his neck and up to his cheeks.

'I was thinking about the murders...' Julia said, keeping her tone light and casual. 'How did you tie them to the arsonist?'

'Ah, well, that's Superintendent Grave for you, he's a clever fellow. He made the connection. The timing, you know. DC Carson on the case, and then her being murdered.'

'Yes, yes, that makes sense. It's just...'

'What?' Walter asked.

'Just a hunch. He just doesn't seem like a murderer. He seems unstable and destructive, but not violent in *that* way.'

'That's it though, isn't it? You just can't tell with people. Especially when they're unstable to start with.' Walter Farmer's face was a picture of earnestness. 'That sort of person is unpredictable. And like Superintendent Grave said, you can't just take his mother's word for it. I mean, she's his mum, she doesn't want to believe her son's a killer. Of course she'd say he isn't violent. And as for the alibi, well. It was weak, like Grave said. And he's the senior officer.'

'So there was an alibi?' asked Julia, but their conversation was interrupted by three sharp taps from Albert's gavel on the table.

'Attention, please!' His voice was more tentative than usual, and he had to shout once more before the hum of voices and clinking of glasses died down. He cleared his throat and said, 'I've no doubt you've all heard the tragic news about our pub quiz member Lilian Carson.' A subdued wave of tutting and headshaking spread amongst the crowd.

'It's very hard to... I can't...' He fumbled over his words and then said, 'She will be missed. May she rest in peace.'

'They should hang that man!' came a woman's voice from the pub.

'I second that!' said an answering voice, male this time. Julia turned to see a burly red-faced fellow at the next table. 'Burning those buildings, and all. And then what he did to poor DC Carson.'

'Please...' Albert said weakly, raising his hand. 'It's very... I know we're all... Let's settle down, please. The best way we can honour her memory is to carry on, to be here together and...' His voice tailed off.

The first round commenced in a sombre atmosphere. The usual excited chatter and banter was largely absent, the police-woman's death fresh in everyone's minds. It had often occurred to Julia that people were unable to remain aware of the brutal and transient nature of life for ever, and true enough, by round three the noise level had risen. By round four and five, it was punctuated with shouts of laughter. By round six, there was a loud but friendly altercation about whether a red pepper was a vegetable or – as Albert main-tained – a fruit.

At the end of round seven, Felicity Harbour arrived, looking flustered and apologising. 'So sorry, very sorry. I got held up...' So, she hadn't been scared off by Nicky's assumed curse, then.

Felicity looked at the table that usually hosted her team, and then back at the tables. 'I didn't know if I should come.' She seemed older and frailer than when Julia had last seen her – hardly surprising, given that her elderly husband was serving a sentence for manslaughter. Julia had got to know Felicity during the course of that case, when it had turned out that the local historian was in fact helping the victim, a famous author, with his books.

'I was the same. I didn't want to let Smarticus down. In case. I mean, I didn't know if anyone would be here,' Walter said. 'It was just me, so I'm just sitting in for Agatha Quizteam. Pippa had a dog problem.' He looked mildly guilty, as if his alle-giance to Team Smarticus might be in question.

Felicity hesitated, looking back at the door as if she might flee.

'Do come on in, Felicity,' Albert said, beckoning towards her. 'I'm sure, under the circumstances, we could find a place for you.' He scanned the tables. There was a little buzz as contestants looked at their own teams. Julia imagined that at least a few of them wondered wistfully how they might jettison one of their weaker links in her favour. As a historian, and someone with a wide general knowledge in very many areas, Felicity was a sought after teammate.

'Take my place,' Kevin said, getting quickly to his feet. 'Sebastian is with my mum, and it's a school night, so I should fetch him, really.'

Nicky was briefly and uncharacteristically speechless as she processed the implications of this offer, and judged what her response should be. Julia watched the emotions play briefly over her face as she weighed up the opposing benefits of keeping Kevin at her side, and gaining a valuable team member for the rest of the night.

Felicity hesitated, and then said, 'Well, I suppose, if you're sure.'

Kevin nodded. Julia could sense his restrained eagerness to escape the quiz. He'd presumably been dragged there by the more forceful Nicky – a statement that, from what Julia had heard, seen or surmised, held true for their relationship, from the first date, to the trip down the aisle, and for much of their subsequent decision-making.

'Well, all right then,' said Nicky reluctantly. 'I'll see you at home. Make sure you remember Sebastian's—'

'Got it, I will.' Kevin gave her a quick kiss on the head, leapt to his feet and headed for the door. Felicity took his seat.

Albert came over. 'Everything all right here? Can we continue with the questions?'

'Yes, sorry I'm so late,' said Felicity. 'I found the garden door open when I came home earlier from the shops. I was absolutely sure it was locked. I always lock it. I think someone might have broken in, and I had a weird feeling that someone had been in the house.'

'Ooooh,' said Nicky, with a shudder. 'Had they?'

'I'm not sure.'

'I hope nothing was stolen?' asked Julia, not that she could imagine how one might tell. She had visited Felicity a few times, when the author Vincent Andrews had been murdered on his book tour, and knew that the place was chock-full of books and objects, layer upon layer of them on every shelf and surface. A few missing bits and pieces would be impossible to spot.

'That's why I was late. I was checking. Nothing obvious. I have a lot of artefacts and specimens, you know, some of them quite valuable.'

'Like what?' Nicky asked, rather rudely, Julia thought.

'Some early Saxon tools that Harry found with his metal detector, Stone Age flints, and a number of rare first editions, a small oil painting, which I believe is by a fairly well-known Renaissance painter, although Sotheby's disagrees.'

Nicky looked disappointed at the exceedingly dull nature of Felicity's alleged treasures.

'Maybe I was mistaken about the break-in. As far as I could tell, everything seemed to be there. Thank heavens my laptop was still there with the new book half finished, the one on the gang activity from the turn of the century until the 1980s, and all the research notes, except for the ones that Monica was working on, of course.'

There was a brief moment of silence for the late Monica. Albert cleared his throat, eager to get back to the business of the quiz.

'Which reminds me, I must get those back,' said Felicity

absent-mindedly to herself. 'I don't want them thrown away. They must be in her house.'

'Actually, her cousin came to the village to sort out her things. She brought a lot of her personal things to Second Chances,' Julia answered. 'But she left all her work papers with DC Carson. Lilian lived next door. She'd promised to find out who might need them and hand them over, but, of course...'

Now the ghost of Lilian Carson descended on the table. Not the actual ghost, obviously, but a quiet sadness at the thought of the young woman's death.

Albert cleared his throat again.

DC Walter Farmer patted Felicity's hand. 'I'll speak to Charles Carson and see if I can get them back for you,' he said. 'I can pick them up and bring them straight over.'

'Would you?' She smiled. 'I'd be very grateful.'

'Round eight, everyone,' Albert shouted over the chatter.

16

Julia watched the video for a fourth time, focusing on the last part in particular, the man-boy crying and screaming on the ground, babbling and sobbing. She listened to the snatches of his words: 'I just wanted to see...' and 'Everyone's fine. It's all okay as long as everyone's fine...'

What did he mean? That no one was hurt in the fire? She thought back to the press conference. As far as she recalled, that was the case – no deaths or injuries. Was that just dumb luck? she wondered. She considered phoning DC Walter Farmer, to pick up on their conversation of the previous evening. She wanted to know more about what the young man's mother had said about his mental state and his alibi. Would Walter talk to her? There was only one way to find out.

Julia picked up her mobile and phoned Walter.

'Hi, Walter. I was thinking about the arsonist. You mentioned his mother...'

'I didn't mean to. I shouldn't have said a word.' Walter sounded like he might cry, not for the first time in Julia's acquaintance with him. 'Superintendent Grave is very strict about what we say.'

'There's nothing to worry about, Walter. You didn't give me any information, and besides, I'm not going to mention it. It's just, I was wondering...'

'Mrs Bird...'

'Julia.'

'I can't tell you anything more. Not that there's anything more to tell.'

'Well, the thing is, I don't think that he was the killer. Lilian's killer. Hear me out, please.'

'No. No, Mrs Bird. I can't talk to you about this. Superintendent Grave was very clear. I have to go. Goodbye.'

Frustrated Julia decided to try another line of enquiry.

Jim McEnroe answered on the second ring. 'Hey, Julia, how are you doing?'

'Very well, thanks, Jim.' There was a brief awkward pause. The two of them hadn't spoken since the aftermath of a rather frightening run-in with a murderer who was trying to seduce Jim, and they weren't exactly call-for-a-chat friends.

'I saw the press briefing on the arson case, and spotted you there, and I thought I'd give you a call.'

'Well, it's good to hear your voice. Yeah, the arson case. What's your connection?'

'Oh, just an interested local, really.'

'Uh-huh.' He said it with exaggerated scepticism.

'Well, to be honest, Jim, I have some doubts about the man's involvement in Lilian Carson's murder. I wondered what was in the press pack, and what else you'd heard. I thought there might be something.'

'You want information from me?'

Julia didn't even try to deny it. 'Yes, Jim.'

'Well, I want something from you too. Let's meet.'

. . .

A large group of birders had taken over three tables of the Buttered Scone. Even Julia, a non-tweeter – or was it twitcher? – could identify them by their appearance and habits. Their colouration was distinctive. They were kitted out in sombre earthy tones of brown and green, with sensible walking shoes, also commonly brown. In the winter months, they were adorned with large puffy outer layers to protect them from the cold. In summer, long sleeves guarded against the sun. The female of the species had sensibly cut hair, all the better to spot the birds, Julia presumed. The males were often bespectacled, and even more often bearded. Further clues – and key differentiators from the more common hikers and ramblers – were the presence of high-end binoculars around the neck, and birding books stuffed into pockets or, in this case, laid on the table of the Buttered Scone.

Julia squeezed past a full table of them, catching snippets of conversation – something about 'a Red-crested Pochard in the reeds on the Westerly shore' – and claimed a small table in the corner. She checked her watch. Jim McEnroe was due in five minutes.

'Morning, Julia.' Flo put a menu down in front of her. There was a flyer tucked inside it, printed with a photograph of their daughter, Fiona, and the words 'Vote for Berrywick, Vote for Fiona Johns as Leader!'

'Hello, Flo.'

'I'll bring your coffee. You might have a little bit of a wait for your breakfast. The kitchen is busy with this group's order.' She tossed her head in the direction of the birders.

'Thanks, Flo. I'm in no rush. I'm waiting for someone.'

At that moment, as if summoned by her words, Jim appeared in the doorway and looked around, peering past the flock of birders. She waved, and he came over.

'What can I bring you to drink?' Flo asked, her pen poised

over the little pad she carried with her at all times, either in her hand, or in the pocket of her apron.

'Just coffee, please.'

Jim thanked her and sat down opposite Julia, reaching into his pocket and taking out his phone and a spiral-bound notebook with a pen clipped to it. He placed them next to him at the table, just as he had some months ago, when she'd first met him in the course of another informal 'investigation'. Jim's hair was neatly tied back, and he looked ready to work – it all felt like they'd just met yesterday.

Jim must have felt the same sense of familiarity, the two of them across the table at the Buttered Scone. 'So, here we are again,' he said.

'Yes, indeed. So, you're working on the arson story?'

'I am. It's a big local story.'

'What do you know about that boy, the arsonist?' Julia asked, taking her own notebook from her bag. She opened it and removed the pen that was tucked into the spine.

'He has a name now – Martin Ardmore. And he's twenty years old. The police are keeping pretty tight-lipped about him, beyond that, but I've found out a few things.'

He paused, pushing an escaped hair back from his thin face. His expression was serious – and expectant. *Ah*, thought Julia, *I see, we're trading*. It was her turn to give him something.

'I watched the video of the arrest. I think he has problems. I think he's the one who set fire to those buildings, but I'd be very surprised if he killed Lilian.'

'What makes you say that?'

'From a psychological point of view, it's a very different crime. The impulse to start the blaze, the desire to watch a building burn – it's very specific. Finding and stabbing the investigating officer, in order to avoid arrest, that's something else entirely. Killing Lilian is too direct, thought through, premeditated. I don't think Martin—'

'Marty, he calls himself.'

'I don't think Marty Ardmore killed her.'

'Because you think the two crimes are too dissimilar?'

'Yes, that and what I saw on the video. His whole demeanour seemed distraught and anxious. He was all over the place. I don't see him planning and committing a murder to protect himself. And then there's what he said, something like, "Everyone's fine. It's all okay as long as everyone's fine." It was as if that's what he was concerned about. That no one was injured in the fire.'

Jim nodded. 'Okay, what you say makes a certain amount of sense. Let's watch it again.'

He fiddled with his phone until it brought up the YouTube video. He turned the sound down low, so as not to disturb the birders, and they watched it together. Despite having watched the video a number of times, Julia felt disturbed by the boy's obvious trauma, his writhing and sobbing. She leaned in to hear his words:

'I just wanted to see...' and 'Everyone's fine. It's all fine...'

The video ended, and Jim turned off the screen.

'And when he said, "I just wanted to see." What do you think that means?'

'He wanted to see the scene of the destruction, I suppose. That was the barn that burned last week. It's not uncommon, returning to the scene of the crime or the disaster. Either to appreciate it, revel in the devastation, or to heal somehow, to come to terms with something.'

'Hhhm,' he said. 'Okay, well, I must say, I tend to agree with you. The kid looks like a bit of a nutter, really.'

'Well, I wouldn't say that...'

The younger man waved her objection away. 'Disturbed then. If we're going to be PC about it.'

'Agitated, certainly.'

'Right. Not like someone who could – or would – track down a police person and kill her in order to avoid arrest.'

Flo put their coffees down on the table, and looked rather alarmed to catch the tail end of the conversation.

'Poor Lilian. She was a regular here, you know. I was just saying to Albert this morning what a shock it was. To think we'll never see her here again. Or anywhere for that matter. Thanks to some murderous maniac, right here in our little village. Poor Albert was quite upset, too. He's usually rather a stoic sort, but he got quite teary about Lilian, he did, and told me he didn't want to hear any more about it. Couldn't bear it. He had to go off for a walk to calm down, poor chap. Anything to eat?'

'No, thanks,' they answered in unison, eager to get back to their conversation.

There was a scraping of chairs and clattering of cups and saucers as the birders got up to leave.

Julia watched them go – no doubt to alight in some marsh or field, where they would settle in an orderly flock for the rest of the morning – and then got quickly back to the job at hand. Which was to press Jim for information. 'So,' said Julia. 'Marty Ardmore. What do we know about him?'

'Not a lot. Lives locally, on the outskirts of Edgeley with his parents.'

'And what do you know about them?'

'I've only just started working on the background story, but I've found out a few things, mostly on social media. Zero privacy settings, of course.' He shook his head sadly at the naivety of the older generation. He picked up his notebook and flipped over a couple of pages. 'His dad, Dominic, is an engineer. Works all over. Dubai, Egypt. One or two posts about the family, but mostly golf and engineering. His mum doesn't seem to have a social media presence, but I did find out her name. It's Molly. Molly Ardmore. What do you know?'

'Walter let slip that the boy's mum denied the murder vehemently, she claimed he had an alibi, but the police – or, I think I should say Grave, because he's the one running this show on a very tight rein – didn't believe it.'

'What was the alibi?'

'Walter clammed up at that point. I probed for more, but he stood firm.'

'Are you thinking what I'm thinking?'

'If you're thinking it's time to call on Molly Ardmore, then, yes, Jim, I'm thinking what you're thinking.'

He nodded and raised his hand to get Flo's attention and the bill.

17

The Ardmores lived in a large barn that had been converted into a very large house. It sat at the end of a gracefully curving gravel driveway, amidst meticulously cut lawns edged with deep flowerbeds. Julia parked next to a bed of hydrangea bushes as tall as her little car and covered with blooms the diameter of the steering wheel. The two of them got out, and Julia let Jim lead the way to the enormous front door with a floor-to-ceiling plate-glass windowpane either side. Jim bounded eagerly up the three steps to the door, but she hung back. Some combination of the size and perfection of house and grounds, and the unofficial nature of her mission, made her feel awkward. Jim, at least, was doing his job. She was just a nosey retired lady tagging along.

Her anxious ruminations were cut short by the appearance of the lady of the house, who had opened the door before Jim had even rung the bell.

'Can I help you?' she said brusquely.

'Mrs Ardmore? Jim McEnroe, I'm a reporter with the *Southern Times.*'

'No.' The huge door made its slow way back to the door

frame, eclipsing their brief view of the thick Persian carpets on the floor of pale, broad wooden planks.

'We think your son is innocent,' Julia said quickly, into the small gap between door and frame, just before it closed. The gap widened enough to reveal Molly Ardmore's face. She was a pale-skinned ash-blonde, with grey-blue eyes and small, even features.

Julia continued. 'Innocent of the murder, at least. We don't think Marty killed Detective Constable Carson. May we come in?'

Mrs Ardmore opened the door and stepped back to give them entry. She was shorter than Julia and slim, dressed in soft trousers and a silk shirt in the same pale-silvery tones as her hair and eyes. She looked like someone from an advertisement, perhaps for a ruinously pricey Scandinavian skincare brand.

Julia wiped her dusty walking shoes on the doormat, surveyed the pristine interior, gave them an additional wipe for good measure, and followed Molly Ardmore in. Two King Charles Spaniels yapped excitedly at their heels. 'Sorry, they get a bit excited with company,' she said. 'Shush, now, George. Maggie.' She addressed the little dogs, calmly and quietly. Rather surprisingly, they obeyed and sat down at her feet in silence. Julia imagined what success she'd have with Jake in a similar situation. The answer was none, of course.

They sat in the kitchen, which was the approximate size of Julia's entire house. Light streamed in from enormous windows and imbued the room with a golden glow. It struck Julia that everything about the place was vast, from the hydrangea blooms and the front door, to the enormous iceberg of a centre island with its big bowls of lemons, tomatoes and peppers, to the Aga the size of a small car. She imagined that there must be an equally outsize inheritance somewhere, or the Dubai engineering business was doing massively well.

Jim and Julia sat at the eating area at the end of the island.

Molly Ardmore brought them small bottles of Italian sparkling water from the fridge – double-doored and huge, of course – and offered them glasses, ice and slices of lemon. She didn't speak until they were all seated, their drinks in front of them.

'What are you looking for, specifically?'

'I'm writing about the arson case for the local paper,' Jim said. He didn't mention Julia's role, which was rather more difficult to explain. 'I wanted to get your experience of it, hear your family's side of things.'

'My family's side of things. Well, I'm not sure we have a side. Something of an explanation, I suppose. For Marty. For his behaviour.'

Molly Ardmore was quiet for a moment, as if deciding what to say next, and then continued. 'I will speak to you for a story, on certain conditions. It will be off the record, for now. I'll need to approve anything you write from what I tell you this morning. I need your word.'

Julia saw a pained look pass fleetingly over Jim's face, but he nodded his assent.

'You have my word.'

She stared out into the garden. The silence built. Julia waited, resisting the urge to break it. She sensed a similar pent-up energy from Jim. Finally, the woman spoke.

'He's not well.'

Another extended silence filled the great white kitchen.

'But he's not a killer.'

'I believe you,' Julia said. 'I watched the video of his arrest. His response. What he said. I don't think he killed Lilian Carson.'

Molly Ardmore's shoulders relaxed a little. 'Thank you. Finally, someone is listening. I tried to tell the police, but that superintendent wasn't interested in what I had to say. He seemed convinced that he "had his man" as he put it. He was just waiting for the forensics to prove it. Well, they won't prove it. Because it wasn't him. Marty would never do something like that.'

'But the fires...' Jim said.

'Yes, I admit that he lit those fires, I'm not denying that, but that doesn't mean... I know it's hard to believe, but the fires... They are something different. A compulsion. He has these compulsions. Always had, well, since he was three or four. Tics. Repetitive behaviours. He's had years and years of interventions and treatments, we've tried it all. Everything from psychiatrists to equine therapy to body stress release to the keto diet.'

'Did anything help?' asked Julia.

'Yes, for a bit. This thing or that thing seemed to relieve his symptoms or help him focus or dampen down the tics, or whatever. But he was always just... different. He was never just an easy, normal kid. He was edgy, anxious, odd. But not troublesome, or violent.'

'So what do you think changed? Why did he start the fires?'

'I don't know where that came from, he's never been destructive like that. Not to that degree. And we thought things were better. He's been doing a course at the local college on business admin, and we thought he was really excited about it. Focused. But a month or two ago he started playing with matches. Just striking them and putting them out. It was one of his weird little habits. He didn't burn anything, just lit the match, let it flame for a minute, and then shook it out. It was a little odd, but not *dangerous*. Not *destructive*. And then the fires... I read about them in the papers, but I didn't know it was him, of course. Never thought for a minute... Not until the police arrested him.'

Molly's grey-blue eyes brimmed with tears. She brought the knuckles of her forefingers to her eyes and carefully wiped under her lashes, drying the tears without disturbing her mascara. She sniffed and lifted her chin, saying with calm determination, 'But I assure you he did not kill that police officer.'

Jim did his best to keep his expression neutral, but Julia could see that he wasn't completely convinced by the mother's protestations. As for Julia, well, what Molly Ardmore said aligned broadly with her own instincts when she'd seen the video – that Marty was definitely disturbed, but he wasn't the killer.

'He wouldn't kill a woman with a knife,' Molly continued. 'I promise you that. Marty can't swat a fly. Literally, he's incapable of doing it. He can't even bear the sight of blood. I cut my finger on Monday, peeling potatoes, and when he saw it he nearly fainted. He had to sit down with his head between his knees.' She held up her left hand. There was a Band-Aid wrapped around the tip of her index finger, her pale-pink painted nail peeking out of the top of the plaster. 'Do you understand what I mean? That there's a difference?'

Julia nodded. Molly's lips twitched in a small smile of relief.

'Okay, so let's assume you're right, he didn't do it. Where was Marty on the night of the murder? That would be...' Jim flicked back in his notebook. 'The police report says between nine and midnight last Thursday night. Does Marty have an alibi for that night?' Jim asked.

'Yes, he was with me and his father. Dominic – my husband, Marty's dad – came home from Dubai that evening. We ordered in from Mi Sushi. It's our favourite treat. Marty and Dominic both order the mixed sushi and sashimi platter – they never deviate – and I get the salmon rolls. Dominic picked it up on his way from the airport, and we ate it at home together. After supper, Marty went down to the pub to meet a friend for a drink. He was home an hour and a half later.'

'You told that to the police?'

'I did. That man said he didn't take a mother's word as an alibi. I asked him to look into it for himself. I told him about the sushi and the pub. He said he'd get one of his officers to come and take a statement and follow up. No one has been yet.'

'Which pub did he go to?' Jim asked.

'The Ball & Claw. It's our local.'

'And who was the friend?'

'A chap he was at school with. Jonathan Fern.'

Jim scribbled in his notebook.

'Jonathan has moved to the States, and he was home for a visit. He invited some old school friends to meet up at the pub. Marty doesn't have many friends. I was pleased that he was invited, and that he went.'

Her voice wavered almost imperceptibly when she said that, and Julia's heart broke a little for the woman. She seemed to have everything – buckets of money, good looks, the ultimate barn conversion, obedient glossy dogs, tiny bottles of Italian sparkling water – but it didn't matter. What she really longed for was for her adult son to have friends.

Jim stopped writing and lifted his head to ask, 'How did he get there?'

'He walked, there and back. It's not far.'

'Did you hear him come in?'

'Yes. It was about quarter to eleven. He's not very sociable, so he had one drink and came home. Dominic and I were still awake, we'd just finished watching a movie.'

'So you saw him?'

'Yes, he came in and said goodnight.'

'And he looked fine? His usual self? Nothing unusual?'

'He was fine. He said he had a nice time. He went to bed.'

Julia opened the driver's door and, as she got in, turned back to see Molly Ardmore staring sadly after them.

'What do you think?' Jim asked, slamming the door behind him. Molly raised her hand in a small wave as Julia put her foot to the pedal, the tyres crunching over the gravel. She turned into the little lane before she answered.

'I think she's telling the truth. Or perhaps I should say, she's telling us what she believes is the truth. And I suspect it is. As you know, my instinct is that she's right about Marty not being a killer. Grave is not wrong about the fact that an alibi from a mother isn't exactly watertight, but it would be a simple matter to investigate the Ball & Claw story.'

'Except that Grave doesn't seem in any great hurry to check his alibi.'

'You know what Hayley said. He talks a big game, but is rather slapdash on the particulars. What my grandma used to call "all foam and no beer".'

Jim barked with laughter. 'That's a good one. I'll be using that.'

'I suspect you'll find it quite useful. There's rather a lot of it about. Anyway, I suspect your article will put a bit of a fire under Grave... Oh gosh, a fire, wasn't that a terrible slip!'

'Awful. But I get your point, it will shake things up, I'm sure. On the day that the paper comes out, he'll have a team down at the Ball & Claw before breakfast.'

'Speaking of breakfast, I was thinking...' Julia fell quiet while she waited for a break in the traffic on the main road. She turned left towards Berrywick, and resumed her thought. '... I was thinking that we didn't even get so much as a muffin at the Buttered Scone. I've had nothing but that coffee and Mrs Ardmore's fancy water all morning. I wonder if we might pop along to the Ball & Claw for a bite. It's not half a mile from here, if I remember correctly.'

She glanced over at Jim, who grinned at her and nodded. 'It is indeed. Next road on the right, and about half a mile. Have to say, I am pretty peckish myself. A Scotch egg, that would do the trick. A nice fresh Scotch egg from the pub. And while you get us there, let me see if I can find Jonathan Fern.'

18

The waitress wrote down their order. Her whole right arm, right down to her fingertips, was tattooed in a mesmerising sleeve of flowers, tendrils and insects. It was rather lovely, but still, Julia was pleased that Jess didn't have any tattoos. Well, not as far as she knew. For two years, she'd only seen her daughter from the shoulders up on the screen of her iPad. Who knew what happened below the shoulders? The thought made her sad, but the waitress's voice jolted Julia out of a slide into melancholy.

'Anything to drink?'

'Water for me, thank you.' She peered at the girl's name tag. 'Thank you, Lily.'

Jim ordered a ginger ale. 'And we'd both like the Scotch eggs, please.'

'I'll be right back with the drinks.'

While she was gone, Jim continued googling Jonathan Fern, narrowing his search to the area, and then trying to find possible Jonathans, or Ferns, of an appropriate age, and whose phone numbers were available on the net. After a couple of false starts, he found a number that was answered by the young man's mother, who told him that Jonathan had left that very day, and was on an aeroplane back to Chicago.

Jim thanked her, and ended the call.

'Well, that's bad timing. I'll try to get him later, or tomorrow,' Jim said with a sigh. The waitress arrived back with the tray of drinks.

'There you go, a water for you, and a ginger beer for you. Your Scotch eggs won't be long, they're in the fryer. We fry them fresh here, not like some places that serve them freezing cold from the fridge.'

'Gosh, freshly fried, that does sound good,' said Julia. 'Have you worked here long?'

'About a year and a half. I'm studying, so it's part-time. I don't have classes on a Friday, so I work lunch, but it's mostly evenings.'

'I don't suppose you were here last week Thursday?'

'Thursday evening? Yes, I worked Thursday. Why?'

'My friend here is a journalist, and we're investigating a news story. One of the people we're interested in might have come here.'

'Oooh, a crime, is it? What happened? Do tell.' Lily sat down and looked eagerly from Julia to Jim and back again.

'Well, we're not sure at this stage, but we are looking for possible witnesses. We're wondering if you might remember some people who came in.'

'You're asking the right girl. I've got a very good memory for faces. I've always thought I'd be an excellent witness. Not like those people you see on the telly shows who can never pick the right guy from the line-up. I'd be great. But I've never needed to till now. Go on, who are you looking for?'

At this point, Julia realised that she didn't have a photograph of Marty or of Jonathon.

'Jim, can you find a picture of Marty, from the news, or social media, to show Lily? See if she recognises him?'

'Sure,' he said, reaching for his phone.

'Marty Ardmore?' the waitress asked. Jim looked up from his typing and nodded in a stunned sort of way. 'Yes, Marty Ardmore.'

'Well, Marty was here for sure. Him and Jonathon Fern, and a couple of others. Jonathan was visiting from somewhere – Australia, I think, or maybe America – and they were having a bit of a reunion. Anyway, they were a year above me at school, so of course I recognised them. And then, of course, it was in the news about Marty... I couldn't believe it when I heard.'

'Well, we're not so sure about that either. What time was he here, do you remember? And for how long?'

'It must have been about nine, I'd say. And I reckon he stayed an hour or so. They weren't big drinkers. As I recall, Marty only had a beer. And he probably left around ten, maybe ten thirty?'

Jim and Julia exchanged a glance.

The waitress looked over to the bar counter where two plates had been deposited, each holding a golden orb.

'Ooh, the Scotch eggs are ready. You want them while they're nice and warm. I'll be right back.'

A fragrant steam of hot oil greeted them as she placed the plates before them. Julia's mouth watered in anticipation.

'Anyway, Marty left first. The others stayed until closing time. He always was a bit of a quiet one, Marty.'

'What was he like at school?'

'A funny sort of chap. Or unusual, you might say. Marched to his own drum, as the saying goes. He had a bit of a twitch. Usually, the kids would tease someone for something like that, but they mostly left him alone.'

'Why do you think that was?' asked Julia.

'I suppose because he was a sweet enough fellow. Kind, you know. He always had loads of really good snacks – crisps, sweets, big strawberries, donuts and so on, and he would always share.'

It sounded like Molly Ardmore's attempt to win friends for her son, Julia thought with a pang.

'Do you think...' The girl frowned. 'Do you think he did the things they said he did?'

'I would be surprised if Marty Ardmore is a killer,' Julia answered carefully. 'And the fact that he was here when you say he was, makes me even more certain.'

Lily smiled, a sweet smile of relief and satisfaction. 'Well, good. I'm glad he's not a murderer. And I'm glad I could help. Now you get on and enjoy those eggs.'

The Scotch eggs were every bit as good as promised, and polished off in minutes. Jim and Julia didn't hang about. They were eager to get going – Jim to the office to get to work on his piece, Julia home to make sure Jake hadn't dug up the entire garden. As they exited the pub, they ran smack into DC Walter Farmer.

'Mrs Bird! What a coincidence. What are you doing here?' he exclaimed in astonishment. Walter noticed Jim, and she watched the light dawn in his eyes. 'Oh, I see. You were... Oh my goodness. Gosh, well, Superintendent Grave won't be pleased. He said—'

'We've been having lunch,' Jim said firmly. 'What are you doing here?'

'I'm following up on the suspect's claim that he was here on the night of the murder. He said he was having drinks with friends. We've been so busy, what with processing the suspect, and the press briefing, and photographing the sites that I've only now got the chance to come over here and check out the so-called alibi. Tie up the loose ends. Not that Superintendent Grave thinks there's much room for doubt. The mother, you know, well, she would say—' He stopped suddenly, blushed and stammered, 'Anyway, I've said enough.'

'Well, good luck with everything. I recommend the Scotch eggs. Lily will help you, she's lovely. She knew Marty Ardmore at school, can you believe the coincidence?' Julia said.

Julia offered to drop Jim at the *Southern Times* offices, seeing as she went right past. As they pulled into a parking bay outside the building, she felt her phone vibrating in her bag. She'd forgotten to take it off Silent.

'Give me a sec,' she said to Jim, and answered the call.

'Hi, Julia. It's Rosie. Hayley's sister.'

'Oh yes, of course. Hi, Rosie. How are you? And how's Hayley?'

'Oh, she's getting on. The leg is much better. She's got one of those braces, you know, to keep the knee at an angle, so she can't drive. But she's pottering around the house.'

'So glad it's getting better.'

'Well, yes, the leg's improving, but...' she lowered her voice to a whisper, 'not the mood, I'm afraid. I'm a bit worried about that, to be honest.'

'I can imagine it's very hard to keep cheerful, under the circumstances. It's very boring.' Julia felt a stab of guilt. She'd been so busy with her amateur sleuthing around that she'd rather neglected the actual detective. 'I will come and visit.'

'Well, that's why I was phoning. I was wondering,' Rosie said, in a normal volume, 'whether you and Doctor Sean might come for dinner tonight. Just an early one, catch-up with news.'

'Oh, well that sounds nice. I'd like that, thank you. I'll check in with Sean and let you know about him.'

'Super,' said Rosie, with determined good cheer. 'We'll see you at about six thirty, shall we? Hayley will be delighted, I'm sure.'

Delighted was not an adjective often attributed to DI Hayley Gibson, but Julia hoped her visit would at least take her mind off things for a bit and ease the boredom. She never phoned Sean during working hours. There was no point, he had his phone off when he was seeing patients. She sent him a text message.

Invited for supper at Hayley tonight. 6.30. Can you make it?

Jim, by now, was out of the car. He leaned down to her open window and said, 'Thanks for the lift.'

'No trouble at all,' said Julia.

'So, we'll talk if we think of anything or hear anything. Right?'

'Of course.' It seemed they were somehow partners now.

He straightened up and patted the roof of the car in farewell.

Julia turned the key in the ignition and put the car into reverse. As her foot touched the accelerator, she felt a sickening lurch in her gut. The lurch that came with a horrible thought bubbling to the surface of her consciousness.

'Jim!'

He turned around at her call, frowning into the afternoon sun.

'Jim, if Marty didn't kill Lilian, who did?'

He walked back the few steps to the car. 'Damn. I was so caught up in Marty, I hardly thought...'

'Me neither. Oh dear, Jim, I think that Hayley might be in danger.'

19

Jake had not, in fact, destroyed the garden, eaten the outdoor furniture, or got himself into any other trouble as far as Julia could tell.

'Good chap, Jakey,' she said, patting his firm, brown flank and setting him all a-wriggle. 'What a good boy you are.'

Jake looked up at her with his great pink tongue lolling out of the side of his mouth and his little white teeth giving the impression of a grin.

'I'll get everyone's supper, shall I?'

Jake seemed fully in support of this suggestion. His tail bashed against a poor chilli bush in a pot, scattering flowers and leaves. Julia slapped her thigh and he moved a step forward, placing the plant out of range of the tail.

On the kitchen table, her phone was ringing.

Peter.

Julia maintained cordial relations with her ex-husband, but their communication usually took place over text, occasionally longer emails. The tone was friendly enough, but the distance of written communication suited them both. She felt a stirring of worry. Was Jess all right?

'Hi, Peter, is everything all right?'

'Why, yes, of course. All fine. Why did you—'

'Jess, I just, I don't know. Just me being silly.'

'I spoke to her this morning, actually. She was in good spirits. Off to Thailand soon.'

'Yes, two weeks' time, I think.' Julia rather lost track of the timing of her daughter's activities, although she had a firm grasp of the substance. She waited for Peter to come to the point of the call. There was a brief silence, which he broke with that nervous cough he had, and said, 'I phoned her. For the same reason I'm phoning you. I have some news.'

Another little cough. 'Christopher and I are going to get married.'

'Married?' This she had *not* expected. She felt the shock in her chest.

'Yes. Julia, I hope this isn't sad news for you. I realise it might be a shock. I would have told you in person, but—'

'Not at all!' she said, recovering her composure. 'Goodness me, no. I just wasn't expecting it. But congratulations! I wish you all the happiness together.'

'Honestly, Mouse?'

Her heart gave a tiny squeeze when he used his pet name for her, the one he'd coined for her when they were first in love, and which had remained a term of endearment in subsequent years. He'd not used it since their divorce.

'Honestly, Peter. I'm delighted for you both. It was a moment of surprise, that's all. Although, why I should be surprised, I don't know. I have only good wishes and congratulations for you both.'

Not a word of a lie, not one. Seeing Peter with Christopher made her realise the limitations of their own marriage, happy as it was. And she was happy too. Happier, if the truth be told.

'Thank you, Mouse. And I mean, it is a bit of a surprise. At our age.' He gave an embarrassed laugh. 'I never thought I'd marry again. It does seem a bit ridiculous at sixty-three. But it just feels right, for some reason.' He made a strangled sort of noise and squeezed out the words, 'The reason, I suppose, is that we love each other.'

'Well, that's all that matters. You are so clearly happy together. He's a lucky man. As the first Mrs Bird, I can testify to your excellence as a husband.'

'That's very kind of you. You are the first and *only* Mrs Bird, you know, Julia. And you were a wonderful wife to me. I will never not be grateful to you and for you.'

Julia felt unexpected tears spring to her eyes.

'Oh, Peter, that's a lovely thing to say.'

'Only the truth.'

Julia breathed deeply to calm herself, and moved on to practicalities.

'So, what are your plans?'

'Well, there's no point in hanging about. Sixty-three and all. So we thought we'd plan it for later this year. We're looking at autumn. A country wedding. It'll be something small and intimate, just the family and a few close friends – you, of course, and Jess.'

'Lovely. Well, you let me know when and where.'

Her eyes fell on Jake, who was sprawled out on the kitchen floor. The light was getting low and she wasn't wearing her glasses, but he looked a bit... odd. Peter was still talking, but she wasn't listening with a hundred per cent attention; she was squinting and peering at Jake who seemed slightly misshapen. Any aberration as far as Jake was concerned was cause for alarm – that he'd brought in something horrible, or broken something or hurt himself, or invented some new way to get into trouble that she couldn't think of.

Julia looked closer. The lump resolved itself into something chicken-shaped. Not chicken-shaped. A chicken. Henny Penny. Snuggled up against Jake.

'Jake, I said NO chickens in the kitchen,' she exclaimed, causing Jake to scramble to his feet, and Henny Penny to emit a loud squawk followed by a series of clucks. From the phone at her ear came Peter's deep guffaw.

'OUT!' she instructed firmly. And then, to Peter, 'I must go.'

'Well, I must say, things have changed rather a lot for both of us, haven't they, Mouse? You go and roust the animals from the hearth. We'll chat soon about the wedding arrangements.'

Julia considered a glass of wine to settle her nerves. The dog bringing the hen into the kitchen, her ex announcing his marriage, all in one fifteen-minute period. On top of her busy day of amateur sleuthing – or perhaps snooping. It all felt slightly mad and rather exhausting.

She rather reluctantly decided against the glass of wine, knowing she would be driving. Instead she had a cup of Earl Grey tea, which she drank out on the patio while Jake and Henny Penny enjoyed their evening meal.

'What an odd couple,' she muttered under her breath.

Jake looked up from his bowl with a quizzical expression.

'Yes you, Jake, I'm talking about you and Henny Penny,' she added for clarity. 'Where are you going with this relationship, hmm?'

Peter and Christopher were a good couple, but then so had she and Peter been. She felt stirred up and a little sad and something else – maybe grumpy, although she wasn't sure why. She tried to sort through her emotions. It had been nearly two years since she and Peter had separated. She was fine and happy on her own in Berrywick. She had no illusions about their marriage. She didn't hope to get back together with him. Nor did she loathe and resent him. So why was she feeling so strange after his news?

Speaking of couples, where was Sean? She remembered that she hadn't heard from him about supper with Hayley. She went back inside and fetched her phone, which showed a missed call from him, and a message. *Hi, Julia. Sorry, I can't make supper this evening. Let's chat when you get home, or in the morning. Make plans for the weekend.*

Okay. Phone you later. x

She texted Rosie. *Just me this eve. Sorry for short notice. On my way.*

With that, Julia drained her tea, lured the hen into the coop with the promise of a handful of corn – under the baleful stare of Jake – and went in to put on some lipstick and fetch a cardigan 'for just in case' as her mother used to say. Her mother never left the house without a cardi, even in the most sweltering heat. In fact, it was a perfect Goldilocks evening – not too hot, not too cold, just right – but old habits die hard. And old habits inherited from your mother generally don't die at all.

She drove towards Berrywick, which looked particularly beautiful, bathed in the soft glow of the golden evening. The honey-coloured limestone that Cotswolds houses were famous for gleamed luminous. The gardens seemed to zing with colour. She still couldn't quite believe that she lived in such an English fairy-tale village, set in a gorgeous landscape of gentle hills and fields and woods. People came from all over the world to visit, and she *lived* here. She glanced at the river now, and the path that bordered it, where she and Jake walked most days.

The traffic slowed – some hold-up up ahead, presumably, it was just about what qualified as rush hour in Berrywick – and she caught a glimpse of Aunt Edna passing under the elm trees, her layers of clothes and scarves fluttering against her bony frame, her mouth moving, saying who knows what wisdom of nonsense. And there was the Border collie lady, the one with the bouncy black ponytail, and much better dog whispering skills than Julia herself. She felt calmed by the gentle familiarity of it all.

And then, another familiar figure.

Sean?

It was just a flash of a sighting of a man roughly Sean's height and Sean's colouring. He was amongst the trees, but it certainly looked like him. It was strange, though, to see him here. His house and his surgery were on the other side of the village, and he seldom walked this route unless he was with her and Jake.

As she passed him, the trees blocked her view. She wasn't going fast, in fact she was crawling along, but with cars ahead and behind she couldn't stop. She looked in her rear-view mirror and saw him through the gap. Yes, it was definitely Sean. She even recognised his shirt, a blue one with white stripes – it brought out his eyes. And he had Leo standing at his feet, and there was someone else with him. Someone blonde.

Gina McFarlane.

The car behind her gave a polite little toot to alert her to the fact that the traffic had begun to flow. Julia moved the car jerkily forward. She was annoyed to find that her heart was pounding nineteen to the dozen. Her palms damp and slippery on the wheel.

What was Sean doing with Gina McFarlane, the flirty blonde from the pub quiz?

Was this why Sean couldn't come to supper at Hayley's? He had a liaison with Gina?

Of course not.

The thing was, she couldn't imagine a likely explanation for it. Yes, Gina was a patient of his – she'd mentioned a bout of pneumonia the previous year – but that wouldn't explain a riverside amble with him and his dog. And then there was the fact that Gina so obviously fancied him. The 007 jokes. The wide eyes and the tossing hair and the simpering 'Oooh,

Doctor...' comments. That woman was very annoying. There was no way that Sean would be interested in someone so...

The slow stream of traffic stopped and Julia slammed on her brakes just in time to avoid rear-ending the car in front of her.

Concentrate, she told herself, sternly. *Don't be so silly about Sean. And don't be so bitchy about Gina. You're a sixty-something retired professional woman, for heaven's sake, not a love-struck teenager in a jealous panic.*

She had never been the jealous type. Never checked Peter's phone or wondered why he was late back from the office or got hot under the collar when he was seated next to someone beautiful at a dinner party. She wasn't going to start now in what she liked to think of as her late middle age.

But as it turned out, she'd been wrong to trust Peter. Although, admittedly, the eventual affair hadn't been quite what she'd expected.

Anyway, it's a public footpath. It's not as if you caught them in bed together.

Julia shuddered. She wished she'd never thought of that.

The traffic freed up a bit, and they crawled along a little more smoothly. She consciously relaxed her shoulders, and calmed her breathing. That was better. She was going to put the whole thing out of her mind and just get to Hayley's house where she would be greeted with that blissful thing – a meal she had not cooked herself. And see her friend, of course. No more fretting about Sean and Gina. None.

The other thing about Gina though – and this really rankled – was her utter obliviousness to the possibility of Julia as Sean's partner. First she didn't recognise Julia, or remember meeting her at the pub quiz, and then she expressed something close to astonishment that Julia and Sean were together. It was infuriating and – truth be told – hurtful. Julia was a clever, trim, more than averagely attractive woman, she told herself, and it was absolutely...

A jolt and a loud noise brought Julia out of her musings. For an instant, she had no idea what it was. It could have been a meteorite for all she knew. Except that it wasn't. Julia had failed to notice that the van in front of her had stopped and the loud noise was her front bumper connecting with its rear end.

Oh damn and bloody hell, she muttered to herself.

She pulled to the side of the road, as far onto the shoulder as possible, and turned off the car. The van had done likewise and out of it came a huge shaven-headed fellow with a belt full of tools and two arms full of tats. His friend got out of the passenger side. He was a tall skinny fellow with a gormless expression and what seemed to be the almost complete absence of a chin.

She felt a prickle of fear as the two men advanced on her little car. The big fellow was shaking his head. The skinny one was following gormlessly.

Julia got out.

'I'm really so sorry,' she said, in her most calm and conciliatory tone. The tone she'd used on cowering teenage runaways, and boozed up step-dads. 'Let's take a look. Maybe there's not much—'

'Ah, will you look at that,' said the driver, who was now on his haunches between the two cars, his gaze flicking from one bumper to the other.

Julia's heart sank.

'Is it bad?' she asked, craning to peer past his bulky torso to assess the damage herself. 'Gosh, I just lost focus for an instant, it was...'

He stood up and reached for her. She felt the urge to cringe away from him.

'Ah, now, don't you worry, love, you can barely see anything,' he said, laying a large hand on her shoulder in what seemed to be a comforting way. It was rather like having a pound of sausages resting on your shoulder. 'Our van's fine.

There's just a little bit of a scratch there on the left of your bumper. Let's see if we can sort that out for you, shall we?'

He removed his hand, which was a relief, because although his intentions appeared not to be violent, it was quite heavy. He turned to shout to the long chap, who was hovering by the van. 'Oi, Jerry, bring us a cloth, would you? There's a good lad. There should be a shammy in the cubbyhole.'

She could see now that there was a graze of sorts on the top of her bumper.

Jerry arrived and handed over a pristine shammy. The driver got to work, rubbing away at the mark with a circular motion. With each circle, his bicep bulged and released, bulged and released. It was oddly fascinating to watch.

'There you have it. Good as new,' he said, handing the cloth back to Jerry. 'No need to report the accident, I wouldn't think. Seeing as there's no damage done.'

'You are quite right,' said Julia. 'Thank you for getting the mark out, and for being so kind and understanding. It really was my fault, I should have been more careful.'

'Now, don't you feel bad about it,' he said, momentarily placing the pound of sausages back on her shoulder. 'We all make mistakes, don't we, Jerry?'

Jerry nodded wordlessly.

'And no harm done. Now you drive carefully home, love.'

20

Ten minutes later Julia was on the sofa at Hayley's house, nursing a tiny sherry – 'For the shock,' said Rosie. 'Just a wee one.' The shakiness had subsided and as long as she put Sean and Gina out of her mind, she felt calm enough to take in the scene.

Hayley looked much improved. Her colour was better, and her face was no longer fixed in an ashen mask of pain and anger. Her leg was in a shorter cast – it reached to the knee rather than to the hip – and she had a sort of shiny silver orthopaedic walking stick for support instead of two crutches. She was quite nimble on it, and had even managed to fetch the sherry glass from the kitchen.

In contrast to what her sister had said on the phone, Hayley's mood seemed quite buoyant. Julia soon found out why.

'I'll be back at work on Monday!' she announced cheerfully. 'I had to send in a whole load of paperwork, doctor's notes and all that. Ridiculous, honestly. Anyway, I heard this afternoon. Just before you arrived, in fact. My God, I can't wait to get to my desk and get stuck in. I've already emailed Grave to ask him to put me on the Lilian Carson murder case. I know they've made an arrest, but they'll need someone to gather the evidence, make it watertight for the trial.'

'I need to talk to you about that,' Julia said.

Hayley registered her serious tone and matched it with her own. 'What's up? What do you know?'

They both looked instinctively towards the kitchen door. Rosie was inside, humming rather tunefully while she clattered about.

'The guy they've got in custody—'

'The arsonist?'

'Yes. He didn't do it.'

'And you know this how?'

Julia related her collaboration with Jim McEnroe and their visit to the boy's mother, and then the pub.

'His alibi checks out.'

'So it's back to the drawing board,' Hayley said. Julia could almost see her quick, clever brain at work on the next steps. 'If it wasn't him – and we'd need more than just your and Jim's say-so – but let's say it checks out, then we need to look at other suspects. I'll need to go over all the forensics, once I get my hands on them. Repeat some of the interviews. I'd go back to the husband first, make sure he's properly ruled out. Because husbands, you know. And then...'

'Nico Gordon. You know he's been in the village. I saw him myself.'

'That was *after* Lilian was killed. Days after. If he killed Lilian, why would he hang around?'

'Hayley, I do not know the mind of a violent criminal, but I do know that he came looking for you at the police station. And he bought a tyre iron. I think you need to think about that.'

'You are right. It's too much of a coincidence that Lilian was killed just days after he was released. I'll look into the Nico situation.'

Rosie bustled in with a tray holding three bowls – a larger one of crisps, and two smaller ones of olives and a beige dip which Julia thought was probably humus, given the ubiquitousness of the smashed chickpea. 'Here we are! Some nibbles to keep you going. Supper won't be a minute. I've got a lasagne in the oven.' She put the tray down in front of Hayley and Julia.

'Gosh, isn't the sky lovely!' Rosie exclaimed, as she turned to go back to the kitchen. It was indeed. The window opposite them held a vivid rectangle of orange, gold and red, thick swathes of them, like oil paint applied with a broad brush. A scattering of swallows wheeled past, black as type against the glow.

'How magnificent!' Julia stood up and moved to the window to see the full extent of the sky, with the black blocks of the houses opposite silhouetted against it.

She let her eyes wander over the scene, and tried to still her mind of the thoughts of Sean and Gina. And Nico Gordon.

Except she couldn't put Nico out of her mind, because there he was! Right there in the street. It was so outrageously unlikely – Nico Gordon walking slowly down the street at the very moment she looked out of the window – that she thought she must be imagining it. Her brain had somehow come up with the likeness, and the man was someone else altogether. But no. She'd tailed him long enough to recognise his large round head, the stocky body. He was carrying a black shopping bag over his shoulder with something sticking out. She couldn't make out what it was.

'Hayley!' she said, trying to keep the panic from her voice. 'Come here.'

'I can see it from here, it's beautiful, and pink and red and all,' said Hayley, glancing up with disinterest, and then down at the ring bound reporter's notebook she had picked up from the table in front of her. She was making notes.

'I'm serious, come.'

Hayley caught her tone. She held on to the armrests and rocked herself up from the chair and onto her feet. She steadied herself, picked up the walking stick that was leaning against the sofa and walked slowly towards the window.

Julia pointed to the man who was now only a few houses away, and walking towards them. 'It's Nico Gordon.'

'Rosie! Come quickly,' Hayley shouted.

Her sister appeared in the doorway, her face even rosier than usual. On her hands were two large oven mitts patterned with Scottie dogs. 'It's nearly ready, the cheese needs a moment to brown.'

'You need to call the station. Tell them you're with me and they need to send someone urgently. There's a man... I can't explain now. But we might be in danger.'

'*Danger?*' Rosie brought her Scottie-mitted hands to her face in shock. It would have been comical, except that it wasn't.

'He's coming in the gate!' Julia said, from the window. 'Up the path.'

'Do it, Rosie!' Hayley shouted. 'Lock yourself in your bedroom and call the police.'

Rosie hesitated, looking from Hayley to the window to Julia, her wet pink lips slack and parted in confusion.

'The bedroom. NOW!'

She discarded the mitts and ran down the passage, her blonde curls jiggling, her hand scrabbling in her pocket for her phone.

They could hear footsteps and they were getting louder.

'Julia, you too. Go on. To the bedroom.'

Hayley held up her walking stick as if checking it for heft.

'No,' said Julia. 'I'll be here.'

She looked around the house for something, anything, she could use to protect herself. She'd not had much experience of hand-to-hand combat – none, in fact – but she knew that something heavy and solid was her best chance of defence. She picked up a wrought-iron door stopper.

The doorbell rang.

'Who is it?' shouted Hayley.

'Is Detective Inspector Hayley Gibson there?'

The voice that filtered through the letter box was rough and deep, as if from a lifetime of cigarettes.

'Who are you and what do you want?' Hayley repeated.

'I'm a...' He hesitated. 'I know her from a while back. We have unfinished business.'

Julia and Hayley looked at each. Julia felt the pitter-patter of fear running up her spine. This man was dangerous. But at least he was on the other side of the door.

He spoke again. 'Is that you, DI Gibson?'

Hayley seemed unsure of how to answer the question. Instead she asked again, 'Give me your name?'

'I don't want... It would be better if we could speak face to face. If you could just open the door, I can explain.'

'Are you Nico Gordon?'

There was a long beat of silence on the other side of the door. Nico hadn't expected that. He clearly didn't know that Julia had seen and identified him days before, and that Hayley was anticipating his arrival.

'DI Gibson, I can explain. Please, let me in.'

He banged on the door, just one smack of his hand against the wood, but both women instinctively drew back. Hayley looked up towards the bedrooms, where they hoped Rosie had already followed her instructions, contacted the station and set the wheels in motion.

'This is Julia Bird speaking. I'm a colleague of DI Gibson. Leave the property immediately. This is trespassing and harassment. You should know that the police are on their way.' Julia spoke with a certainty that she didn't feel.

'Harassment? The police? What did you do that for? Ah,

no. My parole officer is going to hear about this and I'm going to be in trouble. I meant no harm, I swear it. I just wanted to talk.'

He sounded sad and desperate and scared and, to Julia's mind, not aggressive.

'What is it that you want to talk about?' she asked.

He sighed. 'I came to say sorry. I just want to say sorry.'

Julia and Hayley looked at each other, trying to read what the other was thinking. Julia could see the fear and stress beginning to seep out of Hayley's face, the colour coming back to her cheeks.

'Take two steps back. I'll open up.'

'Right.'

She slid the chain into place and opened the door a crack.

Nico Gordon appeared in the gap. He was indeed a step back from the door. His hair was neatly combed and his big battered face wore an expression of nervous anticipation. Over his shoulder was the black bag they'd seen from the window.

'DI Gibson, I wanted to say... I just...' he stammered and blushed. 'There is something I need to give you...'

He reached into the bag.

'STOP,' the two women cried in unison.

He raised his hands. In his right was a bunch of pink carnations wrapped in plastic. A sad little bouquet, the sort you can buy at the train station.

'Please, let me explain.'

Hayley leaned against the doorframe and said, 'Go on, then.'

'I hit you. I'm sorry. I was a thug, but until you and DC Carson arrested me, I'd never raised a hand to a woman. I would never. A man should never, far as I'm concerned. I feel right bad about the way I roughed you two coppers up when you tried to cuff me. I was drunk, and the way I saw it, I was fighting for my life, my freedom.'

'You sprained DC Carson's arm. And I had bruises for

weeks.' Hayley paused, then continued softly. 'Bruises and nightmares.'

'I'm sorry. I'm proper sorry. But I'm a changed man, DI Gibson. It was that stint in prison that did it. I realised I wasn't the man I wanted to be. It was the drink, at least in part. I started as a kid, with a nip of Dad's beer, then helping myself to a swig of his whiskey. And then, well, it was downhill from there. But I have given it all up. I did the twelve steps in prison. Worked the programme. Five years clean. That's why I'm here.'

'What do you mean?'

He looked down at his hands and said softly, 'Step nine. Making amends.'

Hayley reached for the door chain. Julia touched her hand. Hayley nodded and withdrew.

'Okay then, Gordon, say what you have to say.'

'I'm sorry. I'm sorry that I hit you. I'm sorry I scared you. I was drunk and out of control. I can't take back what I did to you and DC Carson, but I want you to know that I'm truly sorry. I won't do anything like that again as long as I live.'

He brought a rough hand to his heart and said solemnly, 'I give you my word.'

'Okay,' Hayley said slowly.

'If you wouldn't mind letting me know where I can find DC Carson, I'd like to say the same to her.'

The sound of a car screeching to a halt in the road.

Next, running footsteps on the path.

DC Walter Farmer bellowing, 'Police! Step away from the door and put your hands on your head.'

21

Julia lifted two books out of her basket and placed them carefully on the table. Not carefully enough, it seemed, because Tabitha Too opened her eyes a slit, and gave her a narrow affronted glare.

'Sorry, Too,' she said. 'I didn't mean to disturb you.'

The cat turned her head away and ignored her pointedly, closing her eyes and settling herself down to resume her nap.

'She has got the whole library to sleep in, all those nice comfy chairs, but she *will* come and lie on the check-out desk where I'm actually working.'

'For attention and strokes, I assume.'

'Well, yes, she likes the strokes, but she also gets cross if she's disturbed. I have been oppressed into silent stamping.' Tabitha-the-human mimed stamping a book with exaggerated gentleness.

'Well, *I've* been bullied into having a chicken roaming around the kitchen, if that makes you feel any better.'

'It does. Much!'

They laughed, but quietly, lest they bother the sleeping Tabitha Too.

Tabitha picked up the two books Julia was returning to the library. 'That was quick!'

'I spent most of Saturday lying on the sofa reading and drinking tea. I was exhausted after Friday.'

'I'm not surprised! You certainly have adventures, Julia. From what you told me on the phone, I couldn't believe what you'd got up to on Friday – the snooping and sleuthing and then the scary drama with that ex-con.'

'Nico Gordon. Yes, it was after ten by the time the police finished taking statements and I couldn't leave until things were sorted out.'

'So, it's sorted then?'

'Yes, I heard from Walter Farmer yesterday. Nico's transformation story has been corroborated by his parole officer. And he had an alibi for the night of Lilian's murder – apparently he was at an AA meeting in the next town over, which is rather apt if you think about it – so he's off the hook. He got a stern warning not to make further contact, and went on his way.'

'Hopefully to lead a crime-free, booze-free, happy life.'

'I hope so,' said Julia. She thought of herself as an optimistic sort of person, but her long career dealing with the troubled and troubling had left her a little jaded about people's ability to change. Still, the meetings were a good start, and he did seem genuinely remorseful. She wished Nico the best.

'What was the tyre iron and rope for though?' asked Tabitha.

'Seems he's starting a small DIY business,' said Julia. 'He was buying things for a job he managed to land. The guy he was doing the work for corroborated it all.'

'I see. Ready for some tea?' asked Tabitha, looking at her watch, as if it made any difference at all when they had tea. 'I was about to make some. And then you can tell me all about Peter and Christopher.'

'Yes, please. Although there's nothing much more to tell

than what I told you on the phone,' Julia said. 'They'll be getting married in a few months.'

Tabitha walked the three steps to the little tea station behind a little screen towards the back of the librarian's desk and put on the kettle.

'Do you think Peter would like me to be bridesmaid? I did a great job at his first wedding. To you.'

Julia laughed. 'I'm sure he'd love that, Christopher too. I do hope you kept the yellow satin bridesmaid's dress my mum made you. With that fetching bustle.'

'Yes, and the puffy sleeves and the yellow satin roses at the waist. I would only have to lose about thirty pounds to get into it.'

'Oh, that won't be any trouble,' Julia said, with a dismissive wave of her hand. They cracked up at that. Tabitha had been trying – in a rather hypothetical sense, as in, talking about it as opposed to changing her behaviour – to lose five pounds for about ten years.

'Funny how things turn out, though, isn't it?' said Tabitha, her bangles clanking as she took two mugs out of the cupboard, and then reached into a drawer for teaspoons. Julia found the gentle soundscape of her friend's movement in the world familiar and cheering. 'Who'd have thought you'd be giving him your blessing thirty years later. Him with a new love, and you with lovely Sean.'

Julia gave a non-committal sort of shrug.

'What's up?' Tabitha asked. 'Are you feeling weird about Peter getting married?'

'No. I mean, I was a little surprised, and somewhat weird – just a tad, and only for a moment, but I'm over it. Actually, it's Sean. I'm a little... I don't know... I guess it's a long while since I've been in a new relationship.'

'And?'

'It's very silly.'

'Spit it out.'

'Well, I invited him to come for supper at Hayley's and he said he couldn't make it. No explanation.'

Tabitha said nothing. Just waited quietly for Julia to continue.

'Of course, he doesn't have to give me a reason. Well, I don't think he does. Or does he? You see, I don't know. The Rules of Dating had been updated significantly since the 1980s.'

Julia tried for a laugh at her own little joke, but it died in her throat.

'Did you ask him what he was doing?'

'No. It's not my business. Or is it? Maybe it is? You see, this is the sort of thing I don't really know.'

'Well, I suppose that would depend on you, and on him, and what your expectations and commitments are.'

'You're right, of course.'

Although she was a highly trained social worker and Tabitha was a librarian, Julia often felt that Tabitha was a lot smarter than her when it came to matters of the human heart. Maybe it was all the reading that did it.

'The thing is...' Julia hesitated.

The kettle came to the boil and clicked off, but Tabitha didn't go to it. She waited.

'The thing is, I saw him talking to that Gina McFarlane. The one who comes to the pub quiz. Do you know her? Blonde. Pretty.'

'Oh yes, I think I know who you mean. She's on the Quiz Wizards team?'

'Yes. Well, she's a patient of Sean's and she's all googly-eyed over him when she sees him at the quiz. "Oooh, Doctor," you know, that sort of thing. Flirty. He's never been anything other than polite and professional to her, but then I saw them together.'

'Together?' Tabitha raised her eyebrows. She had very

expressive eyebrows, and they were currently expressing a nuanced mix of disbelief, disapproval, and 'tell me more'. Which Julia did.

'On the footpath by the river when I was on my way to have dinner at Hayley's. The dinner that he said he couldn't make. They were standing there talking. She was smiling doing this flicking thing she does with her hair.' Julia illustrated with some wrist action near her head – her own hair wasn't long enough to properly demonstrate. 'I realise it's hardly damning evidence of infidelity.'

Tabitha poured the hot water over the teabags. 'Well, there could be lots of explanations for them being there.'

'Could there?'

'I'm sure there are.' Tabitha didn't sound very sure, nor did she offer an example of what those explanations might be. 'What did he say they were doing?'

Julia felt somewhat abashed when she answered. 'I didn't ask him.'

'Well, you know what to do, Julia,' Tabitha said, with a small smile. 'You don't need me to tell you.'

'Yes. Of course. You're right, I need to talk to him. It's just that I don't want him to think I'm jealous. It's so ridiculous, at our age.'

The eyebrows again. Julia's interpretation of their message was interrupted by the opening of the front door, heralding the arrival of a library user. 'Oh hello, Tabitha. Hi, Julia!' It was Pippa, who Julia still thought of as 'the puppy wrangler', even though the puppies she had been fostering had all left her, and gone on to be trained as guide dogs. All except for Jake, of course, who had been better suited to civilian life with Julia.

'Gosh, this book was gory!' she said, shuddering dramatically as she handed over a book with blood spatters all over the cover and the title, *The Knife of Death*, printed across the top with the capital T made in the shape of a dagger. It hardly seemed possible that Pippa was surprised by the bloody contents. 'I couldn't get to sleep last night after I'd finished it. Well, it was only partially the fault of the book, I suppose. But also because of the break-ins.'

'What break-ins?' Julia asked. 'I haven't heard anything about break-ins.'

Tabitha looked equally mystified.

'I only heard because my sister lives next door to the Carsons, and it was their house that was broken into. Poor Charles. As if he hasn't had enough, what with losing Lilian, and now a single dad.'

'I hadn't heard.'

'It's very new news,' Pippa said proudly. 'And, of course, you know that just a few days ago Felicity Harbour's house was broken into. And she on her own, now Harry's in— Well, you know,' she looked around and said under her breath, 'prison. After you know... that poor girl. Remember?'

Tabitha and Julia nodded. Julia certainly remembered what had happened, given that it was she who had worked it all out, and it was hardly ancient history. Pippa continued at normal volume. 'Two break-ins. Same MO. That's modus operandi,' Pippa explained, slightly pompously, as if they didn't all know the police lingo from the telly and from the police procedurals they all read avidly. 'First the arson attacks and no sooner is he behind bars, than this! I don't know what this village is coming to. Luckily no one was home when it happened.'

'What did they take?' Tabitha asked.

'Nothing, as far as my sister knows. They think the person was disturbed and ran off before he could get anything.'

'It was the same with Felicity,' Julia said thoughtfully. 'Nothing taken.'

'Probably some naughty teenagers mucking about. Let's

hope that's the end of it,' Tabitha said, reaching for the books that Pippa was returning.

But somehow Julia didn't think so.

22

'Speak of the devil and he shall appear,' Julia's mother used to say. Not that she was a superstitious woman – on the contrary, she was a sensible no-nonsense sort of person, rather like her daughter. She simply enjoyed a dramatic turn of phrase. And it was true that very often when one spoke about someone, they would indeed appear – as Felicity Harbour did now, on Julia's mobile phone. Well, not her personally, but a missed call and a message.

Julia stopped outside the library to listen to it, putting her basket with its two new books down at her feet.

Felicity's voice was reedy and the message rather rambling and tentative.

> Hello, Julia. I hope you're very well. There's a matter that's, well, it's something a little concerning, and I thought you might be able to advise. Or discuss. As a, um, friend. And your experience with... Well, I'd like to chat to you in person. Are you free this evening? I could make us an early dinner, and we could have a talk. Oh, it's Felicity here, Felicity Harbour.

Julia wondered what it was about. Something to do with Harry? Or the break-in? Or it could be some entirely unrelated matter. As a social worker she was used to being asked about tricky family problems. A daughter's toxic divorce. A son's worrying drinking habits. Sean had a similar problem as a doctor and the two of them joked about which was worse – having to weigh-in on a wayward teenager, or being required to discuss someone's uncle's knee replacement that went wrong.

She didn't know Felicity's family – other than Harry, of course – and she couldn't recall hearing anything about children. Perhaps she was just lonely, without her husband, and the 'concerning matter' was something entirely trivial, an excuse to have Julia round for a visit. Well, she'd find out soon enough. Julia texted her back. *Sorry I missed your call. Happy to chat. Dinner would be lovely. What time?*

Good! Come at 6?

See you then.

By the time the message ended, another had appeared. Peter. *I had a thought about the wedding plans. Want to bounce it off you. Phone when you have a mo? X*

Julia noted that the X, which had ended their text messages to each other since the dawn of mobile phone messaging, and by mutual silent consent had disappeared from their correspondence at the time of their separation, was back. They simply stopped adding it. And now here it was again. She felt there was some amusing joke to be made about the ex and the X, but she couldn't be bothered to think it through, and besides, who would she tell it to?

. . .

She'd had enough of standing about outside the library in a rather chilly breeze. She felt sure Peter could wait an hour or two to 'bounce' his wedding ideas, preferably somewhere warmer, and with a cup of tea. Julia pocketed her phone and set off for home, and lunch.

What would be really helpful, Julia thought to herself from her horizontal position on the sofa, would be if dogs had opposable thumbs and could do small, useful tasks like putting the kettle on for you. Of course, they would need common sense, too. And to be able to walk upright on their hind legs, so they could use their forepaws for the small, useful tasks. She laughed at the image in her head – Jake up on his hind legs at the sink, turning on the tap with his big clumsy paw to fill the kettle. She wouldn't let him near the good tea set, that's for sure.

She settled back into the cushions that she'd banked up against the arm of the sofa to rest her head on while she attended to her messages. Tea could wait another few minutes, she would phone Peter first.

'Christopher had an idea about the wedding,' he said, having answered on the first ring. There was something tentative about his voice. 'He fell in love with the Cotswolds when we visited you. He loved everything about the area, the village, the river, your charming house, everything. He wants us to get married there.'

'Here?'

'Yes. Well, not at your house, of course. But the general area. The Cotswolds. What do you think?'

What *did* she think? Good question. She thought it made her feel mildly disconcerted and unaccountably annoyed, but she almost immediately second-guessed her response. After all, she didn't *own* the Cotswolds.

'Of course, if he has his heart set on the place, that's where you should do it. And there are lots of options for venues.'

'We thought we might look at that nice country hotel we had lunch at, remember?'

'You mean The Swan?' The Swan was rather closer than she'd expected. As in, right on her doorstep.

'Yes, that's the one, just outside of Berrywick, down by the river. What do you think?'

'It's a lovely venue,' she said, taking the narrowest interpretation of his question. 'Lovely garden. Good food. There's the river, which is pretty.'

'That's what I thought,' he said, sounding relieved. 'We could have it outdoors, depending on the season, and that rather depends on when Jess can come over from Hong Kong. It's important to me that she's here, and meets Christopher, and she's going to let me know her timing within the week.'

Julia felt a flush of longing for her daughter's presence, and of excitement at her arrival.

Peter carried on. 'So, depending on the weather. We were thinking of just a short ceremony in the beautiful gardens down by the river – there are all those hydrangeas, remember? – and a nice lunch afterwards. We do want to keep it small. Perhaps thirty people. The closest friends and family.'

'It sounds lovely.'

'So you think it's a good idea? You are fine with it?' His tone was both eager and grateful.

'Of course. It's your wedding, you must do what you want. And Christopher is right, the place is lovely. It would be lovely for a wedding.'

Why couldn't she stop saying 'lovely'? It was an almost meaningless word that generally annoyed her.

'I'm so glad you think so. It's Christopher's first – and I hope *only* – wedding. You know how he adores gardens and flowers, and it's his fantasy to have the country garden setting, with the river running by. I'd like him to have that.'

'Of course.' She lost her edgy, grumpiness, and felt only warmth for Peter. He was a kind man. He wanted the best for his husband-to-be, just as he'd wanted the best for Julia when they were married. She decided to take her cue from his book, and be open-hearted. 'Why don't you come and stay one weekend and go and look at venues and options. I could give you some local intel, introduce you to a few people and places.'

'That is a very kind offer, Julia. Thank you. You've been really kind and helpful. I'll speak to Christopher and propose some dates.'

'Lovely.'

As Jake had failed to develop fine motor skills, and turn on the kettle, Julia got up and did it herself. While the water boiled, she scavenged for leftovers. It was reasonable pickings – a bit of cheese, some rye crackers, Tabitha's garden tomatoes, her own fresh basil, a dollop of the home-made chutney that had been lurking at the back of the fridge for months. She put it all on a plate and made her tea.

Julia wondered if it was warm enough to eat her lunch out in the garden, where she could admire her plants, murmur encouraging words to the bees, and watch the hens go about their bossy business. She opened the door, stepped outside, and stepped rapidly back indoors. It was one of those English summer days that had decided it was just going to be autumn, and there's nothing you can do about it. She went back inside and had her lunch at the kitchen table, scrolling through her emails and messages with her free hand. The nice thing about living alone is that you could do that sort of thing without guilt or judgement.

There was a much belated reply to the message she'd sent to

Hayley that morning. *Wishing you well for your first day back. Don't overdo it!*

Hayley's message said, *Oh, I'm overdoing it all right! On a mission to find Lilian's killer. Marty in the clear. Alibi checked out. Starting from scratch – evidence, interviews, etc. Hope I'm not crushed by the tower of case files on my desk!*

If she was, at least she'd die happy, thought Julia as she popped the last baby tomato into her mouth. Nothing like a giant pile of case files and evidence to go through to cheer up a workaholic police detective. Maybe Hayley's sharp eyes and brain would find something Grave and his team had missed. Julia certainly hoped so.

23

Julia could hear the yapping and barking and whining of dogs on the other side of the door. She remembered, from the first time she'd visited the Harbours, the pack of assorted tiny rescue mutts that moved in a seething mass of fur and feet and noses and noise. While Julia waited for Felicity to answer the doorbell, small dogs hurled their bodies against the door and scratched their claws against it.

There was no answer – well, no human answer – from inside. Julia knocked hard, setting off a further round of dog activity. But there was still no sign of Felicity. Not a sound or even a light shining in the twilight. Had she forgotten and gone out? It hardly seemed likely, given that she'd only made the arrangement that very morning, but she was quite flighty.

After another press of the bell and another firm knock, Julia tried the door handle. It turned and she pushed the door open. The wave of dogs spilled out onto the doorstep, lapping at her ankles. When she went inside, the tide turned, and they followed her, leaping and yapping in ecstatic welcome.

'Felicity?' she called into the dark house.

She thought that she heard a door slam somewhere in the

bowels of the house. 'Felicity,' she called, louder. 'I'm here.' There was no answer.

The dog mass led the way into the sitting room with its display cases and bookshelves packed with books and artefacts. Ancient tools, fossils, bones, ceramics, masks, globes and papers covered every surface, just as Julia remembered from her previous visit. And there was Felicity Harbour, in her usual spot on the red velvet wing chair, in a small patch of relative calm amidst the clutter. Her slight frame seemed dwarfed by the chair, her face obscured by the wing. Julia could see her slippered feet on the floor, and her hands resting on a green-checked pillow. At her elbow was a table with a lamp – unlit – a small pile of books and a notebook, and a small copper pot filled with her preferred green pens.

'Oh there you are!' Julia said. 'I let myself in, I hope you don't mind. I rang and rang, but don't think the bell's working.'

Felicity didn't turn to her. It seemed she was asleep, her head resting on one of the chair's wings, her fluff of grey hair mussed up into the corner.

'Felicity, it's me, Julia!' she said loudly, to wake her.

She was directly in front of the woman now. Felicity lay slumped in the chair, her hands resting on the cushion. Her head was leaning against one side of the chair, as if she was in a very deep sleep. But her colour was off, and something about the way she was lying made Julia worry. In the distance, Julia heard what sounded like quick footsteps, and the dogs took up their cacophony of barking again, running towards where the sound came from.

'Felicity,' said Julia, taking hold of the woman. 'Wake up!'

For a moment, Julia thought she must be dead, so inert was her body. Julia felt a wave of nausea rise in her throat. She couldn't bear it – another loss. But when she placed her hand on Felicity's throat, she thought she could detect a faint heartbeat.

She almost fainted with relief, before quickly reaching for her phone. Time was of the essence!

Her hand shaking slightly, she called the ambulance services, telling them to hurry, and having the presence of mind to give them not only the address, but the closest corner. It was only after she got off the call that she realised she wasn't in London any more, and that the local chaps could probably have found the house if she had just said, 'The Harbours' place'. She quickly felt Felicity's neck again – the pulse was still there. Not being at all sure what to do next, she removed the cushion that was on her lap, placing it to the side, and covered her with a blanket. Then she called Hayley.

'It's not really police business,' she said, 'but, Hayley, I heard something when I came into the house. It might have been nothing. But there was a slam, and I could swear I heard footsteps.'

'You're not a fanciful woman, Julia,' said Hayley, in what might have been the highest compliment that she could pay anyone. 'Don't touch anything – we're coming now.'

Once again, Julia felt for that faint pulse. She knew it had only been a few minutes, but it was feeling like hours. She thought of what Hayley had said about not touching anything. Any minute now the ambulance would arrive, and touch everything. Julia pulled her phone out again, and quickly took a few snaps of Felicity, before once again checking her heartbeat. Where was the ambulance? Would it arrive in time? Almost as she had that thought, she heard the dim wail of the siren in the distance, growing closer and closer to the house. She hurried out, and stood on the step, waving her arms, as if she needed to flag them down.

A tall young woman leapt out of the passenger door as soon as the ambulance stopped.

'She's in there,' said Julia, before the woman could even speak. The older man who had been driving joined her, and the two of them went into the house, carrying their emergency equipment. As Julia turned to follow, she heard a second siren, and saw the familiar shape of the Berrywick police car careening into the driveway, parking to the side so as not to block the ambulance.

DC Walter Farmer stepped out of the driver's seat, walked round to the passenger side, and opened the door for DI Hayley Gibson. She waved away his offer of an arm, and grabbed the door frame to hoist herself out of the car. She reached in for her stick, and hobbled over the gravel to the door.

Only the cast and a slight tightening around the lips as she put her weight on her right foot acknowledged her recent injury. For the rest she was all business.

'Lead the way,' she said.

Julia showed them into the sitting room, where the two paramedics had put an oxygen mask over Felicity's mouth and were loading her gently onto a stretcher.

Hayley went over to the medics and asked, 'What do you think?'

'Seems like a heart attack – but they'll do a full exam at the hospital,' said the younger of the two without looking up from her tasks.

'She's stable, but she's not in good shape, let's get her to the ER,' the older one said, taking hold of the stretcher and gesturing to his partner to do the same. 'We're taking her to South Fields Hospital.'

'Nothing really for us to do here, by the looks of things?' said Hayley. She sounded ever so slightly accusing, as if Julia shouldn't have called them.

'There were footsteps, Hayley,' said Julia. 'And a door slammed. Someone was here.'

At that point, Walter Farmer came into the room, having done a check of the house. 'Nothing that I can see,' he said. 'No sign of forced entry and nothing seems disturbed, that I can tell.

It's all a bit strange though. Masks and things on the wall.'
Walter paused, as if thinking. 'But that's not a crime,' he finally
stated, in a decisive voice, as if someone might challenge him.

'Well, if someone was here, they're gone now,' said Hayley.
'And nothing seems to have been disturbed.'

'Except for Felicity,' said Julia. 'Felicity was disturbed.'

Hayley gave Julia's arm a quick squeeze. 'You heard what
the paramedic told us,' she said. 'It looks like a heart attack.
Felicity's been through a lot recently.'

'That's true,' said Julia. 'But, Hayley, I know what I heard.'

'I'm sure you do,' said Hayley. 'And I also know you're
seldom wrong.'

The medics left, trundling Felicity's stretcher between
them.

Hayley had a frown on her face, looking around the room,
as if trying to see the answer to the riddle of Julia's footsteps.

Walter was shaking his head sadly.

'I can't believe it. Poor Mrs Harbour. I saw her just yesterday, you know? I had those papers she was looking for. The
ones Monica Evans had been working on. You know the
researcher lady who had a heart attack?'

'Yes, I didn't know her well, but I remember,' said Julia.
'Gosh, two heart attacks...'

'Monica was doing some work for Felicity when she died.
Anyway, Lilian Carson was going to give the papers back to
Felicity. I got them from Charles.'

'Yes, I remember from the pub quiz night,' said Julia. 'The
Carsons and Monica were next door neighbours.'

'That's right. So I got them and I brought them over for
Felicity. She needed them for her work. Nice lady, she insisted I
have a piece of her apple spice cake. Delicious, it was.'

Walter looked around, as if wondering if there might
perhaps be another slice of apple spice cake in the house. 'I just
hope Mrs Harbour is going to be all right,' he continued. 'Life

can be so unpredictable. You never know when it's your time. Alive one minute, and the next...' He made a palms-up gesture somewhere between a shrug, and a magician releasing doves above the heads of a gasping audience. He shook his head sadly. After a moment, he added, a little more cheerfully, 'But she might be fine. My mum says that I always think the glass is half empty, so she does.'

Hayley was still pacing around the room, looking thoughtful and mildly grumpy.

She gestured for Julia to follow her out. They sat in the dining room next door, at the one end of the dining table not covered in books. They could hear the scratching and whining of the dogs, whom Julia had shut in the kitchen when the paramedics arrived, and who were none too pleased about it.

'You found her?' Hayley asked Julia.

'Yes. About half an hour ago.'

'What were you doing here?'

'She phoned this morning and asked me to come round for supper.'

'I didn't know you were friends.'

'We aren't really. I liked her, but we didn't socialise. She said she had something she wanted to talk to me about.'

'Did she say what?'

'Why are you asking? You don't think somebody might have done this to Felicity?'

'A hunch. I've got a feeling... I hope I'm wrong. I probably am. But take me through it anyway. What did she say, exactly, when she phoned?'

'I can play you the message if you like. It's still on my phone.'

She found the voice message, and Felicity's voice filled the room.

Hello, Julia. I hope you're very well. There's a matter that's, well, it's something a little concerning, and I thought you might be able to advise. Or discuss. As a, um, friend. And your experience with... Well, I'd like to chat to you in person.

'Does she sound rattled to you?'

'I didn't know her very well, but, yes, I do think she sounds... let's say, concerned.'

'Do you have *any* idea what she wanted to talk to you about?'

'I've been wracking my brains, but nothing comes immediately to mind. There's Harry, of course. He's in prison. Something to do with him?'

'Could be. Accessing services or something. It sounds like she wants your input as a social worker.'

'It could be completely unrelated to Harry. Some other family member in trouble. I get that a lot. Or it might be about Felicity herself. Something personal. But I had another thought...'

'What?'

'The last time I saw her – that would have been Thursday, at the pub quiz, she was a bit rattled then too. She arrived about half an hour late. She had found the garden door to her house open. A break-in, she said. She said she got the feeling someone had been in the house.'

Hayley raised her eyebrows. 'She didn't report it, as far as I know.'

'There was nothing missing. She did say she might have forgotten to lock the door. It wasn't locked when I arrived today, so I wonder if she wasn't just getting a bit forgetful about locking up. Still, it could be that she was rattled by that. Felt insecure, wanted someone to talk to. And then when I got here, Hayley, I swear, someone else was in the house. Honestly, I don't know what to think.'

She didn't know what to think, but she did have that funny fizzy feeling in her chest that she got when something wasn't right. She didn't get it often, but when she did, it seldom let her down. And it seemed Hayley was feeling her own version of the funny fizzy feeling.

'Right. Well, you get home. DC Farmer and I will see what the doctor says.'

'Do you want me to forward the message to you? In case you need to listen to it again, or to play it for Grave or someone.'

'Yes, send it. But didn't I tell you? Grave is gone! He left yesterday. Back to Regional Headquarters with his tail between his legs and egg on his face.'

'And his heart in his mouth?'

'Something like that. Of course, being Grave, even as he left the building, he was still strutting about, making out like he was the hero who had completed his quest and saved the whole region from certain fiery death and destruction. Even though he was one hundred per cent wrong about Marty Ardmore killing Lilian, and that her killer's still on the loose.'

'Well, you're back now, so maybe...'

'There's no "maybe" about it. I'm going to find Lilian's killer if it's the last thing I do. That is my promise to her family.'

'I hope so. Well, I'll be off then.'

'I'll need to talk to you again tomorrow, I should think. You'll be around?'

'Yes, home all day, I think. Call me any time.'

'Thanks.'

24

'Grapefruit?' Julia asked. 'Toast? Or I could make oats.'

'Oats would be good, but I will make them,' Sean said. 'You've got the livestock to take care of.'

Jake was already lumbering about in anticipation of the first meal of the day, turning in clumsy circles, smacking his tail against shins and furniture. The tea in their two mugs sloshed about dangerously when he bumped the table. Sean's Leo sat and waited politely and patiently at the door, looking up at her with eager eyes, his tail brushing the floor.

Julia opened the door. 'Out!' she said. Jake dashed out, ready for breakfast, and Leo took the hint and followed him. Julia closed the door behind them, saying, 'In a minute.'

She smiled at Sean. It was strange – strange in a nice way – to have him in her kitchen on a weekday morning. He seldom stayed over because of Leo. Sleeping at her place meant he would either have to leave the dog at home alone for the night and dash back to feed him in the morning, or bring him to Julia's and drive home to drop him off. Either option meant a very early start if he was to get to his surgery in time for his first patient, usually scheduled at nine.

Today was an exception. She had phoned him from the car, driving home from Felicity's house the night before, to tell him about the day's events. He had insisted on coming over with a takeaway chicken korma. And Leo.

He had been so kind and concerned about her after her awful discovery – and especially coming so soon after the other grislier discovery of the murdered Lilian Carson.

'I called the hospital, and they said she's critical. In a coma. It didn't sound good,' she'd told him, and he'd promised to phone the hospital himself later and see if he could get any more information.

Sitting together on the sofa after supper she'd told him about Peter and Christopher and the upcoming wedding, and her slightly complicated but mostly okay feelings around it.

'You were married for nearly thirty years. You had a child together. A life. That doesn't change when you get divorced. It's no wonder you feel a bit weird about him getting married to someone else. It's different for me, of course, because Annie died, but even so I have had complicated feelings about moving on, finding love again.'

Love. It was the first time the word had been used in relation to the two of them. It seemed to float there between them, light and heavy at the same time, with a warm glow. It felt good.

He took her hand. 'It's a funny thing to say, but I sometimes wish you could have met each other. She would have liked you, I'm sure. And you her. She said she wanted me to find someone after she'd gone and I know she'd be happy that I am with someone as kind and clever and funny as you.'

Julia blushed – yes, blushed like a teenager – and laid her head on his shoulder.

'Well, I'm sorry not to have known her. But happy that we found each other.'

They sat in companionable silence for a few minutes, until

Sean spoke. 'I didn't tell you, but it was the fifth anniversary of her death last Friday.'

'Oh, Sean, I'm sorry.'

'That's why I didn't come with you to Hayley's for supper. I felt I needed some time alone with my thoughts, and besides I didn't think I'd have been much good in company.'

'Well, I completely understand that. As far as being good company goes, as it happened, I doubt that would have been an issue. But it's a good thing you weren't caught up in the Nico Gordon misunderstanding. That's the last thing you needed.'

He smiled. 'True. Anyway, I took a walk along the river, a walk we often took together, and I sat on her favourite bench and enjoyed the view and watched the ducks and the water, the way we used to.'

'That sounds like a good way to remember her.'

'It was. The only mildly annoying thing was that I ran into that patient of mine who comes to the pub quiz. Gina. I really did want some quiet reflective time and she can be quite hard to shake once she's got you in her sights.'

'Oh, she has you in her sights, all right!' Julia laughed. 'I can see she fancies you.'

'It's not me, per se. It's the white coat effect.'

'Were you wearing your white coat?'

'No, I was not walking along the river in my white coat and stethoscope, you'll be pleased to hear. But the white coat effect, it's a well-known thing. People fall for their doctors.'

'That doesn't happen with social workers. People just want to tell you their problems. Anyway, I think in your case, it's more likely that you were experiencing the 007 effect.'

Now it was his turn to blush. 'Ah now, I don't look at all like him.'

She took a more serious tone. 'Sean, I'm glad you told me about Annie's anniversary. Thank you.'

'I should have told you before. It was silly, I felt awkward and a bit tender.'

'And I should have told you that I saw you by the river. I drove past on my way to Hayley's house and I spotted you and Gina talking. I felt awkward and a bit jealous.'

And now here he was on a Tuesday morning, stirring oats into boiling water while she dug around for a suitable bowl in which to give Leo his breakfast. Sean had phoned his receptionist and she had rescheduled his early appointments to later in the day. They had time for a leisurely breakfast.

'Come outside with me and admire the hens,' said Julia. 'Bring the mugs.'

She had already put on her garden shoes and a long shape-less cardigan she kept on a hook by the door. Sean put on his boots and grabbed his own jacket that was hanging up on another hook.

'Stylish get up,' he said, looking her over with a twinkle in his eye.

She didn't feel embarrassed at all in her odd combination of pyjamas and outdoor gear, without make-up or even a shower. 'I'm a farm girl. Not like you city slicker, gentleman-doctor types. Here, you can carry the egg basket for a bit of authenticity.'

She handed it to him and nodded approvingly. 'Yes, that's better.' She picked up the bowl of food scraps and opened the door.

They were greeted by a most peculiar sight. Jake was crouched down and growling, a low warning growl, in the direction of Leo.

Leo gave a little pounce, as if he thought it might be a game.

Jake growled back.

'Jakey, stop that, what are you doing?' Julia had never seen him like this. She'd barely even heard him growl.

Leo barked a sharp, confused bark.

'It's the chicken,' Sean said, pointing. Behind Jake was Henny Penny, all puffed up.

Sean grabbed Leo's collar. 'It's okay, boy,' he said soothingly, stroking him. Julia passed him a lead that she kept by the door.

'We'd better introduce them. Henny Penny is a Houdini chicken who knows no boundaries and observes no rules, and she's Jake's new best friend. He's defending her.'

Sean shook his head in astonishment.

With Leo calmer, and at heel, they approached. Julia stroked Jake and spoke calmly to him and Henny Penny who was tucked under the lavender bush behind him. Leo edged forward and rolled onto his back in a submissive posture. Jake gave his face a lick. Penny came to inspect him. Julia and Sean moved back a step to give them space, the lead light in Sean's hand. Leo rolled over onto his front and leopard-crawled closer to the hen. She let him touch her with his nose. Jake looked relieved that everyone was getting along so nicely. He thumped his tail gently.

'Well what do you know?' Sean said quietly, and then, a whole lot louder. 'Oh heck, the oats!'

The oats were fine and the dogs were fine and the hens were happily eating their breakfast of kitchen scraps and corn. There were five warm eggs in the basket, and Sean was at her kitchen table. The sun was coming out, promising a bright and beautiful day. All was well in Julia's world.

Her phone rang. After a scrabble to locate it behind the sugar bowl she answered.

'Hello, Hayley.'

As usual, Hayley skipped the polite preliminaries and cut straight to the chase.

'I chatted to the doctor at the hospital. There was some skin under Felicity's nails on admission, and there's some bruising on her face and neck. It looks like she was attacked.'

'Oh no, Hayley.' Julia reeled in shock, slumping into a kitchen chair. 'Oh that's horrible, poor Felicity.' Even in the midst of her shock, she realised that she wasn't actually *surprised*. She'd known, somehow, in her bones if not in her conscious mind, that this was the case. There was something dark happening in Berrywick, something dangerous.

'I think you'd better come in. I'm going to need you to go over everything again in detail and make a full statement.'

25

Hayley's desk was piled high, as always, the file trays stacked to capacity with bulging files, sticky notes plastered on the computer, the surface of the desk itself awash with slips of paper, notebooks, pens. The only difference was that Hayley had taken the sturdy visitor's chair, on account of her leg, and left the visitor – in this case Julia – with the less stable swivel chair. The chair's movement, although minor, made Julia feel a little seasick. Or perhaps the queasiness wasn't from the chair at all, but from the words coming out of Hayley's mouth.

'Samples from under her fingernails show evidence of human skin and blood. It's usually a sign of a struggle, of a victim clawing her attacker in an attempt to free herself from his grip.'

'There was no sign of a struggle around her, though, Hayley. She was just sitting in her chair. She looked so calm, so peaceful, her hands resting on the cushion on her lap. It's hard to believe she was attacked.'

'Here's my theory, Julia. Whoever attacked Felicity Harbour came up behind her. She didn't see or hear him coming.'

'So there was hardly any struggle.'

'Exactly. That's why it looked like a heart attack or a stroke.'

'Do you know anything more?'

'The doctors think she was suffocated. Only whoever did it stopped too soon. She wasn't quite dead.'

'The footsteps,' said Julia, aghast. 'I heard the murderer leave, Hayley. I let him get away.'

'Actually, Julia. I suspect that you saved her life. I think that your arrival is what stopped him from finishing the job.'

Julia hoped that Hayley was right.

'I want to show you a photo,' said Hayley. 'See if it jogs any more memories, if that's okay?'

Hayley pushed the photograph across the desk. There was Felicity, in her chair, just as Julia had found her. Julia stared at the photo for a moment, her brain snagging on something. She made her head empty of everything except what she was looking at, until she could zero in on what was bothering her.

'The cushion,' Julia said. 'That green-checked cushion on her lap is from the chair by the patio door. I noticed the fabric the first time I visited the house, because I've seen it before – my aunt had the same fabric on her cushions – but I didn't register it yesterday. The cushion is out of place. He must have picked it up when he walked in, come up behind her, and had it over her face before she knew he was there.'

'The cushion. Of course! You're probably right. He held the cushion against her face but you interrupted him. He must have quickly put the cushion on her lap and her hands on the cushion. Which is how she was when you found her.'

Julia thought back to her discovery with horror. It was awful to think of Felicity struggling for breath and then succumbing... It was appalling. Whoever did this was a monster. But who was it?

'Do the doctors think she'll recover? Wake up?'

Hayley sighed. 'It seems it could go either way now. But for now, they're keeping her comfortable and hoping for the best. I do hope she wakes up, and when she does, I hope she knows who did this to her.'

'Can we do anything in the meantime?' asked Julia, hating the idea that someone had attacked Felicity and was now just walking around Berrywick, nobody knowing who they were and what they'd done.

'The lab is running DNA tests on the skin from under her nails, but that takes a while, so we don't know anything about who it might belong to. And forensics went this morning to see if there's any evidence at the scene. Footprints, fingerprints, anything like that.'

'Good luck to them. That house must be a forensic teams worst nightmare. The chaos! And all that stuff everywhere. The artefacts, the books and papers. And now the green cushion.'

'I wouldn't want to be looking for fingerprints in that lot. I wouldn't put much hope on the cushion though. Fabric is usually a bust when it comes to fingerprints, but there might be something – a hair, or something to link to the attacker. Yup, it's a tricky scene for forensics. But that's their problem. Mine is to work out who wanted Felicity dead, and why.'

'It's hard to imagine anyone wanting to kill an elderly historian. She's practically a recluse. She barely goes out, especially since Harry was locked up.'

'Indeed. Hard to imagine...' Hayley glowered into the distance. Julia was sure that if she really listened, she might hear the whirring of the detective's brain.

'Except that Lilian was killed. A murder and an attempted murder in one little village in a week. They must be related,' Julia said.

'Yes, there's got to be a connection. I just need to work out what it was, and I've got the killer.'

'Sounds simple enough,' Julia said, with an ironic shrug. She knew that nothing was ever simple.

Hayley shifted uncomfortably in her chair and massaged the knee of her injured leg.

'How's the leg?' Julia asked.

'Ah, you know, just a bit stiff...' Hayley stretched it out and winced. 'But on the mend. And happy to be off the sofa and back at work.'

'Do you know if Lilian and Felicity even knew each other?' Julia asked.

'They lived in the village, it's not big. They must have been acquainted.'

'And they were both at the pub quiz. Both in the competition.'

'That's the truth. In fact, they weren't just at the pub quiz, they were on the same team. So they must have known each other fairly well! But if someone is attacking old women and police over the Berrywick Pub Quiz Championship, then the world has gone mad and I'm handing in my badge.'

Julia snorted with laughter, in spite of herself. 'It does seem a bit of a stretch, but I can't think what else they had in common.'

'In the absence of more sensible leads, or some other connection between them, I'll be looking into the pub quiz link,' Hayley said. She seemed to think hard for a moment. 'You know, we joke, but there's got to be something to it. It's really too much of a coincidence, two members of the same quiz team... What if there was a competitor? I don't know, some mad ambitious quiz team fiend who'd go to all sorts of lengths.' Hayley stared off into the middle distance as if trying to conjure up an image of said pub quiz fiend.

'Hayley!'

The urgency in Julia's voice made the DI stop her musing and muttering.

'Hayley, I have an awful feeling...'

'What?'

'I've an awful feeling that it isn't two team members this person has targeted. It's three.'

The expression on Hayley's face went from disbelief and confusion, to sudden understanding.

'Monica Evans.'

'Yes. I think you'll find it wasn't a heart attack. It was something else.'

'Something premeditated and deliberate.'

'Right.'

Hayley reached for the phone.

It was only when the flurry had died down, and information and instructions had been relayed up and down the chain of command, and permission was being sought for Monica's body to be exhumed, that Julia came to another awful realisation. If pub quiz contestants were being killed off – and it seemed almost certain that they were – then it was quite possible that more of them were in danger. Julia and Hayley still had no idea what the motive for the murders was, or if the killer had finished this killing spree. Whoever had killed the two women and attacked Felicity might be preparing to take another victim. And if the pattern held true, it would be someone from the pub quiz, and likely someone from Team Smarticus. She shared her theory with the detective inspector.

'Other pub quiz members could be in danger. *You* could be in danger, Hayley.'

'Me? I was a stand-in for one night, and I think I got the answers to about two questions. I seriously doubt that I'm going to be killed by some psycho who desperately needs to win a village quiz and win a free supper at the pub, or whatever the prize is.'

'Monica and Felicity were top competitors, but Lilian wasn't.'

'That's a good point,' Hayley said. 'It doesn't make sense to kill Lilian, if the motivation is competition. Maybe there was something else they had in common, some other motive. I just can't see it.'

She ran her fingers through her hair in a familiar gesture of frustration. 'What could it be?'

'I don't know, but until you find out, don't you think it's best to warn the other quiz team contestants?'

'I suppose it's a sensible precaution, just to be on the safe side. I don't like the idea of hosting it again unless we know what the connection is. Why Felicity was attacked, and Lilian – and possibly Monica – were killed. Although, I don't know... It might spread panic and make the investigation more difficult.'

It wasn't like Hayley to be so undecided.

'Well, there's a quiz scheduled for Thursday,' Julia said. 'So...'

'I suppose I should speak to Albert Johns. Just have a quiet word, and see what he thinks. If he wants to cancel, or reschedule, he can just send a message to the group.'

DC Walter Farmer knocked on the door and came in without waiting. 'Don't mean to interrupt, but I've got the lab on the line for you. It's about Felicity Harbour. They want you to come down to talk about it in person, if you can.'

'On my way.' Hayley swung into action, pushing herself up onto her feet. Only once she was standing, and started towards the door, did she remember her condition. 'Damn it. I can't drive. And I don't have a car. Can you take me, Walter?'

He held up his car keys with a smile. 'I'm on it, DI Gibson. Ready and waiting.'

Hayley nodded her thanks, and made her surprisingly nimble way to the door.

'What about the quiz on Thursday?' Julia asked. 'Will you speak to Albert?'

Hayley had already turned her attention to Walter, and the

lab, and Felicity Harbour. 'I've got my hands full right now, Julia. Would you mind having a word with Albert? Tell him our concerns about the quiz, and see what he thinks about cancelling.'

'Okay, I'll speak to him. I don't have a number for him, but I can go home via the Buttered Scone and ask Flo where he is and how to get hold of him.'

'Good. Thanks. Later,' Hayley said over her shoulder.

Julia gathered up her things, to the sound of two uneven footsteps and a walking stick disappearing down the passage.

26

The Buttered Scone had just a smattering of customers at this hour. It was just after noon and the mid-morning coffee drinkers – mums after school drop-offs, locals catching up on the gossip with friends, gym-goers in activewear, occasional business people with their laptops – had largely vacated the place. They would soon be replaced by the lunch crowd, which included fewer mums and more tourists.

Julia took a seat and waited for Flo, who was at another table, busy with a bill and what seemed to be a long and animated story. She used the time to mull over her refreshment options. She was here for information not nutrition, but on the other hand the Scone did a mean cheese toastie and it was almost lunchtime.

She hadn't come to a firm decision when Flo arrived.

'Morning, Julia. And how are you today? I heard about Felicity. A heart attack, they're saying. In a coma, poor thing.'

'Very upsetting,' said Julia, deliberately neither confirming nor denying what 'they' were saying about the cause of Felicity's illness.

'Poor dear. It was the stress of Harry being put away that

caused it,' Flo said with confidence. 'And poor you, first Lilian and now this.'

'It was rather awful, I have to say.'

'I don't know what the world is coming to. Our Fiona is going to make safety a priority for the council if – *when* – she gets elected. We were talking about it last night. Good heavens. The arson, and then Lilian's murder.' Flo gave a dramatic shiver.

'I must say, it's hardly what I expected when I moved to a little cottage in a Cotswold village.'

'Exactly. What's more important than being safe in your own home? In your own village. Our Fiona is going to prioritise the fight against crime in the Cotswolds.'

'Well, that's a very important issue.'

'It is that. And do you know, our Fiona is top of the pops, you know. Top of the polls, I mean to say, got my words all muddled up.'

They chuckled at her mistake. 'Anyhow, they do a poll, like a survey, asking people who they think they'll vote for, and it seems that she's just ahead of the other fellow. Imagine, Fiona Johns, Leader of the Cotswold District Council. And not even thirty! Albert is beside himself with pride, I can tell you.'

'Marvellous news, Flo. That's just wonderful.'

Flo nodded and smiled in quiet pride, then whipped out her pencil and got back to business. 'Now what can I bring you?'

'A coffee to start, please, and I haven't made up my mind about food. I'll take a look at the menu, see what tickles my fancy.'

Flo handed over the menu with a smile. 'You know the cheese toastie always tickles your fancy, Julia. But if you want a change, there's nice smoked trout just come in, so we've got a trout salad as a special.'

'That sounds good. Oh, Flo, I want to get in touch with

Albert. It's about the pub quiz. I realise I don't have his phone number. Could you give it to me?'

'Of course!' Flo opened the notebook where she wrote down the orders, scrawled Albert Johns and a number on it in big loopy handwriting, tore it off and handed it to Julia with a flourish. 'There you go. You'll likely be able to chat to him in person, though, if you hang about a bit. He's on his way over here. He has been fetching the lovely free-range farm eggs for me from old Farmer MacDonald.'

'Old Farmer MacDonald?'

Flo grinned at Julia's raised eyebrows and her delighted expression. 'I know. Can you believe it? He's a chicken farmer and his name's Jamie MacDonald. He tried to go by Jamie back in the day, but of course everyone calls him Old MacDonald.'

'Of course. It's irresistible, isn't it? How old is he?'

'He's getting on a bit now, so it fits, but the poor chap has been known as Old McDonald since he was about thirty.'

They shared a laugh.

'I'll be getting your coffee and be back for your order.'

'Thanks, Flo. No need. I'll have the smoked trout. No eggs for me, I'm egged up to the eyeballs thanks to my hens at home. Much as I'd like to support Old MacDonald. Ee i ee i o.'

Albert arrived at the same time as Julia's coffee, coming in the front door with a pile of trays of eggs. It looked like the set up for some comedy skit in which things did not end well for the eggs, but he made his way through the swing doors to the kitchen without incident. Minutes later he came out again, heading in Julia's direction.

'Hello, Julia. Flo said you were looking for me?'

'Yes, Albert, I was going to phone you, but this is better. Can you sit for a minute? There's something I'd like to ask you.'

He pulled out the chair opposite her and sat down.

'It's about the pub quiz.'

He waited.

'Felicity Harbour is in hospital in a coma.'

'Yes. So I heard. Very sad,' he said, looking down and smoothing the tablecloth with his square hands and stubby fingers. His hands were trembling slightly. Poor man, he was taking this very hard.

'It's not been officially reported yet, but the police suspect that she might have been attacked. It looks like someone might have been trying to kill her.'

The colour drained from Albert's face. 'Ah no, is that what they think? That she was attacked? Did DI Gibson say that?'

'Yes. In fact, it seems she's pretty convinced of it, although the forensic results aren't in yet.'

'Forensic results?'

'You know, DNA, fingerprints, that sort of thing. You'd be amazed what they can do these days to identify the attacker.'

'Ah no,' he said again, shaking his head. 'What a terrible business.' He looked properly worked up by the news. His hands trembled. He tutted his tongue against the roof of his mouth.

'In fact, it was Hayley who asked me to have a word with you. She's been run off her feet...' As the words came out, Julia recognised their strange double meaning – Hayley had in fact been literally run off her feet by a crazy motorist. 'What I mean is, she's busy with the investigation into Lilian's death, and Felicity's attack. But we... she... well, it seems like a very strange coincidence that there were two people targeted...' she didn't mention Monica, as there was so far nothing to confirm Julia's suspicion that her death was anything other than natural '... and both of them are on the quiz team.'

'That's true, it is an odd coincidence.'

'If it is in fact a coincidence. DI Gibson is wondering if there's some connection between them, something – or someone – to do with the pub quiz.'

'That's just ridiculous. It's got nothing to do with the pub quiz,' Albert spoke with a sudden flare of anger. 'I mean, it's just a bit of fun, is the quiz. Who attacks people over a pub quiz?'

'You're probably right. It could well be unrelated.' Julia spoke calmly. Albert was clearly very defensive about his beloved pub quiz. 'But she has to investigate all the possibilities.'

He nodded. 'Yes, of course she does. Tell you what. I could give her a list of the team leaders and their contact details, if that would help. The police could contact them, get the details of the people on each team, and check up on them, I suppose.'

'That sounds like a good idea, Albert, thank you.'

'I'll get it done today and send it to her. Strange that you'll be on the list, of course, and Doctor Sean, and DI Gibson.'

It was a bit odd, come to think of it. Three people to cross off right away.

'Can you give me DI Gibson's email?'

She tapped her phone, lying on the table. 'I'll check and write it down for you. And I'll let her know to expect the list. Thank you for your help.'

'You can email it to me if it's easier,' he said, pulling a card from his wallet.

'I'll do that. Oh, and Albert, one more thing. It's just that, under the circumstances, DI Gibson thought it might be better to delay the pub quiz finals, just by a week, until things are a bit clearer. Just to be on the safe side, you know.'

'Yes. That makes a certain amount of sense. I wouldn't want people to think I'm putting them in any danger. It's not as if I don't care about their teammates. Because I do, I really do...' His voice faltered. He was clearly deeply distressed by the whole matter. 'You're right. I'll send out a message to all the teams and let them know that the final will be pushed out by a week. Out of respect.'

'Good idea, Albert, I think it's for the best.'

He nodded, grimly, and got to his feet.

'Thanks, Albert. I'll let Hayley Gibson know,' Julia said,

and added, for a change of topic onto something more pleasant. 'And good news about your Fiona, from what Flo tells me. You must be very proud.'

A hint of cheer came to his stricken face. 'That I am. That I am.'

The smoked trout was deliciously moist and flaky, swimming smokily atop a bed of lettuce and peppery watercress and rocket. Alongside was a small jug of creamy lemon and dill dressing, a doorstopper of a slice of seeded bread, which Julia recognised as the work of Bob the Berrywick baker, and a pat of golden farm butter. All in all, it was a fine spread.

In the past year, Julia had come first to accept, and then enjoy eating alone in a coffee shop or restaurant. When she got divorced, it was one of the things that she had viewed with some alarm, imagining the awkwardness she'd feel. She had gone solo to an establishment reluctantly, armed with a book and a phone as protection. These days, she was happy to sit alone with her thoughts, to eat what she felt like at any time of day irrespective of conventional meal times and choices, to enjoy the food without guilt or embarrassment, to chat if she felt like it and there was someone to chat to, or, yes, to read a book or a news-paper, which she brought with her not to shut out the world, but to read if she wanted to.

Today was a day for thinking, not reading. At her table at the Buttered Scone, Julia buttered her bread slowly and mused on the murders. It seemed almost certain that the two victims must be connected somehow. The pub quiz was the obvious connection. But if they hadn't been attacked by a rival quizzer, what else might they have to connect them? Aside from the pub quiz, Felicity and Lilian had little in common, as far as Julia could see.

Not age – Felicity was about two decades older.

Not work – you couldn't get further apart than an academic historian and a copper.

Friends and family? Julia couldn't say for certain, but to the best of her knowledge the two women had neither in common.

But Monica...

Julia felt the familiar prickle that came with the sudden arrival of instinct, of a good guess, or a dawning realisation.

If the tests showed Monica to be a victim, too, *then* there was something to investigate.

Julia knew that there was a real and current connection between Monica and Felicity. They were working together on a project. What was it, though? The details were frustratingly vague. What had Felicity said? Monica was helping her with research. For what, a book? On what? Felicity had mentioned it the other night, but Julia couldn't for the life of her remember. '*Something something turn of the century... something 1980s...*' It was no use. If the information was rattling around in her brain somewhere, it wasn't floating to the top where she could scoop it up into her consciousness and put it to good use.

There was talk of papers, that much she recalled. Research notes that Monica had been working on. Felicity had mentioned she needed to get them back. It was coming back to Julia. The papers! When Monica died and her cousin had come from London to sort out her effects, she had left them at the neighbour's house. The neighbour was Lilian Carson. And Lilian Carson was dead.

27

Julia had hailed Flo for the bill, gobbled the last of the trout, and dashed out of the Buttered Scone. The police station was close by, and since Hayley was immobile, Julia figured she'd be there. As indeed she was. Julia rattled off her story – Monica's research notes and papers, which had gone from her, to Lilian, to Felicity. All three of them ended up dead – or would have, if the attack on Felicity had been successful.

With each new piece of information, each new connection, Hayley nodded, or muttered, 'Yes, right.' Her quick mind was already reaching for connections, for what to do next.

'I need to know what was in those papers,' she said, when Julia was finished. 'Whatever was in them is key to this whole investigation. Whatever it is, it got two people killed, and one in a coma in the hospital.'

'DC Walter Farmer delivered the papers to Felicity's house remember, so maybe he can...'

'WALTER,' Hayley bellowed in the direction of the open office door.

She picked up the desk phone and barked, 'Get DC Farmer, I need to see him now.'

Either the bellowing or the terse instruction to the desk sergeant had an almost immediate effect. Walter almost skidded into the room, looking red-faced and anxious, and about eighteen years old. He was one of those skinny, baby-faced chaps who never quite seemed to exit adolescence into full manliness. He had a new young wife, and must be at least twenty-eight, but you wouldn't know it to look at him.

Hayley gave him the brief rundown of what they'd found out, then asked, 'What exactly did you deliver?'

He chewed his lower lip and raised his eyes to heaven in the hope of divine inspiration. 'Errrr, um, notes. Papers, at any rate.'

Hayley flushed red and looked as if she might explode. Instead, she let her breath out in a controlled, audible exhale, breathed in and said patiently, 'Yes, I know they were papers, Walter, but I want to know what kind of papers. What did they look like? What was the subject matter?'

He looked blank, and stricken.

'Walter,' Julia said gently. 'What do you remember about the papers?'

'I didn't read them. Just fetched them and delivered them. They were in a plastic bag.'

'Can you recall anything? Anything at all? For instance, were they in a file?'

'Yes! They were in a folder.' He beamed in relief at having some piece of information. 'It was blue. You know the ones, made of card, or thick paper. It was not a lever file or anything, the papers inside were loose.'

'How thick?'

He held his thumb and forefinger an inch or so apart.

'And what do you remember about what was inside? Were they stapled?'

'I think some pages were stapled, like they belonged together. There were some loose ones too. I remember they slid about a bit on the passenger seat when I went to deliver them.'

'Were they photocopies of pages from books? Or printouts, like from a computer? Were there pictures? Photographs?' Hayley demanded.

He shook his head. 'I don't remember... Could they have been articles? I think I saw some newsprint? And, yes, maybe photocopies?'

Julia tried again. 'Was there handwriting?'

The poor chap scrunched up his face, and with great effort came up with, 'Yes, I think I saw some handwriting. Scrawly handwriting. Terrible.'

It was clear that this line of questioning wasn't getting them very far.

'Is there any chance the papers are still at Felicity's house?' Julia said. 'We should at least go and see.'

Hayley rested her elbows on the desk, her face in her hands, her fingers massaging her temples as if to ward off a headache. 'I'm certain that whoever attacked her would have taken them. I imagine that's why he was there. To get the papers, and to stop Felicity talking about whatever was in them. But there might be something else that will point to the subject of the research. Walter, go out there, see what you can find.'

'There could be a notebook, a laptop, something like that,' said Julia.

'Exactly. Unfortunately, I have been put on desk duty. Not allowed to go out, which is ridiculous, but those are the rules,' Hayley said. 'When the big boss discovered I'd been out to Felicity's, he had a fit. Something to do with liability. Or the union. God knows what, but I'm stuck here until I get a doctor's sign-off for active duty.'

'Should I go with DC Farmer?' The words came sponta-neously and rather surprisingly out of Julia's mouth. 'Not to interfere, but I was there... I found her... I know the house a little. An extra pair of eyes.' She didn't want to say out loud that

Walter hadn't exactly shown himself to be an astute observer of papers.

She worried that she'd overstepped, but Walter looked quite pleased at the idea. He looked from Hayley to Julia and back again, waiting for his boss's decision.

'Take Julia with you,' Hayley said. 'And bring me back something I can use.'

'Will do.' For a moment Walter seemed about to salute, but he thought better of it. 'Oh, and one more thing, DI Gibson. I just remembered, there was something written on the folder.'

A storm of emotions passed over Hayley's face – confusion, disbelief, anger, resignation. She breathed deeply and said, 'What was written on the folder, DC Farmer? Do tell.'

'A word...' He scrunched up his face in deep thought. 'SEW, I think it was.'

'S-O, as in "so what"?'

'No, sew, like, with a needle and thread? S-E-W. It was written in big capital letters, so I thought it might be important.'

'What else?'

'Nothing. Just doodles. A star, maybe. And a sort of arrow thing.'

Julia pushed a piece of paper towards him. 'Walter, could you write down what you saw? Whatever you remember.'

Walter did as she asked. The arrow thing turned out to be a line with arrows at either end, indicating swapping one thing with another. The star was an asterisk. S.E.W had full stops between the letters, indicating that it might have been an acronym.

'Oh, I remember now. There was an exclamation mark after the initials, so it must have been important.'

'Great, Walter, thanks,' Julia said, although there was no knowing whether any of it would be useful.

. . .

The Harbours' house was strangely desolate. It was only a day since Felicity had been taken to the hospital, but already it had a sad and abandoned air. They walked to the front door. The place was eerily quiet.

'The dogs! Walter, where are all the little dogs?' Julia couldn't believe that she was only thinking about the dogs now.

'Don't worry. There was a niece, apparently. Mrs Harbour's niece. She's looking after them. All I can say is that she must be a very nice lady.'

'I hope she's got a big garden and poor hearing,' Julia said, and then felt bad for making a joke, under the circumstances. 'Come on, let's go in.'

They started in the room in which they'd found Felicity, the room where she worked and read. The seat of the red wing back held the imprint of years of use in the seat cushion, and the arms were worn. A small oriental rug lay in front of it, with two scuffed patches where Felicity's feet would have been. To the right was a table with a lamp, a very large dictionary, a little notepad, a little pile of books, and a small copper pot filled with pens. Would it be too much to expect to find a blue file with HELPFUL EVIDENCE! printed in large letters on the front? Apparently so. There was nothing of the sort on the table, or on any other surface.

In the absence of the blue file, it was hard to know what might be useful. There was just so much *stuff*. Walter was wandering around, hopefully picking up books and other items in the hope of uncovering the elusive folder, and putting them down again.

'No blue folder,' he said dispiritedly. 'I've looked everywhere.'

'Whatever was in the file, it is likely to be related to Felicity's work. Knowing Felicity, there would be other sources of research on the subject. Other books. Notes. Anything she was currently reading or working on could be a clue.'

'The tech guys have got her laptop, there might be something on that. As for books...' Walter gazed around at the floor-to-ceiling bookshelves.

They did a brief sweep of the rest of the house, with no success.

'Waste of time,' said Walter, as he locked the front door behind them. 'We're leaving empty-handed.'

'Not entirely. We have information.'

'We do?'

'Yes we do, Walter. The fact that the blue file is missing confirms our theory that whatever information it contains is key to the attempt on Felicity's life.'

'So, if we can find out what it is that she was working on, we will have a big clue to who tried to kill her, and why.'

'Exactly.'

'I'll tell DI Gibson,' Walter said, looking slightly less dejected now that he had at least something to take back to his boss.

Julia turned for a last look at the house. Harry and Felicity were clever, eccentric, gentle people who for decades had made a happy home there. In the past year, there had been so much tragedy. She hoped that Felicity would recover and return to her books and artefacts and yappy little dogs, and finally be able to write her own books in peace.

'Mrs Bird?' Walter's voice from inside the car interrupted her sad pondering. She pulled herself together and answered.

'Sorry, Walter.'

As Julia turned towards the car, a glimpse of white caught her eye. There, at the base of the azaleas, was a piece of paper. Could it be...? Her heart was all a-flutter. It felt too good to be true, that they might get a break like this. Julia walked over to the shrubs, which still held the last of the spring blooms, looking rather tired now.

'What is it? What have you found?' Walter was out of the car now, and heading towards her.

'A piece of paper, it might be from the file.'

She bent down and grabbed the paper. It was a sheet of lined foolscap.

It was blank. Julia turned it over. Nothing.

'Damn, Walter. False alarm. There's nothing here.'

Her arms dropped to her sides, dangling the useless piece of paper. The rush of adrenalin that had accompanied the discovery dissipated, leaving her feeling weak and sad.

'Sorry, Mrs B. Well, let's be going, shall we?'

'Yes. Of course.'

Julia took one last disappointed look at the non-clue and there, just a couple of feet from where she stood, was another sheet of paper, just like the first. She walked over to pick it up. You shouldn't leave trash lying about, after all. As she bent down, a blue scrawl caught her eye and set her heart racing all over again.

Success! There was writing on it. She pushed her glasses up her nose and peered at it eagerly. The only thing she could say for sure was that there were squiggles on the page, and at least some of them seemed to be words. The words appeared to be arranged in lines or sentences, and the lines or sentences were arranged vertically.

'What is it?' asked Walter again.

'I'm not sure. It seems to be some sort of a list. It isn't in Felicity's handwriting, and it's not in the green ink that Felicity used.'

'Would it be from Monica?' he said, wide-eyed.

She handed it to him to look at.

'I can't swear it, but I think it could be the same handwriting I saw on papers in the folder. Absolutely terrible writing, you can't read a thing. I don't know, Mrs Bird, it might as well be in Greek.'

'It's not in Greek, I assure you of that, Walter. About the only thing I can say about it is that it's in the Roman alphabet.'

'The Roman alphabet? Do you mean the writing is in Italian?'

He was a good chap, Walter, but not overly quick on the uptake.

'No, the Roman alphabet is... Never mind. I'm sure it's in English and I'm sure we'll be able to decipher at least some of it if we sit down and put our minds to it. If you're right, and it's Monica's writing, it means our murderer dropped it from the folder on his way out of the house.'

'Mrs Bird, we might have a crucial piece of evidence right here!' he said, waving it about.

'We might indeed. If we can only read the damn thing.'

'Come on, get in. DI Gibson needs to see this right away.'

With a spin of the wheels, and a glimmer of hope in their hearts, they turned into Heath Hill Road, and headed back to the station.

28

It is a strange contradiction in life that a slow day is usually more tiring than a busy day. When there's lots to do, time whizzes by, and you're amazed to discover the day is over. But when there's not much going on, you look at your watch at what must surely be noon to discover it's ten a.m. So it was at Second Chances that Wednesday morning. While Julia sorted out the coats and jackets, making sure they were in the correct size order, customers trickled in at a rate of two or three an hour. Every time the little tinkling bell announced a new arrival, Julia looked up in the hope that it might be Walter Farmer, with news. It wasn't. Neither did her phone offer anything interesting, no matter how many times she pulled it from her pocket and glanced at it to check on her messages. He had promised to let her know when he heard anything so she had to assume there was nothing to report. Nor was there any word on Felicity's condition. It wasn't entirely surprising – Sean had said that you could never tell how long it would take for someone to regain consciousness in a situation like this, and it could be slow – but it was worrying.

Even Wilma, not known for her sensitivity to other people's lives, noticed her constant checking of the phone.

'Have you joined Tinder?' she asked, sort of teasing, when Julia picked up her phone for the tenth time.

'Tinder? Goodness, no.' Julia reddened at the very idea.

'Why would she be on Tinder when she's got the dishy doc?' asked Diane. 'You haven't broken up, have you?'

'Gosh, no, nothing like that. I'm just waiting for something. Nothing important.'

'Lord knows you'd be mad to give Sean the boot, but if you ever do and you want to start online dating, speak to me first. I could TELL you things.' Wilma gave a little shudder that set off a ripple through her smooth bob. 'None of them good.'

'I think I'm all right for now, but I'll bear it in mind. Thanks.'

Julia got no news the entire day, did a rather desultory job of her work, and was yawning and practically dead on her feet when she left, more than an hour early. The walk to the library got the blood flowing and she felt rather more energised when she was sitting with Tabitha, drinking a cup of tea and eating a chocolate digestive biscuit.

She had shared everything she knew about the murders and Felicity's attack with her friend. Tabitha was a chatter, but not a gossip. Julia knew that whatever she told her in confidence would remain so. She updated her on yesterday's developments – the dogs' temporary new home, the missing folder, the page she'd found under the azalea bushes – and the message that had finally arrived from Hayley, just as Julia had arrived at the library. She was her usual chatty self. *F stable. No change.*

Julia had texted back, quick as a flash. *Thanks. Any ideas about the paper we found??*

The message had gone through, but the double tick

remained stubbornly grey. Clearly Hayley had put her phone away as soon as she sent her message. Julia looked at it again, just in case. She stared at it a few moments longer, willing the ticks to turn blue. Willing Hayley to send her an update on the page they'd found. Nothing.

'Well, I'm all ears. What was on the paper?' Tabitha asked.

'Hard to say. Lots of scrawling, mostly. Not easy to read. I took a photograph of it before we handed it in as evidence,' Julia said, feeling a bit shifty. 'I haven't really had a chance to have a proper look.'

Tabitha peered at the tiny phone screen, pushed her glasses further up her nose and squinted. Julia watched the back of her head hopefully. The curls shook as Tabitha raised her head in defeat. 'Heaven help us, do you think I'm twenty-five years old? I can't read that!'

'Whoever wrote this had an awful scrawl. We think it might have been Monica. And the screen—'

'Could use a good clean! Well, let's print it out. Here you go, give it here.' Tabitha grabbed the phone and did some clever thing – forwarded or shared or put it on the network – and the next thing, there it was, in the tray of the printer as clear as a bell on an A4 size sheet of white paper.

'That's better.' She looked again.

Julia peered over her shoulder. 'It's a list. Short sentences. Whoever wrote it was making quick notes. Then there are some words or initials in capitals. It looks like some of them are abbreviated.'

'Yes, and some could be acronyms, I think. What for, I don't know.'

The two of them went through, deciphering the words they could.

'Criminal... H-ford... gong... violin... what on earth would they want with gongs and violins, I wonder... 80... review... July... grabbed or is it grubbed?...' Julia said.

'The letter SE. Someone's initials? Or for something else. South East?'

'And I think this says Weekly. Someone called SE Weekly?'

'Or South East Weekly. That sounds like a local newspaper. And this word could be Herald... That could also be a newspaper,' said Tabitha.

'I think what we have here is a list of references to do with her research. Articles related to whatever she was working on. These might be the first few words of headlines of the articles she was looking at. Yes, look!' Julia ran her finger over one of the slightly more legible items. 'It's not "gong", it's "gang". Something about "gang violence".'

'So no gongs or violins, then,' said Tabitha with a smile. 'That's a pity.'

'Sorry, no violins. But progress, Tabitha! Information. That's it, that's what you're looking at. A list of articles and references, from a bunch of local newspapers. If I could find the articles, I would know what Monica was researching. And that might lead us to find what it was that got her killed. We don't have dates though.'

'Unless you count "July",' Tabitha said wryly.

'Not very helpful without a year. God knows how many years, how many papers... If we could narrow it down...' Julia stared at the scrawls and scribbles, as if willing them into sense. And one of them suddenly sort of did. 'SEW!'

'So what?'

'S-E-W. Those letters were written on the outside of the folder, according to DC Walter Farmer. With an exclamation mark. And some other scrawls. Arrows, apparently. They must stand for *South East Weekly*.'

'Well, if she noted them on the folder, maybe they have some special significance.'

'It's a start. Where would one find that sort of thing? I

suppose I have to go to a university library. A trip to Gloucester, or perhaps even to London...'

'The British Newspaper Archive.'

'Yes, that's what I need? Where's that housed?'

'It's the 2020s, Julia. It's on the internet.' Tabitha tap-tap-tapped her computer keyboard. 'Here you go.'

She shifted her laptop so that Julia could see.

'*Over 40 million searchable pages, from more than 1,000 newspaper titles from UK and Ireland...*' Julia read. She leaned back, looking up to the ceiling and raising her arms dramatically. 'Praise the Lord, and hallelujah. I could kiss this screen right now!'

'You've still got a lot of work ahead of you,' Tabitha said. 'Why don't we do it together?'

'Would you?'

'Of course. I love researching and investigating. What are your plans for this evening? I could come to you, bring my laptop, you use yours, and we see what we can find out?'

'Brilliant idea. I'd better get back to Jake. Hope he hasn't wrecked the place. I'll pick up something simple for supper and see you later. The British Newspaper Archive. God, I love the digital age!'

Tabitha laughed. 'Off you go. See you later.'

Jake practically took her out at the knees when she arrived home. Fortunately, she'd seen him coming round the corner of the house like a bear in full charge, and had time to put down her shopping bags and steady herself against the bench at the front door before he reached her. It was nice to be missed, and to be welcomed home, but she would prefer not to suffer any major orthopaedic damage.

'Who's a good chap, then?' she asked rhetorically, giving him a good few hard pats to the shoulder and the rump. He did his cute little bounding and bouncing thing, and then his wiggling and squirming thing, brushing against her, smacking her with his tail, all the while grinning at her with his big silly tongue hanging out of his mouth. Her heart gave a little squeeze at the sight of him. 'Good boy, Jakey. I'm happy to see you too.'

He had not wrecked the place. Henny Penny was hanging about the garden, walking her bossy walk and pecking officiously in the undergrowth for unsuspecting insects. Since she'd decided on a free-range life, Jake was less destructive when Julia left him. She seemed to have had a calming influence on him. Or perhaps he was just less bored and lonely.

Pippa the Puppy Wrangler had suggested that a companion – another dog – might calm him down and keep him occupied. Julia recognised the logic but was having none of it. She could only see a sort of corridor of mirrors like you get in a dress shop changing room stretching into infinity with additional dogs being adopted to calm down the dog ahead of them in the long line of dogs, from Jake until who-knew-where, getting smaller and smaller and more and more numerous.

A single over-attached chicken seemed like rather a bargain in comparison.

Julia put the infinite dog image out of her head, and fed the lone actual dog, as well as the chickens. She scoured the vegetable garden for the wherewithal to make supper. She hadn't been able to face the menu-planning or the shopping. She had stopped on the way home for a loaf of fresh bread from Bob the Berrywick baker, and trusted there would be enough odds and ends to provide the rest.

She was in luck in her scrounging in the veggie patch. A few courgettes, on their way to becoming marrows. A green pepper and a red one. A large eggplant that had been nibbled by something, but was definitely salvageable. The last of the tomatoes. All the herbs you could want. She was never without onions and garlic in the pantry, so ratatouille it was. While she was about it, she picked three big blowsy roses, in a deep apricot tinged with pink.

Fifteen minutes later, the vegetables were chopped and simmering on the stove, and the roses were in a little blue china vase on the kitchen table, filling the room with their thick, sweet scent. *Pretty efficient*, she thought smugly. She imagined the Julia of two years ago looking at her now. She would be astonished at how lucky she was, and how competent in this country life. Her whole existence had been completely turned upside down with the divorce, but she had somehow managed to find herself in the classic retire-to-the-Cotswold fantasy. The cottage and its garden ablaze with summer flowers and vegetables. The chickens. Jake. Lovely Sean. Her friends.

Her moment of gratitude was interrupted by one of the aforementioned friends – Tabitha – who had come in the open front door and appeared behind Julia, giving her quite a start.

'For afters,' Tabitha said, pulling a punnet of raspberries from her basket and putting them on the counter. 'Now, shall we get started?'

Julia rubbed her hands together in anticipation and said, 'To the keyboards! We have a killer to catch.'

29

They set up their laptops on the kitchen table and got down to business. Julia took out the printout of the photograph of the paper. 'Let's start with the *South East Weekly*. That seems to me to be our strongest lead.'

She'd no sooner opened her laptop than her phone rang.

'Hi, Walter.'

'Hello Mrs... Julia. DI Gibson said I should phone. She thought you'd like to know that we've got an update on Felicity's condition. It's good news.' There was a rustle of papers. 'It seems she's turned a bit of a corner, her vital signs are good. She is off the critical list, and out of danger.'

'Is she awake?' It would certainly save a whole lot of time if Felicity could just wake up and tell everyone who had tried to kill her, and why, and thus save Julia the trouble of working out what had been in the papers that each victim had briefly had possession of.

'No, she's still heavily sedated. They have to bring her round slowly, from what I hear. Reduce the medications. They hope to take her off the ventilator tomorrow or the next day, and then, of course, DI Gibson will be having a word with her as soon as possible.'

'That's good news, Walter, thank you.'

'Right then, bye, Mrs Bird.'

'Walter,' she asked quickly. 'One more thing. Any news on Monica Evans?'

There was a brief uncomfortable pause while DC Farmer struggled between the competing forces in his life at that moment. In the silence, Julia could hear the tap-tap-tapping of Tabitha's fingers on the computer keys, and the tinkle-tinkle-tinkle of her bangles on her wrists. Walter sighed, and opted for compliance with Julia's request.

'Monica Evans was exhumed this morning.'

'Ah, I see. And do you know if...'

There was another sigh from Walter. 'We have the initial results.'

Julia waited patiently, although she was ninety-nine per cent certain she knew what the results would be – they would turn up something deliberate and deadly.

Walter gave up the info. 'It seems she ingested a high dose of Benzodiazepines, which resulted in a heart attack. Her death is being treated as suspicious. We're going back to her flat in the morning to look for medications, prescriptions, and so on. To see if anything has been tampered with, DI Gibson says.'

'Thanks for letting me know, Walter.'

'About Monica Evans...'

'I won't breathe a word. And, Walter, any news on the paper we found?'

'Now then, Mrs Bird. You know I can't talk to you about an ongoing investigation.'

He spoke sternly, and seemingly without a drop of irony.

'Of course not, Walter, I quite understand.'

While Julia had been chatting, Tabitha had established that

there was indeed a newspaper called *South East Weekly* and fortunately for them – if not for the proprietor – it had closed in 1988. 'If
we assume that the number "80s" refers to the time frame, and the
paper stopped publication in 88, that narrows the search quite a bit.'

'That is good, although we've still got our work cut out for
us. It is still almost a decade,' said Julia, pulling up the same
information on her own screen. 'Ah, but lookie here! It gets
better. In its latter years, *South East Weekly* was in fact not a
weekly, but published every second week.'

'Well, that helps.'

'We must always be grateful for small mercies,' Julia said.
Jake grunted in agreement. Or perhaps it was a snore.

'So, what's next?'

'Let's look at the words we can decipher on the paper, the
ones that seem to have something to do with SEW, and search
the *South East Weekly* to see what turns up, and see what we
get.'

Julia looked again at the paper and read the words out,
'"Gang" and "violence" and "grabbed"'

Tabitha, who was nimbler around the computer and the
search engine, put them into the search bar.

Twelve articles appeared in seconds. It never ceased to be
amazing, the speed and availability of information in this digital
era. Of course, you had to know what to look for, which is
where common sense, intuition and good old-fashioned
snooping proved essential.

They started from the top, clicking on the first link, and
were disappointed to discover that the article was about a
teenager who grabbed a hot pie from the hands of an old lady
outside a bakery in Grange. A neighbour had nabbed him and
dragged him off to the police, saying, 'It's a hop and a skip from
nicking pies, to gang violence.'

Not to be deterred, they made their way through the articles
that their search had brought up.

'It's odd how something can have all the right words, but none of the meaning,' said Julia, at number four, which had to do with reformed gang members who voluntarily came out on the first Saturday of every month to clear alien vegetation from a local waterway to allow a naturally occurring and threatened aquatic plant to thrive.

'Hardly the sort of thing that would lead to two murders, I would think.'

'Nothing for it but to keep going,' said Tabitha.

'Yes. If we don't turn up anything useful from this lot, we'll have to think of something else.'

Headline number six, which seemed interesting at least. Julia read the lead article out loud.

MASSIVE SEARCH FOR MISSING BOY

William Hunter (7), son of well-known local businessman Gregory Hunter and his wife June, went missing on Friday 4 July from the shopping precinct in Hudderwold. The boy was having lunch at Happy Hamburger with his au pair. He was playing in the play area when she went to make a phone call. On her return, she couldn't find him, and raised the alarm. Police and dogs combed the area yesterday to no avail. The search will continue today.

The boy's mother appealed to anyone who has seen the boy to come forward, and offered a substantial reward for information that leads to his return. 'The worry is unimaginable. We think he wandered off, but it's been a day since he disappeared and he hasn't been found. My only hope is that some kind person will see him and help him, and return him to us. In my nightmares, I worry that he has been grabbed.'

'How very sad. I do hope that little William was found.'

'One way to find out,' Julia said, tap-tap-tapping on her keyboard. 'Here we go. FOUR ARRESTED IN HUDDERWOLD HORROR.'

She pulled up the article. 'Oh no.'

'What?'

'The boy was found dead.'

Tabitha's face was aghast. 'They killed him?'

'Let me read it... It says here it was an accidental death. The cloth that had been tied around the boy's mouth was too heavy. He couldn't breathe. Oh my God. How awful.'

'Read the whole thing.'

Julia did. It was a tragic story. The boy had been grabbed to be held for ransom – his dad apparently owned a chain of car dealerships in the area and had plenty of money – and the kidnap had gone horribly wrong. At least two of the kidnappers had been recruited from a gang of local good-for-nothings with a propensity for violence.

'The whole thing is just too terrible. Listen to this: "*In a dramatic turn of events, local maths teacher Gary Alberts arrived on the scene and tried to grab his own son – himself a minor – from the police. 'John was never in any gang. He's innocent!' Mr Alberts shouted as he was led away and charged with interfering with police business.*"'

'When did this happen?' Tabitha asked.

'It must have been 6 July, 1986. This piece was published the week of 20 July. Two weeks after the first article.'

'Do you think this is what Monica found? What got her killed?'

Julia looked again at the list of words she'd deciphered from Monica's handwritten list. 'July. 80s... gang... violence... Hudderwold... And the SE Weekly, of course. The words match up. But how it all fits together, I don't know. What about this could possibly get a person killed now?'

'It's so long ago. Almost forty years.'

'I wonder what happened in the end. Let's see if we can find anything about the four who were arrested.'

Their two heads lowered over two keyboards, four hands went to work. Julia was the first to find a hit. 'Here we go. THREE CHARGED IN HUDDERWOLD HORROR. That's odd, I wonder what happened to number four.'

'Maybe the maths teacher was right.'

'Huh?'

'The maths teacher who said his son wasn't a killer, or something.'

Tabitha brought the page up. 'Gary Alberts, he was the maths teacher. "John was never in any gang," he said.'

'Oh yes. Do they give the names of the three?'

'Dennis Falmouth, Gerry Kerry...'

'Gerry Kerry? That's his name?' Julia smiled.

'I'm afraid so. And Larry Greenway.'

'So no John. Lucky for Mr Alberts.'

'And for John Alberts.'

'Indeed. Now there's a follow-up piece from a few weeks later. Two of the men – Greenway and Kerry – were charged with manslaughter, and were sentenced to twenty years each. They were the ringleaders, apparently, and part of a gang called, what was it, oh yes, here it is, The Greenway Brothers. The third chap, Dennis Falmouth, was an accessory, and he got five. It says here that eyewitness testimony put them away.'

Tabitha wrinkled her forehead. 'Still, Julia, I don't see how any of this can be relevant. The case was solved. There's no secret piece of information.'

The table was cleared of laptops, and set with mats and cutlery. The ratatouille was delicious – plenty of olive oil was the key, Julia had discovered – but the mood was somewhat sombre. They had made great strides in their research, and turned up what they thought might well be relevant information, but they couldn't make the links between the papers and the killer. They were proud of their sleuthing, but felt no closer to solving the crime.

'We're stuck,' Julia said dejectedly, mopping up the garlicky tomato gravy with a crust of Bob the baker's sourdough. She popped the tasty morsel into her mouth and chewed slowly, hoping for a brainwave.

'It's just so frustrating! I'm sure there's something there, Julia, but we're missing a vital piece of information.'

'Well, we've done our best. I'll take everything to Hayley Gibson in the morning, explain how we got to what we found, and see if she can make sense of it. And it sounds as if Felicity will be conscious in a day or two, and she will be able to identify her attacker – or at least fill in the gaps in the story.'

30

Jake and Julia occupied their usual table just outside the door of the Buttered Scone. It was only nine thirty, but it was warm enough to sit outdoors. Julia's mood was greatly improved from last night. In fact, she felt quite buoyant. She always felt better once she'd made a decision. And last night she had made a significant one. As soon as she'd had her morning coffee, she would be on her way to the police station to hand over the articles she had found to Hayley. And she would have no more to do with it.

She was looking forward to letting go of her obsession with these crimes. Julia had enough insight to know that she had a tendency to get involved in things that weren't actually any of her business. She liked to think of it as helping, but it could be construed as meddling. It was just that she didn't like to see a mystery unsolved, or an injustice not rectified. But true, she did get carried away. She just had to work it out. Well, today was the end of that, for a while. She'd hand over the information and let the proper authorities get on with it. And she would get on with her own life. Maybe Hayley would figure out whether there was anything useful in the articles.

It was shaping up to be another lovely summer's day. The countryside was at its finest, the grass and trees a green so vivid, you could hardly believe it was real, and the fields bursting with wild flowers and buzzing with bees. She should take advantage of the glorious weather. She'd spent enough time beavering away at her computer yesterday. Today, she was going out and about.

She messaged Sean. *What are you up to today? Pub supper at The Riverside? My treat. We can go early, bring the dogs.*

Inspired idea. I'll come to you after my last patient. About 5.00ish. xxx

The three little x-es gave her a flutter.

'A penny for them?'

'What?' She started at Flo's voice. She'd been so busy with her own thoughts about Sean that she hadn't noticed her arrival.

'Your thoughts! A penny for your thoughts. You had a little smile, is all?' said Flo.

'Oh, gosh, nothing...' Julia felt herself blushing. 'Just that it's a lovely day, isn't it?'

'That it is. Going to be a hot one. I'll bring Jake some water when I bring your coffee, shall I?'

'Thanks, Flo. I think I might treat myself to a slice of your carrot cake, too.'

'Ah, something to celebrate?'

'Not really. Just in a good mood this morning. And actually, I did get some good news. Well, it's early days, but it seems like Felicity Harbour is going to be fine.'

'Oh, that is good news! Goodness, last I heard the poor woman was at death's door. That's remarkable. I'll be sure to let Albert know. He's been in such a state about her, you wouldn't believe it. This will be a weight off his mind.'

'Well, you can tell him that she's turned the corner, and they are going to take her off the ventilator in the next day or so.'

'Ah well, isn't that something to celebrate? Definitely worth a treat. I'll get that carrot cake to you right away.'

She looked down at Jake who was gazing at her with the adoration ordinarily reserved for a lamb chop. 'And I might be able to find a little something for Mr Jake here, too.'

His frantic tail wagging set the whole table rattling. Luckily, the coffee hadn't yet arrived or it would be sloshing around in the saucer by now, and likely drenching the folder of papers that Julia had printed out to deliver to DI Hayley Gibson.

'Settle down, Jakey,' Julia said, patting his head. 'You'll get your snack, and then we'll pop in on Hayley, and go home along the river, shall we? And this evening, you have a playdate with Leo. It's turning out to be a marvellous day all round, my friend.'

Fully caffeinated and caked – and in Jake's case, watered and sausaged – they set off with a spring in their step on the short walk to the police station.

'Is that a service animal?' asked the new young copper at the desk, eyeing Jake suspiciously. Jake stayed very still and calm, almost as if he had understood the question and was trying to pass himself off as an official Labrador on official business.

'Well, he was in training, he was going to be a guide dog, but, um...' Julia couldn't lie. 'But, no. He's not a service dog. He has been here before though. Cherise lets him stay.'

'That would have been a violation of health and safety protocols on her part, I'm afraid.' The new copper looked as if he had graduated copper school the previous week, but he made up for it with a spotless uniform, highly polished shoes and an officious manner.

'I'm sure she didn't mean... Oh dear. Well, I won't be long,

I'm going to visit DI Gibson quickly, just a quick word and to drop something off, in fact.' She waved the folder. 'I spoke to her this morning, she's expecting me.' Julia tried to sound very sure of her and Jake's right to enter the inner sanctums of the station. She'd found in her life that often if you say something with enough conviction, people accept what you are telling them. Unfortunately, this new chap was made of sterner stuff than that.

'I can't let you in with a dog.'

'I quite understand. It's the rules. That's fine. I'll tie him up outside. Could you keep an eye on him while I go and chat to her quickly?'

'I'm a police officer on duty,' he said, offended. 'I can't be babysitting random dogs.'

Jake looked from one to the other as if he knew he was the subject of negotiation.

'Okay, then,' Julia said, sighing inwardly. 'Please could you contact DI Gibson and tell her Julia Bird is here. She *is* expecting me.'

'I will do that for you,' he said. 'But health and safety regulations state that—'

'I'll wait outside.'

Julia sat on the bench in the little garden outside the police station with the folder beside her on the bench and Jake at her feet. They watched the birds. Someone had put down a cut-up apple and a piece of bread on the bird feeder, and they were all over it, big ones and little ones, all squawking and flapping their wings as if they hadn't eaten in a month. Once again she tried to remember which was which, and what their names were. Once again she failed, and resolved to look them up again in her bird book when she got home. There were little brown ones and bigger black ones, and some other colour, what was that, a sort of murky khaki green?

Her very amateur twitching was interrupted by a bark from

Jake. It was his 'Oh, look! A friend!' bark and it heralded the arrival of DI Hayley Gibson. She was still walking awkwardly with some sort of orthopaedic boot on one leg, and a stick in her hand.

'Hi, Julia. I see young Masterson wouldn't let Jake in.'

Julia rolled her eyes.

'Just doing his job, I suppose,' Hayley said with a sigh, sitting down next to Julia on the bench. 'They've gone mad for health and safety on the force. It's half the reason why I've been stuck at the desk. So what have you got for me? I'm intrigued.'

'The trouble is, I'm not quite sure. I've found something that could have a link to the murders, but I don't know what it is.'

'Curiouser and curiouser...'

'Let me explain.'

Hayley sat next to her on the bench, her bad leg stretched out in front of her, while Julia went over the theory that the research papers somehow tied the three murders together. First Monica, then Lilian, then Felicity, had had the papers. All three had died – or almost died, in Felicity's case.

'Exactly. So the question is, what was in those papers? The piece of paper you and Walter found at Felicity's house wasn't very useful, as far as we can see so far.'

'No, although Tabitha and I did some digging last night and we found something, a news story, that seems to match the few bits of information on that piece of paper.'

She handed the printouts of the articles to Hayley, who read them quickly.

'God, what an awful story.'

'I know, just awful.'

'So what's the connection between a thirty-five-year-old murder-kidnapping, and this bloody mess that's on my desk?'

'Hayley, I don't know. Mostly likely nothing at all. If there is something, I'm not seeing it. Maybe you can.' She lined up all the papers, put them back in the file and handed them over. 'All yours.'

'Thanks, Julia. I'll take a look. And I should be able to interview Felicity soon, so that should give us more to work with. I can only hope she saw her attacker. Did you know they're taking her off the ventilator today?'

'I had heard that it would be sometime soon. I didn't know it was today, exactly.' Julia was glad that she could be truthful, and vague enough not to drop Walter in trouble for blabbing.

'Just heard from the hospital. In fact, I'm going over there this morning.'

'I hope poor Felicity is able to remember something about the attack. Trauma can take a terrible toll on the memory. But, at the very least, she'll be able to tell you what she was working on for the book. Maybe that will tie it together.'

'I'd be going right now if I could only drive. I'm waiting for DC Farmer, he has been held up. Something to do with sheep.'

Julia didn't enquire further about the ovine obstacles. She got quickly to her feet. 'I can give you a lift. I'm parked by the Buttered Scone. I'll fetch the car and be back in a jiffy!'

'Are you sure? God, it's infuriating not being able to drive. But at least I've argued my way out of stupid desk duty.'

'Absolutely sure. I was intending to drop off some flowers to cheer Felicity up when she comes round. After all, I found her. I feel very connected with the whole case. I'll fetch the car. Back in a mo.'

She was indeed back in a mo – or maximum two mos – with Jake sitting upright in the back seat like his lordship out for a Sunday afternoon drive. She got out and helped Hayley into the car, lifting her bad leg gingerly, then went round to the driver's side, and got in. As she pulled into the main road, DI Gibson got down to business.

'I read the file while you were gone. Good work.'

'Thanks. It might be, it's not clear yet. Have you solved the puzzle?'

'Unfortunately not. No idea how this could possibly be connected. But I'm wondering about the fourth guy.'

'I was too. The teacher's son. John. He just disappeared from the news story.'

'The question is why? He might have been a bystander caught up in the arrests. Innocent like his dad said. All sorts of reasons, I suppose. I made a phone call while I was waiting, a request for information about the case, and for details about the fourth person arrested. It was a long time ago, and the record-keeping wasn't what it is now, but let's see what turns up. There might be something useful.'

Julia pulled up outside Blooming Marvels, a florist in an ancient cottage, beautifully renovated, just off the main road. 'Won't be a minute,' she told her two passengers.

She stepped under a curtain of petunias cascading from hanging baskets, through the doorway into a shop that smelled like heaven. The choice of flowers was overwhelming. It was high summer, after all, and it seemed as if the whole country was ablaze. Great buckets of blooms of every description.

A pretty blonde with the name Angela embroidered on a smart denim apron offered her help.

'It's all so gorgeous,' Julia said, rather overwhelmed. 'It's for a friend who's in hospital. Something pretty and soft, and sort of cheerful, you know...'

'I do know,' the woman said. 'A mixed bouquet, a sort of meadow look.' She picked a lily from one bucket, and a couple of irises from another, and a few more pretty things that Julia didn't recognise, sometimes holding one up and putting it back, reaching for another. In a flash she had the exact perfect soft country bouquet that Julia would have asked for, if she'd known what to ask. 'It is absolutely perfect.'

'For hospital, you'll need a vase. They never have any.' The florist picked a simple white one off a shelf behind her and raised her eyebrows.

'Perfect,' Julia said again. 'Goodness me, you really do have an eye for it.'

'Thank you. I've had lots of practice. Just finished thirty table arrangements for a huge wedding. But I love this sort of thing the best – a simple, natural bouquet. I hope your friend likes it. And that she's better soon.'

Julia handed over an admittedly rather large sum of money, but even so, she was delighted with it. It reminded her of the flower arrangements Christopher did. He somehow made it look as if he'd gathered them in a dewy meadow at dawn and tossed them into a jam jar, but in such a way that they were absolutely perfect.

'Pretty,' said Hayley, and held the vase carefully while Julia drove home to drop off Jake. He looked surprised to see her turn round and get back into the car without him.

'Don't look so hurt, Jakey boy. Go and find your chicken-girlfriend, she'll keep you company. I'll be back soon.'

31

'Here we are again,' Hayley said wearily. It was, of course, the same hospital that she had been in just weeks before, most reluctantly trussed up with wires and pulleys. 'I was hoping for a rather longer break between visits.'

'Look how well you're doing, though. It's amazing. You're basically up and about. It's just the driving. And you are here on official business, not due to injury. You are back in the saddle!'

Ordinarily, Julia would have taken the first available parking spot, but today she drove right to the front, looking for something close so that Hayley didn't have to walk too far. She did not mention this to Hayley, of course.

She found one very close to the big glass entrance and pulled in. 'That was lucky.'

She exited the car and quickly went round to the passenger side to open the door for Hayley and help her out.

'Not to worry. I can manage, thanks.'

Julia took the vase of flowers from her and left her to struggle her way out of the little car. She got her phone out of her bag and checked her messages, taking her time about it, so that Hayley wouldn't have to see her watching the inelegant exit, getting her bandaged leg and her stick to obey orders. When Hayley was on her feet, Julia put her phone away and locked the car.

'It's second floor, ward B, room one,' Hayley said, reading from her notebook. 'I know where that is, I was just down the hall. Her doctor's name is Doctor Hassan. She knows I'm coming, she said to ask the sister to page her when I arrive.'

Julia, of course, had no official business here. She was simply delivering flowers.

They entered the big foyer with its admission cubicles on one side and the coffee shop on the other. Julia glanced at the coffee shop which was sparsely populated. The few tables that were occupied seemed to be occupied by anxious-looking relatives passing the time waiting for news, which made Julia feel sad.

'This way,' Hayley said, leading her to the corridor marked West Wing.

Everything was bright and white and metal and wipe-downable. The sort of environment that gave Julia a headache. She looked down at the flowers and breathed in their scent, masking the antiseptic odour of the hospital.

They went up to the second floor, sharing the lift with a waif-like woman of about Julia's own age wearing a dressing gown and holding a drip stand. She was so tiny, it seemed that without it she might fall over.

'How's the leg?' she asked, nodding down at Hayley's cast. She seemed in remarkable good cheer for someone in a hospital lift with a tube snaking into her arm.

'On the mend, thank you,' Hayley answered. It came out rather brusquely, and she added, 'And how are you?'

'Oh, coming along,' she said, whatever that meant. Julia suspected it wasn't good.

The lift opened to the second floor and they said goodbye to their companion. 'Best of luck to you,' Julia said, rather to her own surprise.

The woman waved slowly in the gap of the closing doors.

Hayley approached the desk and explained her business to the nurse in charge.

'Doctor Hassan did say you would be coming,' she said, pushing one of a bristle of hair pins back into its place in her bun. 'I'll page her.'

She sent a message and turned back to Hayley. 'She won't be long. Would you like to wait in our Visitors' Waiting Area?'

'Yes, thanks.'

'Lovely, aren't they? Just like spring in a vase,' the nurse said, nodding towards Julia's flowers. 'From Blooming Marvels, aren't they?'

'Yes!' To Julia's surprise, she was right.

'We get a lot of flowers in here, as you can imagine, and I can always tell. Angela's are the best, in my view.'

Julia felt curiously proud of herself for picking what was, in the extensive experience of – she read the woman's name badge – Nurse Graham, the best florist in Berrywick.

The nurse showed them to a waiting area with comfortable seats and blandly beautiful posters of the sea and beaches, designed to soothe worried family members. A window looked out over the parking lot. Julia could see her little car there waiting by the entrance. She watched people coming in and out and wished them all good health. She hoped that they were there to welcome new grandchildren or have a routine check-up, not have some ominous lump removed and sent for further investigation.

She noted the familiar gait of an older man crossing the parking lot. It took Julia a moment to recognise the rolling motion of Albert Johns. She wondered if he was visiting Felicity. It would make sense, he was chairperson of the Berrywick Residents' Committee – not to forget Pub Quiz Master – or if he was there on some other business. She had a horrible thought there might have been another attack, on another member of the pub quiz teams, and that was who he was visiting. She quickly pushed the idea aside. There was absolutely no reason to think that anyone else was injured. For a start, if that was the case Hayley would have heard.

'Detective Gibson?'

Julia turned from the window to see a doctor in a white coat and blue headscarf looking at her expectantly.

'I'm Detective Gibson,' Hayley said, coming forward.

'Oh, hello. Doctor Hassan. Felicity Harbour's doctor.'

'Thanks for coming to meet me, I know you must be busy. This is Julia Bird, she's a friend of Mrs Harbour. She kindly gave me a lift to the hospital.' She gestured to her leg.

The three women smiled and nodded at each other, shaking hands being a thing of the past in hospitals.

'I am here to find out about Mrs Harbour's condition, and to see if she might be able to answer a few questions.'

'She won't be answering any questions today, I'm afraid. She's still heavily sedated from this morning's procedure, but she's doing very well. I expect that...'

The doctor looked over to Julia and stopped speaking. 'I'm sorry, I realise... um... this is confidential patient information, would you mind...'

'Of course, I quite understand. I'll go and take the flowers to Felicity's room. Leave you two to talk,' she said. 'Is that okay? I can pop in for a quick visit?'

'Yes, just don't excite her,' said the doctor. 'We want to keep her calm. Down the passage, on your left. Room one.'

'I won't be long. I'll just deliver these and say hello and I'll be right back.'

'Come and find me here when you're finished,' Hayley said.

Vase in hand, Julia hesitated outside Felicity's room, mentally preparing herself for what she might see. She stepped inside to find Felicity lying on her back in the hospital bed, her eyes closed. A white blanket covered her small frame, pulled up to her armpits, and lifting and falling slightly with her breath. Knobbly knees and feet created a folded topography, like snowy mountains, with valleys between. Over the foot of the bed was a typical hospital tray table on wheels, the sort that could serve as a dining table for a bedbound patient.

It would have been a peaceful scene, if not for the oxygen feed into her nose and drips and drains emerging here and there. A bank of machines flashed and beeped, measuring who-knows-what. Julia recognised the jagged up and down of the heart, and the big green numbers indicating blood pressure, but the rest of the lines, dots and numerals were a mystery.

Julia put the flowers on the little table by the window, relieved to be rid of the heavy vase. She fluffed them up a bit, then sat down in the visitor's chair next to the sleeping woman. Felicity looked old and frail and deathly pale, her skin almost translucent, her hair sparse and wiry on the pillow.

Julia felt a surge of anger at whoever had put this brilliant, feisty woman into this state. What kind of awful, violent man would push a pillow over the face of an old lady, and why? Still, here she was, and the only hope was that she would get better and help them discover who had attacked her.

She placed a hand gently on Felicity's shoulder and spoke softly. 'Hello, Felicity. It's Julia.'

She had no idea whether Felicity heard or understood her, but she'd read many stories of people reporting that they'd been able to hear when they were unconscious. 'I'm glad you're going to be okay,' she said, in what she hoped was an encouraging tone.

Felicity's eyelids fluttered briefly, as if they might open, but the effort seemed too much.

'Don't try to wake up, just rest. I'll only stay a minute.'

Julia's anger was replaced by a wave of frustration at herself and her own failure to put all the pieces together. The file with its cryptic initials and arrows, the newspaper articles about the kidnap and murder. Not that the police had been any more successful. The papers *had* to be the key. But how?

Julia sat for a few more minutes, making small talk about the activity of the neighbourhood and how worried everyone was about her, and were sending good wishes. She reassured Felicity that her dogs were in good hands while she recovered – she hoped she wasn't worrying about them. She even found herself telling Felicity about Jake's unlikely friendship with a hen.

'I'm going to go,' she told the sleeping woman, after a few minutes of one-sided chatter. 'I'll come back when you are ready for a proper visit. The doctor says you're on the mend and should be awake soon. Bye, Felicity.'

On her way out, Julia went to the little bathroom and washed her hands which were sticky from the flowers.

Albert was walking into the room as she came out of the bathroom. He jumped when he saw her.

'Oh hello, Albert. Sorry, I didn't mean to startle you. I was visiting, but I'm leaving now.'

'Is she conscious?' he asked. 'Can she talk, do you know?' His brow was wrinkled with concern.

'I'm afraid not, Albert. They only removed the ventilator this morning and she's still quite sedated, apparently. They are taking it slowly.'

'So no information about her attacker?'

'Not yet. Of course the police will want to question her as soon as she's able.'

Felicity let out a small groan. Her right hand moved, as if she was trying to lift it.

'Gosh, Albert. She seems to have perked up a bit, hearing your voice. She was quite still and unresponsive before.'

Felicity's bony, blue-veined hand clawed at the white blanket. She managed to lift it up an inch, one finger pointing forward, before it fell to the bed. She let out another sound, this time a high gurgling whine, from deep in her throat.

The jagged peaks of the heart rate rose higher as Julia spoke. 'Oh dear, I think my visit must have been too much for her. The doctor said she needs to be kept calm. No stress or excitement. Maybe I shouldn't have mentioned the dogs. Oh dear. I'll be on my way. It's probably best to have only one visitor at a time and I was just leaving anyway.'

'I won't stay, I'll be right behind you,' he said. 'We don't want to put her under any stress.'

Julia returned to Hayley, who was sitting where she'd left her, looking through her notebook with a small frown. 'Ready?' she asked.

'Yes, ready. Let's go.'

She painstakingly lifted herself to a standing position. 'It's probably nothing to do with this, but I got a call from my contact with info about the fourth kidnapper in that story you found.'

'You mean John, the maths' teacher's kid?'

'Yes, him. John Alberts. Turns out he was only seventeen at the time of the crime. He gave evidence against the others. That's why his name wasn't in the papers, so—'

'Oh heavens, I haven't got my handbag!' Julia interrupted. She realised, when she reached for her car keys, that it was nowhere to be found. It must be in Felicity's room. 'Goodness, my brain is full of this mysterious... and then Albert. Back in a sec.'

While she walked briskly down the passage of gleaming linoleum, her full brain, although unable to remember her hand-bag, presented her with an odd little observation – Albert Johns, John Alberts. It was almost the same name. A strange little coincidence. John Alberts, Albert Johns. The names just swapped around. An image flashed into her mind. The curved line, an arrow either side. The drawing Walter Farmer had made, that he'd seen on the front of the folder.

What if it wasn't a coincidence? What if Albert Johns was John Alberts? If somebody had discovered that in those mysterious missing papers, would he kill to keep his secret?

Julia's breath quickened, as did her pace. A child had died in the crime he was involved in all those years ago. That might indeed be a thing that he would murder for – and was he about to do it again?

Julia found herself running the last few steps to the room. She pushed the door open so hard it banged against the wall.

'Oh!' Albert let out a yelp of surprise.

He was standing on the far side of the bed, next to Felicity's head, a big, white pillow in his hands. The old woman's eyes were open now, and her fingers scrabbled uselessly at the blanket.

'I thought she might like to be propped up a bit. Another pillow,' Albert said, holding the pillow to his chest and forcing a smile. His voice – usually booming – came out wavering.

A ghastly, ghostly attempt at a scream came from Felicity's pale, dry lips. She managed to roll her head to the side. When her eyes met Julia's, they held pure terror.

'Put the pillow down, John,' Julia said.

'I...'

'You're John Alberts,' Julia said the words calmly. 'Don't make this harder than it needs to be.'

He dropped his hands, the pillow hanging limply at his side. They stared at each other across the bed, neither sure what to do next. He moved first, and surprisingly quickly for a man of his age and build, making a dash for the door. Julia quickly shoved the wheeled tray table at the end of Felicity's bed hard enough to slow him and put him off balance. She gave it another push, forcing him back towards the table by the window. A final shove of the table, and now he was caught between the two tables. He hesitated for a moment, their eyes locked, and then he pushed it back at her, hard, throwing her off balance. She managed to stay upright, but the force of his push rattled the table behind him and the vase of flowers fell over, the water pouring over the table and to the floor, the stems scattering as he struggled to get free of the furniture.

'Hayley. Help!' Julia yelled at the top of her voice. 'Someone help.'

'Let me go!' His shout came out somewhere between a threat and a plea.

'There's nowhere to go,' she shouted back at him.

He gave another desperate push, and the wheeled table connected painfully with her ribs. She pushed it to the side and lunged for the only weapon she could see – the vase lying precariously at the edge of the table. She grabbed it and smashed it over Albert's head.

The blow wasn't hard enough to injure him, but it stopped him in his tracks, water and shards of glass dropping on his shoulders. He scrambled to stay upright, but his feet slid on the wet linoleum and he crashed to the ground.

'It's over, Albert. Just stop,' she said quietly now. In the silence, she could hear footsteps in the passage.

He tried to get to his knees, but slashed his right hand on the broken glass, blood mixing pinkly with the water.

'Good God, Julia. What's going on?' Hayley had run in on that bad leg of hers. 'Albert! What on earth? Why are you on the floor? What's happened in here?'

'His name is not Albert, it's John. John Alberts, not Albert Johns,' said Julia grimly.

'He's the fourth kidnapper.' Hayley looked at Julia, understanding dawning.

'Yes.'

Hayley pushed the wheeled table aside and stood over Albert, as Julia still thought of him, who had crumpled to the wet floor, meek and broken amongst the shattered glass and crushed flowers.

'You stay right there,' she said. 'Don't move.'

More footsteps in the corridor. Dr Hassan came running into the room, with Nurse Graham hard on her heels. She took a moment to survey the chaotic scene and went straight to her patient. Her eyes flicked between Felicity and the monitor, her fingers pressed against her wrist.

'Call security,' Dr Hassan barked briskly at the nurse. 'I want everyone out of here. Now.'

32

'I think the dogs might be back from their stay with Felicity's niece,' Julia said with a smile, over the high-pitched barking and whining that was coming from the other side of the front door. The door opened and a river of small mutts flowed out onto the doorstep, leaping and bobbing at their ankles.

A young woman appeared, wincing at the noise. 'Doctor Sean?' she asked.

'Yes, that's me. And this is Julia Bird.'

'Ah, I've heard all about you, Mrs Bird,' she said, nodding her approval. 'The woman who saved the day. Please, come in. Oh, my manners, I'm Tania. Felicity's niece.'

She stood back and let them into the hallway, whilst deftly blocking the dogs with her foot, saying, 'You chaps can stay outside, I'll give you your supper in a minute.'

'Thanks for looking in on her, Doctor.'

'It's no trouble. I'm pleased she's been discharged. She'll be happier and calmer in her own place.'

'The doctors wanted to keep her in hospital for a few more days, but Aunt Felicity was insistent. She couldn't wait to get out of there after what happened. I do think she will heal better in her own space. Luckily I'm on holiday – I'm a teacher – so I said I would stay a few days. Shall we go through and see her?'

Felicity wasn't in her usual spot in the red wing back, but reclining on the sofa under the window, her head and shoulders propped up on pillows.

'Hello,' she croaked softly. Sean went over to her. Julia and Tania hung discreetly back to give the doctor and patient a little privacy.

'Shall we go into the kitchen to make some tea while they chat?' Tania said brightly.

'That's a good idea. I've got scones.' Julia lifted the tea towel over the basket to reveal the scones, and two little bowls of jam and cream.

'Oooh, those do look good.'

When they came back with the tea tray a few minutes later, Felicity was sitting upright, with Sean next to her. Julia sat on an armchair next to them.

'Julia, Felicity was asking me about Albert Johns. I thought you'd be better able to fill her in on what he did and why.'

'I don't understand why Albert of all people would attack me,' Felicity whispered.

'It's all to do with the research for your book. The one Monica was helping you with?'

'Gangs...' Felicity said, waving her hand around vaguely, her voice hoarse.

'Aunt Felicity is writing about the criminal gangs in operation from the end of the war, through to 2000. She told me all about it last time I visited. Fascinating story. Rackets. Drugs. Guns. Kidnaps.'

'That's just it,' said Julia. 'Albert Johns – then known by his real name, John Alberts – was involved in one of the gangs in the 80s. He was a youngster, only just turned seventeen. He was persuaded by his older cousin, who was a member of the gang, to help with a job. A kidnapping. Albert was a fresh-faced, young-looking seventeen, and his job was to lure the boy from a hamburger place into the car while the au pair's back was turned. The kidnapping went wrong, and the boy died. He was seven years old.'

Tania stopped mid-pour, the teapot aloft, and gasped, 'Oh no!'

'I know, it's just awful. Albert testified against the rest of them, including the gang leaders, in exchange for his own freedom. By all accounts he was really just a child caught up in a situation that he didn't realise would go so terribly wrong. The others all went away for a long time, and he changed his name and moved away to start a new life. He trained as a paramedic, got a job. A few years later he met Flo and came to Berrywick. They had Fiona, Flo started the Buttered Scone, it was all hunky-dory. A fresh start.'

Julia fell silent at the mention of Flo. She felt desperate for the poor woman. Tania came over and handed her a cup of tea, resting a hand briefly on her shoulder in passing. Julia smiled.

'It was Monica who made the connection,' Julia continued. 'She saw the news articles about the kidnapping and the trial, and saw the name – John Alberts. But Monica used to work as an archivist. She went through the archives of the local paper – took a trip especially – and she found an article with a picture of John Alberts. It was unrelated – he'd scored a winning goal in a local match. But there was no mistaking, it was our Albert. She recognised him as Albert Johns, Berrywick quizmaster and put two and two together. It was this photograph that caused all the problems. While the names were close – goodness knows what he was thinking, but I suppose he was young – it was the photograph that was the actual proof. And Monica took the original article; the only known copy. If Albert could have destroyed that evidence, it would have been hard to prove he was John Alberts.'

Julia was interrupted by the doorbell, followed by the inevitable yapping and howling.

Tania stood up. 'I'll get it.'

She was back minutes later with DI Hayley Gibson and DC Walter Farmer, and about a dozen tiny mutts.

'They just barged in, the naughty fellows,' Tania said, smiling indulgently at them. 'Now settle down, chaps.'

What looked like a Jack Russell Terrier crossed with something with significantly longer legs and a piglet tail jumped up and sat next to Felicity. A tiny fluffball of indeterminate provenance leapt onto her lap. She stroked them both, one with each hand, and gave the first smile Julia had seen from her all day.

'We didn't mean to interrupt your tea party. Just came by to check on you, Felicity, and dot a few t's and cross some i's. I mean cross the t's and...' Walter's voice trailed off.

'We should be on our way when we've finished our tea,' said Julia. 'We don't want to tire Felicity out. I told her how Monica worked out Albert's secret past.'

'What did Monica do with this information?' asked Tania, who had finished pouring the tea and was now distributing the scones. She put one on a plate and placed it next to Julia's teacup, on the little side table.

'From what Albert says, she blackmailed him,' Hayley answered. 'Monica had lost her job a few years ago, and things had been tight for her since. I suppose the temptation was just too much for her, when she realised. We haven't got the bank statements yet, but it seemed she took quite a few pounds off him for a few months.'

'I don't understand,' Tania said, in a tone of disbelief. 'It was so long ago, and he was so young when it happened, would anyone have cared?'

'You don't know village gossip!' Julia said. 'It would have been the talk of Berrywick. Probably for months. People aren't very forgiving.'

'Julia's right,' Sean said. 'Albert is a well-known and respected man around here, he's Chairperson of the Berrywick Residents' Committee. An upstanding citizen. A man known for saving lives, not ending them. To be connected to such a crime and implicated in the death of a child, even if it was accidental? The impact would have been significant. On Flo's business too.'

'Albert's real worry was Fiona,' said Hayley. 'She is standing for public office. And a big part of her platform is crime prevention. It would have been disastrous for her if this thing had blown up. Albert couldn't stand to see his only child hurt by his past.'

'Albert killed Monica?' Felicity said, her voice soft and breaking.

'Yes, I'm afraid so,' Hayley said. 'She was becoming more insistent, more threatening. His medical background helped him. He substituted her heart medication with benzodiazepine, and made it look like a heart attack, and he thought his secret was safe.'

'I knew it was something to do with the papers,' said Felicity, surprising Julia. She took a sip of her tea to soothe her throat and spoke quietly, with some effort. 'I was looking at the pile of papers with Monica's scribbles, and it suddenly struck me that everyone who had had them had died. I couldn't see what the connection might be. That's why I called you, Julia. That's what I was going to talk to you about.'

'I'm afraid you were spot on,' said Julia. 'The papers were the common thread.'

'But why kill Lilian? Why not just take the papers?'

'It seems he thought he was in the clear with Monica gone, and her death accepted as natural. But then at the pub quiz, he overheard that Lilian had the documents Monica had been working on. She said that she was going to read the papers and see what they were about. The last thing he wanted was a police officer digging around in his past, and seeing that photograph of him as a young man. And perhaps making the connection between him and Monica's death. He wanted to stop her from looking at the papers.'

'So he stabbed her?' asked Tania.

'Well, first he said that he saw me and Lilian walking home, and just on the spur of the moment tried to run us over.' Hayley looked down at her leg with irritation. 'When that didn't work, he waited till the next quiz, and went to Lilian's room at the inn. His plan was to find her house keys, and then return to her house – knowing that she was at the inn – and steal the papers. He thought he could then drop her keys on the pub floor after-wards, like she'd dropped them there, and she'd never even know that some of the papers were missing. Not a bad plan, actually. But then she came back to her room, and caught him going through her things. He panicked, grabbed a steak knife from the room service tray that was on the dressing table, and stabbed her.'

'And then it turned out that the papers had been handed over to you, Felicity. That's when he...' Julia stopped, not wanting to traumatise the old woman further. She had come within a hair's breadth of death.

'Fortunately, Julia managed to make the same connection.' Sean looked at her with pride. 'And got there just in time.'

'Well, not me alone. Walter played a key role in it – remem-bering what was on the folder, the words, the arrows. It all added up. I only wish I'd got to it sooner.'

'Apparently, when he arrived at your house, and let himself in, he saw the papers lying on your little desk, and the photo-graph was on top,' said Hayley.

'I hadn't a clue that it was him,' said Felicity sadly. 'I had wondered why Monica had got a football article muddled up with my notes, that's all.'

'He thought that you were onto him,' said Julia. 'He took the pillow from outside, and snuck up behind you.'

'But you interrupted him,' said Felicity. 'Just in time.'

'A lucky day for all of us,' said Julia, with a smile.

'It's all so sad. So sad.' Felicity hugged the little dogs to her.

Julia reached over and took her hand. 'That it is. Two deaths, completely unnecessary. And poor you, Felicity, what you've been through. And Hayley's broken leg. And the suffering of Albert and his family. And the little boy, of course, little William and his parents. Tragic. But thank heavens you are still here with us, Felicity.'

'Julia's right, Aunt Felicity. We're all grateful that you are alive. The doctor said there's nothing to worry about long-term, you just need to rest and take care of yourself, and you'll be right as rain.'

Felicity nodded, and gave her niece a weak smile. 'I do feel better. Home.'

'Speaking of rest, you could probably use a nap. Sean and I will be on our way. You call if you need anything, and I'll pop in again in a few days.'

'We will be right behind you. Just one or two questions, if you are up to it?' Hayley said.

Felicity nodded, and then turned to address Julia. 'Thank you. For everything.'

The afternoon was still warm and bright when they got back to Julia's house.

'Let's take the dogs for a quick walk, shall we?' Sean said as they got out of the car. 'Get the blood flowing?'

'Okay, a little stroll along the river might be nice,' Julia said, although in truth she felt rather more like a cold glass of Chardonnay with her feet up.

Sean read her mood, as usual. 'You must be tired. It wasn't an easy day. We don't have to go, but it might cheer us up?'

'I'm a little tired. And sad. I was thinking of poor Flo, with her husband going to jail. And poor Fiona. You know she's withdrawn from the local election.'

'Yes. It is sad. And a waste. I think she would have made a very good leader of the council.'

'All the terrible things Albert did, he did to protect her, and as a result, her future in politics is over before it's begun.'

'Unintended consequences.'

'Although it's hardly surprising. You can't reasonably expect your plan to have a good outcome when your plan includes murder.'

'That, Mrs Bird, is a true statement. You are a wise woman. And a beautiful one.'

'And you are a flatterer.' She patted his arm dismissively, but couldn't keep her lips from stretching in a smile.

'Every word of it the truth. No flattery.'

'Well, you are a very good man. And a handsome one.'

The dogs had heard their voices, and came barrelling round the side of the house to greet them.

'And as for the dogs...'

'The dogs are marvellous,' she said, bending to pat the writhing bodies. 'Will you get the leads?'

Henny Penny came round the corner, following her canine companions at a more stateful pace. 'No walks for you, I'm afraid. You do know you're not a dog, right? You'll have to wait here.'

Living alone, Julia had become accustomed to holding these one-sided conversations with the animals. She suspected that the hens, with their quick, clever little brains and their bright eyes, understood more than they let on. And Jake possibly quite a bit less, poor chap. She continued her address to Henny

Penny. 'I did see a chicken harness in the *Chickenews!* magazine, actually. But don't get any ideas, I'm not getting you one.'

'I should hope not!'

She blushed, rather, to discover that Sean had heard her talking to the hen.

'I don't think it would do for the village doctor to be spotted walking the fowl. But I'd happily be spotted walking the smartest problem solver in Berrywick.'

'And Berrywick's finest dogs?'

'Yes indeed.'

'Well, in that case, Doctor, let's be on our way.'

A LETTER FROM KATIE GAYLE

Dear reader,

Katie Gayle is, in fact, two of us – Kate and Gail – and we want to say a huge thank you for choosing to read *Murder at the Inn*. We have loved exploring more of Berrywick with Julia and Jake. We hope that you have too. If you are a new friend of Julia Bird, please grab a copy of *An English Garden Murder* to read about Julia's first adventures in Berrywick, and then *Murder in the Library* and *A Village Fete Murder* for more of her sleuthing.

And we are not stopping here – we're hard at work creating more adventures for Julia and Jake and the characters of Berrywick. If you want to keep up to date with all Katie Gayle's latest releases, just sign up at the following link. Your email address will never be shared and you can unsubscribe at any time.

www.bookouture.com/katie-gayle

You can also follow us on Twitter for regular updates and pictures of the real-life Jake! (Who is, if anything, even naughtier than Julia's Jake.)

We hope you enjoyed reading about Julia's adventures, and if you did we would be very grateful if you could write a review and post it on Amazon and Goodreads, so that other people can discover Julia too. Ratings and reviews really help writers!

You might also enjoy our Epiphany Bloom series – the first three books are available for download now.

You can find us in a few places and we'd love to hear from you.

Katie Gayle is on Twitter as @KatieGayleBooks and on Facebook as Katie Gayle Writer. You can also follow Kate at @katesidley and Gail at @gailschimmel.

Thanks,

Katie Gayle

 facebook.com/KatieGayleWriter
twitter.com/KatieGayleBooks

Made in United States
Troutdale, OR
09/20/2023